Dirty Weekend

Dirty Weekend

Alan Scholefield

St. Martin's Press
New York

Library of Congress Cataloging-in-Publication Data

Scholefield, Alan.
    Dirty weekend / Alan Scholefield.
        p.   cm.
    ISBN 0-312-05415-7
    I. Title.
    PR9369.3.S3D5   1991
    823—dc20   90-48993
                                                                    CIP

First published in Great Britain by Macmillan London Limited

First U.S. Edition: January 1991
10 9 8 7 6 5 4 3 2 1

Dirty Weekend

1

The men who had come for Jack Benson were waiting near the eighteenth green of the Royal Hong Kong Golf Club.

Come for.

His brain used the phrase, not because it was an understatement and he could not face the truth, but because it was correct. Come for. Not kill. That would happen later.

First, as was the Chinese way with those who owed money and could not pay, they would hold him down and cut off a finger or an ear: a warning shot across his bows, so to speak.

If, when the wound had healed he still had not found the money, there would be a road accident, or a boating accident, or a swimming accident – and goodbye Jack, dear old sport.

He'd seen it happen before. Only last month the chairman of the International and Oriental Bank had been found in the deep end of his own swimming pool with a manhole cover wired to his neck. It was well known that he had come badly unstuck in a development deal in Central.

The eighteenth hole on the Old Course at Fan Ling is a dog-leg to the left. A good tee shot gives a view of the clubhouse terrace and the practice putting green, and Jack Benson had hit a good drive.

It takes approximately ten minutes to play a long hole in golf and, give or take a few seconds, about three minutes to drive, walk to your ball, and whack it a second time.

During those three minutes, from the moment Benson struck his drive down the middle, to the time he reached his ball, he knew (a) that Mr Shao Li-tze, with whom he was playing this round – the last, as it transpired, he would ever

5

play at Fan Ling – was not going to buy his excuses, and (b) that the two men were waiting for him.

He might not have connected the one standing on the empty putting green, but the other was conspicuous. You don't normally see casual strollers standing by the eighteenth green looking down the fairway through binoculars. The glasses were pointed straight at Benson. And Mr Shao was just *too* casual.

To say that he was afraid would be to err on the side of understatement. He had been afraid for months now, in fact ever since he had first read in the *South China Morning Post* that some of the Chinese students arrested after the Tiananmen Square peaceful revolution had been executed.

Even then, even after the executioners from the Peoples' Liberation Army had placed the pistols at the back of the students' heads and pulled the triggers, he had continued to hope and be afraid by turns. Benson was, after all, an optimist. Everyone said so. And things had usually worked out for him. But not this time. The luck, as Hemingway had written, she had run out.

For, from the moment those executions took place, Hong Kong got the jitters. The money markets, the share markets, the commodity markets and the Hang Seng Index, had all gone into terminal decline. The thinking was simple: if the Chinese were doing this to their own people who had had only the faintest whiff of democracy, what were they likely to do to a freedom-loving Hong Kong when they took it back from Britain in 1997?

He was, Benson told himself, a victim of history. And, if he wasn't careful, this Chinese upheaval was going to cost him an ear and then his life, for there was no way he was ever going to find forty million Hong Kong dollars by the end of the Easter weekend. No way at all.

He had used the money he had borrowed from the bank against the business. He had used the unsecured loan from Mr Shao. He had even used some of his own money, because the deal was absolutely one hundred per cent cast-iron and copper-bottomed. It would make him more money than he could count. He would never have to work again in his life.

6

And everything had looked so good. First, Mrs Thatcher had come out and struck a deal with China over Hong Kong. Then Gorbachev had arrived to cement the new friendship that was breaking out all over. And then a lot of bloody twits, students for Christ's sake, who should have been reading books and smoking pot, suddenly started to play at being grown-ups – and screwed everything up. What a mess!

As Benson struck his drive down the eighteenth, he came to the considered opinion that history, politics, and the international situation were not worth dying for.

He was forty-three years old, of medium height with dark wavy hair and a square, good-looking face. One he had been slim but years of the good life, or his version of it, had given him a small belly that overflowed the top of his pants, and a slight mottling of broken veins on his cheeks. But he was still a man who turned women's heads when he walked into a restaurant.

Mr Shao by comparison was twenty years older. He had had smallpox as a child and his face was pitted with craters. But he was as thin as a rail and looked fit enough to run up and down the Kowloon hills – which he often did. For years he had kept in trim by playing tennis and squash on his own courts. He liked to keep healthy, for it would give him longer on Earth to be with his money. The only game Mr Shao could not play, as far as Benson knew – or thought he knew – was golf.

He had played Mr Shao twice before, and both times had purposely lost to him. He knew it. Mr Shao knew it. The caddies knew it. It has caused Mr Shao to lose face.

They had not played for nearly a year. Benson had played little in that time and his eight handicap had drifted upwards through lack of practice. But Mr Shao had had lessons four times a week for six months and was matching Benson stroke for stroke and hole for hole. It had become important for Mr Shao to beat Benson and they both knew it.

But, in the three minutes it took Benson to reach his ball lying in the middle of the eighteenth fairway – during which time he had seen the two men and considered China's past,

7

present, and his own future – he no longer gave a toss who won or lost.

They had not taken caddies because when they set off on their round in the late morning there were no 'A' caddies remaining and neither wanted the hassle of a 'B' caddy. But, more importantly, Benson had not wanted to be overheard. Caddies in Hong Kong were a rich source of information after carrying bags for two talkative businessmen, especially when the deals were on the shady side as they so often were.

Like Mr Shao, Benson was pulling a trolley. The late spring day was hot and the humidity high. He was drenched in sweat.

By comparison, Mr Shao, in fawn sportswear and a Sinatra straw hat, was cool and composed. It seemed incredible, Benson told himself, that it would be this man who would receive the finger or the ear. How would it be presented to him? Gift-wrapped?

Benson waited for Mr Shao to play his shot. He played safe, percentage golf.

Benson said, 'Good one.'

Mr Shao was away to his left and Benson was able to shield his ball from Mr Shao's view. He swung. At the last moment he let his right hand take over. The club head met the ball and cut across it. The ball rose, curved away in a heavy slice and disappeared into the trees.

'Too bad,' Mr Shao said.

Benson went off in the direction of his ball.

'Careful of bamboo snakes,' Mr Shao called after him. 'They coming out now from winter sleep.'

'I'll be careful.'

He left his trolley on the edge of the fairway and entered the rough. It was thick, bushy. He had taken a six-iron in his hand just in case there was a snake. It wasn't the moment to be bitten.

He pushed his way through the branches and leaves to the point where his ball might have dropped. He was out of sight of Mr Shao now. He went on walking.

He walked through the rough until he reached a point where he was also out of sight of the car park and the clubhouse and where a road cut through the golf course. He began to run.

He had no precise idea of what he was going to do, only that he had to get away. He had thought he might stop a car, hitch a ride, but then, like some providential gift, he saw a green New Territories taxi. It was empty. He stopped it. The driver had no wish to go into Central. Benson offered him twice the fare.

The driver shrugged. The *gweilos* sometimes did these strange things. 'OK,' he said.

It took Benson the better part of ten minutes to calm down and take stock of things. His heart was still jerking in his chest but not as badly as it had been. He already had high blood pressure, God knew what this would do to it. He mopped his face with his handkerchief and dried his forearms and hands.

They wound down past Tai Po and Tolo harbour and then the racecourse at Shatin where he'd backed so many losers.

He wondered what Mr Shao was doing now. He would have waited for Benson at the eighteenth green, and then, when he did not reappear, would have walked back along the fairway and into the rough to help Benson look for his ball. There was no reason why Mr Shao should have been suspicious of anything.

When he did not find Benson among the acacias and eucalyptus, he'd search the clubhouse terrace, then the car park. He'd see Benson's Mercedes. Being bright yellow it was difficult to miss. Then back to the clubhouse, the locker rooms and the bars. By then he would probably have sent his two minders back down the eighteenth to the seventeenth. After drawing a blank Mr Shao would probably go to the secretary's office and ask there.

The whole thing would take half an hour, perhaps longer. And then? Then they'd probably postpone any further moves until after dark. They'd come to his apartment in Stanley, and they'd find it fully furnished and fully provisioned. Clothes still hanging in the closets. Only no one would be there, for

9

this was the way he had planned it if things went wrong.

It was a lovely apartment, the best he'd ever had, with views of the South China Sea which would never be repeatable. Nor, of course, would the women.

He told himself they wouldn't rush. There was no need to. As far as they were concerned Benson wasn't going anywhere.

How had he got into a situation like this? He'd always thought that financially Hong Kong would do for him what London and New York never had. Always wheeling, always dealing, always planning. Jesus!

Before they entered the Cross Harbour Tunnel they were passed by another taxi full of Australians clutching flags and cans of lager. And then he remembered that the International Rugby Sevens tournament had finished two days earlier.

He used to go with Richard. It was a kind of tradition; Richard coming out each March and making up a party. One year Maria had come with Richard. Jack had taken . . . Lisa, or Joan, or Mei-Li, or . . . the names escaped him now.

Pity about Richard, but what the hell. It was every man for himself in this life.

They came up into daylight again and stopped at his office on Des Voeux Road, Central. For a moment he thought of asking the driver to wait, but he knew he'd get an argument and he didn't have time. He paid and went up to the twenty-third floor.

A glass door on the left side of the foyer said DUNLAP & BENSON among several of his agencies. This was the only one with his own name on it; the only one in which he had a real share. One day, if he'd kept his nose clean and worked hard, it might have made him moderately well-off. But the word 'moderate' had never interested Benson and already he was thinking of it in the past.

He went into the outer office. His secretary, Mrs Feniman, looked up from her desk and said, 'You finished early.'

'The course was empty.'

She was in her mid thirties, the English wife of a Ministry of Works official. Good-looking in a pale, ethereal way. She wore long chiffon dresses and pale make-up. After an office party two Christmasses before, he had taken her home in a taxi and tried to make her and she'd gently untangled herself and said, 'Don't be crude, Jack.'

He'd been angry at the time. Then, after he had sobered up, he had wondered how she would react at work, but she had never referred to it again either by word or look.

'I was going to make some tea,' she said, rising and floating towards the little kitchenette.

'I'd love some.'

Benson's suite had a small bathroom and a built-in wardrobe. He showered and changed quickly and Mrs Feniman brought him his tea.

He locked the inner door and opened a large wall safe. It contained a soft leather hold-all. He opened it and took out his passport and an open-date airline ticket to London, the rest of the bag was filled with money. There was the equivalent of a quarter of a million sterling in US dollars, Swiss francs, German marks and British pounds, with a couple of thousand Hong Kong dollars on the side.

In terms of what he owed it was not a lot, but it would give him a new start wherever he chose to make one. It would also support him in some style in London until that new start could be negotiated. He put the passport and ticket in the top pocket of his dark blue linen sports shirt, took his cup into the outer office and said, 'Seconds?'

Mrs Feniman smiled palely and said, 'I'll make some fresh.'

She went back into the kitchenette, as he knew she would. He picked up the bag, quickly crossed to the outer door then called, 'I'll be back in a minute, I'm going to get some cigarettes.'

On the street, he thought: no cabs this time, don't leave a trail. So he caught the Star Ferry to Kowloon. It ploughed out into the choppy waters and he felt the cool breeze on his body.

He wondered if they would find the New Territories taxi driver or what they would do to Mrs Feniman. He hoped they wouldn't hurt her.

On the Kowloon side he felt safe enough to pick up a cab. 'Kai Tak,' he said.

11

Although a plane lands at Kai Tak Airport every three minutes, the terminal is run with the same dedicated efficiency as Hong Kong's business life. Today it was more than usually crowded as the rugby supporters took their flights home.

There were Australians, New Zealanders, British, French and Irish – many of whom were partly drunk. Benson went straight to the British Airways desk. There was a long stand-by queue. And an even longer one at Cathay Pacific. He studied the departures board with care, for there were never flight announcements at Kai Tak.

As he stood there he began to feel afraid again. He thought people were looking at him, registering his face, remembering him.

In the next thirty minutes there were departures to Jakarta, Manila and Perth. If he had to disappear, neither Jakarta nor Manila seemed like good ideas. Not with a white skin. Perth, then.

He went over to Qantas. There was one seat left. He suddenly remembered that the only money he had, except for change, was in the hold-all. He couldn't open it now. He thought of going to the lavatories, locking himself in and opening it there.

But the departure light was flashing and someone else was queueing behind him. So he paid by American Express. Even as he did so he knew it was a mistake.

He had to run the last few yards to the departure gate and then he was being shown his seat in Smoking. Everywhere he looked there were Chinese and Japanese faces. They seemed to be staring at him.

He took his seat and the hostess said, 'Your bag, sir.'

'No, I want it with me.'

'I'm sorry.'

'No!'

Next to him an Australian rugby supporter wearing an orange rosette looked at him oddly.

'It's got to be stowed for take-off, sir. You can put it under your seat.'

'Oh. OK.'

12

He put the bag on the floor and gripped it between his feet.
'Where you making for?' the Australian said.
'Iceland.'
The man paused for a moment and then laughed. 'You're
taking the long way round, sport.'
'I'm sorry. I don't speak English.'
He leaned back. His whole body had begun to shake.

2

Terry was only truly happy when he was running. And he was running now. One foot after another, his soft-soled trainers making a light thud ... thud ... thud ... on the cold London pavements.

Day ... lee ... Day ... lee ... Day ... lee ...

He kept up the rhythm of his running. Left ... right ... left ... right ... Day ... lee ... Day ... lee ... The Thames was behind him and he ran up Northumberland Avenue and into Trafalgar Square, a boy of fourteen, small for his age, dressed in a green and black track suit and a phosphorescent green woollen beanie.

The evening rush-hour was in full swing. People pushed and shoved and nearly bumped into him. But Terry was agile. He swerved and jinked and ducked through the phalanxes of office workers at bus queues.

They looked at him curiously. Everyone looked at him. Or so he thought. Could they see the blood? The fingers of his right hand were sticky with it. The knife in his pocket was covered in it. Why were they looking at him? Were there traces of blood on his face?

He rubbed his cheeks and nose and forehead with his arm. This brought a sudden flash of memory. The first day at school when he was eight and they had held him down and rubbed at his brown face 'to see if it came off.'

He rejected the memory but that only caused him to remember why he was running. If he thought about what had happened he became afraid. Terribly afraid. So afraid that he tasted copper in his mouth and felt like vomiting – or 'bringing up' as his grandfather had called it.

He was afraid of what the people could see: afraid of the

eyes, the swivelling heads. Would they remember? Would they tell?

Is that the police? I want to report a boy running through Trafalgar Square. A black boy. All covered in blood.

But he wasn't black. Not true black. 'What we calls a quadroon,' his grandfather had said. 'You the colour of Daley Thompson. Can't be bad.'

He ran under Admiralty Arch and along the Mall. The plane trees were still bare of leaves. The March evening was bitterly cold with a wind out of the east, so dry that he could feel his lips cracking. The sky was leaden and there were freckles of powder snow. The lights were on. Dusk had come to the West End.

He ran beside the windswept, paper-strewn expanse of St James's Park with Buckingham Palace looming up in front of him. This wasn't his London. He'd hardly ever been here. He swung right into Green Park and ran towards Piccadilly.

Leicester Square and Chinatown, with their amusement arcades, beckoned. But he knew he'd be finished if he went there. Too many eyes. Too many street kids who already knew him by sight.

Day . . . lee . . . Day . . . lee . . . went the trainers on the pavement. The moment he began to think of running, the fear oozed away, he was back in his world.

Let's see. Who could he be. Arthur Wint or Herb McKenley. 1948. Gold and silver for Jamaica. What a year! His grandfather said he'd never seen anything like it. Wint with his long legs going into his 'float' after the first hundred metres. Jamaica one and two. The best four-hundred-metre runners in the world. His grandfather had said so – and his grandfather *knew*.

Or he could just be himself. Why not? Arthur Wint. Herb McKenley. Himself. And Garner Maitland. OK. Four-hundred-metre relay final. He, Terry Collins, running the anchor leg.

Into Piccadilly now and heading west towards Knightsbridge. Thud . . . thud . . . thud . . . went the trainers.

Terry! Why couldn't they have given him a proper name? Garner Maitland. His grandfather. That was a name. Don

15

Quarrie. Two hundred metres. Twenty-point two-three. Gold for Jamaica 1976. That was a name. Haseley Crawford. Gold. Hundred metres. Trinidad. That was a name.

Wendell Motley . . . Harrison Dillard . . . Jesse Owens . . . Lee Evans . . . Bob Beamon . . . Hayes Jones . . . Willie Davenport . . . Lloyd LaBeach . . . Norwood Barney Ewell . . . The litany of names acted as a kind of tranquilliser.

'You take Harrison Dillard,' his grandfather had said. 'Finest high hurdler I evah seen. Doesn't make it in the US trials. So gets in the team for his sprintin' alone. Man wins the hundred-metre gold.'

Kipchoge Keino . . . John Akii-Bua . . . Edwin Moses . . .

So, OK, here's the final of the four-by-four hundred. US, East Germany, West Germany, Great Britain, Russia, Cuba, Nigeria *a-a-n-n-d-d – Jamaica!*

Lead-off man, Arthur Wint. Garner Maitland running the second leg. Then Herb McKenley and Terry at anchor. Except he wouldn't be Terry but Huntsman. He'd seen the name on a tailoring shop a few days before and it had stuck in his mind. Huntsman Collins. *That* was a name.

'Now, Arthur, he was like a flagpole,' his grandfather had said. 'Longest legs I evah saw. And after the first hundred, mon, he *floated*.'

Floating across Knightsbridge now with the traffic heavy on the south carriageway of Hyde Park. In among the trees, thudding along Rotten Row, not knowing where he was going, what he was going to do; just running.

Running past the Albert Memorial and into Kensington Gardens. Jamaica on the inside lane. Trailing down the straight. Arthur in his float. Then the bend and the stagger unwinds and . . . 'and there's Arthur coming through like a train . . . '

And then Maitland . . . and McKenley . . . and Huntsman Collins . . . Don't drop the baton . . . ! Clean change . . . ! Now just hang on tight . . . !

The cheers were still ringing in his head when he found himself in strange territory and stopped running.

It was dusk now and he was alone. A pond glittered over to his left. A statue stood tall on his right.

16

Where was he?

He ran back a little way, found a deserted path along the Serpentine and followed it. The water was grey and forbidding. Pieces of stale bread flung to the ducks during the day had broken up into small waterlogged pieces. He came to the statue of a small boy. In the dim light he could make out the words PETER PAN on the stone plinth. Something stirred in his memory. Yes, he had it. A crocodile. And Captain Hook. And the Darling family. He forgot momentarily about where he was and why he was there and stood staring up at the statue feeling an ache in his heart. His grandfather had read him the story when he had first come to stay with them. That's what he desperately wanted now, a family like the Darlings. Somewhere safe and loving.

He could not form this into coherent thoughts but that is what the ache meant.

Behind the statue was a wall. He would be out of the wind on the other side. It was not a high wall and he climbed over it, dropping softly down on the other side. Instantly, he found himself in a strange new world.

The wall enclosed an area of about half an acre. Shrubs and trees had been planted to hide and disguise it further. On one side was a large gate and on the far side to Terry stood a bulldozer.

In the enclosed area were enormous heaps of grass cuttings, piles of paper bags, newspapers and discarded Styrofoam cups. Thin wisps of smoke were rising from some of the grass heaps. It was one of the park rubbish dumps, but a relatively clean one. Terry looked at the grassy mounds with an appraising eye. It was just possible this place might temporarily answer his need.

He went over to a mound of grass and touched it. It felt dry and faintly warm. Now if he had some food he—

'What d'you want, sonny?'

He whirled.

A man in overalls was sitting on one of the grass piles. He had a bottle in his hand. Now he screwed back the top and placed it in his pocket. He rose and picked up a rake. There was something menacing about him in the evening wind.

17

Terry was momentarily stunned. Unable to move his legs. 'Don't you know the park gates are closed at dusk? Can't you read? There're notices everywhere!'

He was in his late forties with a tired face and tired eyes. He wore, over his overalls, a black donkey jacket and a scarf. On his head was a flat cap.

'What are you doing, anyway? This isn't open to the public.'

'I been running,' Terry said.

'Jogging? At your age? You think you're going to get a heart attack?' The man looked at him for a moment and then his face softened. 'Still, I work here and I'm as late as you. Come on, I'll show you something. Just between the two of us, OK?'

'OK.'

The park employee made his way along the Serpentine. On the other side of the darkling water Terry could see thickets of bush and trees.

'That's where the ducks sleep,' the man said, pointing to the weedy growth.

He led Terry to the iron railings along the north side of the park. In the middle of a large rhododendron bush he hid his rake and then he moved a loose railing, sliding it to the right. It created a gap just big enough for the two of them to slip through.

'Remember what I said,' the man said. 'You never seen this.'

'Yeah. OK.'

The man disappeared in the direction of the Lancaster Gate tube station, the bottle making a bulge in his back pocket. Terry ran across the Bayswater Road. Now the streets were unfamiliar. He had never been here before. Everywhere he looked he could see Mercedes, BMWs, and Jaguars. He stood uncertainly, not knowing what to do but knowing he had to do *some*thing.

3

While Terry was running through London, a woman called Maria Dunlap was having tea with a friend. They were in Maria's home near the village of Liss on the Hampshire – Sussex borders.

The house was a large and rather grand red-brick Edwardian villa, with Tyrolean woodwork, and a steeply pitched tiled roof. It had fourteen rooms on two floors if you counted the billiard room, sixteen on three if you counted the attics. It had been modernised five times in twenty years but the servants' bells, although they no longer worked, still hung in their mahogany and glass case above the kitchen door. It stood in two acres of garden at the end of a gravel drive and was hidden from its neighbours by overgrown hedges of laurel.

Maria hated the shiny leaves so much that she sometimes discussed with Richard, her husband, the possibility of having it taken out and a beech hedge planted in its place.

Sometimes he said, 'Fine. Good idea,' and sometimes he said, 'We'll lose our privacy, but if that's what you want then do it.'

That's as far as it ever got. He was too busy and she was too . . . too what? Tired? God knows, it wasn't that she didn't have enough time to organise it, but somehow it never got done.

The English were very private, she thought. But then the Germans were even more so. And being half English and half German she should have been doubly private. In fact, she had always been gregarious, outgoing – until she came to live in this house the year before.

It had been a mistake, especially since she had lost the very reason for coming here. She had wanted her child brought up outside London. It was *she* who had insisted they leave the London house and find something in the country. At that time house prices were so high they had sold their house in Hampstead, the one that Richard's father had left them, to an American multinational, and had been able, with the money, to keep the mews house in Bayswater for Richard to use, and to buy this villa in the country.

They were having tea in the small 'winter' sitting-room on the ground floor where a coal fire burned cheerfully. Maria was in one of the two leather armchairs, her legs drawn up under her. She was wearing black jeans and a loose white polo-neck sweater. Her thin, triangular face was shadowy in the half light of dusk.

In the other armchair was one of her oldest acquaintances in Britain, Jean Carradine. They had been at school together in Hampshire, had never been close friends and now, even though Jean lived less than twenty miles away, saw each other infrequently.

The afternoon had been taken up with whatever-happened-to-so-and-so conversation, with special emphasis on marriages. Many were on the rocks and both women gained secret satisfaction from the fact.

Jean was Maria's age, thirty, but there the resemblance ended. Jean had had two children very young, a boy and a girl, both were at boarding-school. Maria had none.

Where Maria was rakishly thin, Jean had a kind of serene plumpness. Where Maria's eyes were filled with worries and doubts, Jean's gave the feeling that her main concern was what to give the children for their birthdays.

As they talked and as the cigarette butts grew in Maria's ashtray, the light had gone out of the afternoon and grey dusk had crept into the room.

Maria had been fearful of putting on the lights, fearful of moving in her chair in case she precipitated an answering move from Jean. But now they could hardly see each other and finally she stretched to the big table lamp and switched it on.

Jean's reaction was instant. She looked at her watch. 'Is that the time?'

'It's early. When does Jeffrey get back from the City?'

'Oh, not before eight.'

'Well, it won't take you more than half an hour to get home. What about a drink?'

Jean shifted in her chair. 'I don't . . . '

'Come on, just one.'

The telephone rang in the hall.

'Excuse me.'

Maria went out and picked up the receiver. It was a man wanting Richard. His voice sounded foreign.

'I'm afraid he's not here,' she said.

'It is about business.'

As if it was ever anything else, she thought.

'He'll be back next week,' she said.

'He has an office in London?'

'That's right.' She gave him the address and telephone number. He thanked her politely and rang off.

She came back into the sitting-room feeling deflated. For a moment she had convinced herself it was Richard and that he was telephoning to say he was coming home.

'What about that drink?' Maria said.

'All right. Just a sherry, then. A small one.'

Maria gave her an amontillado, and poured a gin and tonic for herself. Now that she was on her feet she put on the other lights in the room and drew the curtains. 'That's better. It shuts out the dark.'

The thought twisted in her stomach like a knife. Soon Jean would finish her sherry and refuse another and she'd go off to get Jeffrey's dinner and Maria would be left in this large empty house – in the dark.

Dusk. Nightfall. The very words frightened her. Things happened in the dark that did not happen in daylight.

They talked about Jeffrey's ulcer and how ulcers weren't so much of a problem these days with the new drugs. And then Jean finished her drink and rose, smoothing down the pleats of her Jaeger skirt.

'Have another,' Maria said. 'You don't have to go just—'

'I really must.'

She fetched Jean's coat and they made their way to the

21

front door. Caesar came out of the kitchen to see what was happening. Caesar was a large Alsatian Richard had given her as protection and company when he was away. Maria had never come across a dog with so little personality. It neither liked nor disliked her and she felt the same about it. All it wanted from her was food. It was supposed to be a guard dog but never barked when anyone came. It would put its head out into the passage and then slink back to the warmth of the kitchen. Apart from anything else, it smelled.

They stood in the front hall, chatting.

'Are you going away?' Jean said.

Maria shook her head. 'Richard's gone to Lisbon.'

'For Easter?'

'It's business.'

She must have spat the word out for Jean's eyes suddenly widened.

'Yes,' Maria said, 'the Easter weekend. He has to go on the Easter weekend.'

'Jeffrey's parents are coming,' Jean said quickly. 'Otherwise . . .'

'No, no, I didn't mean . . . ' She was embarrassed now.

'Never mind, I'm sure it'll be worth it.'

'Worth it? Who for? For me or him?'

'I mean business–wise.'

'Would you like it if Jeffrey said he was going away for the whole weekend?'

'Oh, he'd never do that,' Jean said comfortably. 'The bank closes for the Easter weekend.'

Maria got between Jean and the door and stood with her back to it. 'You know how many weekends Richard has been here in the last six weeks? Two. That's all. The rest is work, work, work. Two weekends! And most of the week he's at the house in London.'

'I'm sure it's only temporary.'

'Oh, you think it's temporary. What if it's permanent? And me stuck down here! What if he's got another woman?'

There. It was out.

Jean's eyebrows shot up. 'Come, Maria.'

'It's true. I'm sure he has.'

Jean smiled, a dimpled plump smile. 'You're sure it isn't imagination? Don't we always think of that when they're late or away?'

Maria suddenly hated herself. She saw Jean now as a kind of vegetable, a marrow perhaps, and she was ashamed. But she had been nursing the thought for so long that it had simply burst through her guard.

'I'm sorry,' she said.

'But if you want to talk about it . . . '

Maria could hear a quickening of interest in her tone.

'No. It's as you say. My imagination. Forget it.'

She switched on the outside light and opened the door and a few moments later stood in the icy wind waving to Jean and watching the red taillights of the car disappear down the drive.

Now she was alone. Really alone. It was Wednesday evening and she wouldn't see Richard again until Monday night. Five nights.

She locked and bolted and chained the front door. Caesar came out of the kitchen again to see what the commotion was. 'Come,' she said. 'Come, Caesar.' She held out a hand. She needed the dog's friendship and she offered her own in exchange. But Caesar stood in the doorway and watched her.

'All right, don't!' She went back into the sitting-room and began to clear away the tea things. She must stop feeling sorry for herself, she thought. There were hundreds of thousands of women like her – divorced or widowed – who would be spending this Easter weekend alone. And probably thousands whose husbands were having affairs. What made her angry was that his woman had started phoning him here, at home. *Her* home. There had been three calls in the past few days. The woman had asked for Richard and when Maria had said he wasn't there and could she take a message the voice had said no, no message, and the receiver at the other end had been replaced.

Don't think about that.

All right, what would these hundreds of thousands of women be doing? They'd certainly be doing something. But what?

Would they be going to the movies or theatres or restaurants

23

by themselves? She had never been to a theatre by herself. There had always been Richard in recent years, and before him, Jack.

Except Jack wasn't a theatre person unless it was something like *Oh Calcutta!*. But they'd had other things to do, other fish to fry.

A lump suddenly formed in her throat as she looked back down the vista of her life to this golden time. Did everyone have a time like that? Had Jean? Had she had a lover like Jack? Had she been taken motor-racing and yachting and nightclubbing when she was nineteen?

People said Jack Benson was a bastard. It was true. But every girl needed a bastard at some time in her life.

So, no movies or theatres or restaurants by herself. She could play billiards by herself. That would be fun. Or she could get into the car and go for long drives by herself. Or stay in and watch television and read and relax. Except that's what she always did. Ever since she'd lost the baby she'd been 'relaxing'.

'Why don't you take it easy?' That was Richard's phrase.

And Dr Hartwell had said, 'It's perfectly natural to be depressed. Most women who miscarry are depressed afterwards. But you must eat. You've lost too much weight.'

She had lost weight. She'd also lost her interest in food. Not, however, in liquor. She'd have to be careful of that this weekend.

She went round the house checking the catches of the windows and the locks on the doors and then came back to the fire.

It was such a cliché, she thought. Wife stuck in the country, husband works up in town. Husband meets another woman and starts an affair.

Maybe she should have an affair too. After all, what was sauce for the goose, et cetera. The problem was she didn't know anyone down here to have an affair with, even if she'd wanted to.

She picked up the paper with the TV listings and began to check the programmes. It was going to be a long, long weekend.

24

4

'Dinner's ready,' Lottie said. 'It's on the table. Where's your father?'

'I heard him a moment ago,' Leo said.

'His last pupil's at five. It's now half past six. Tell him please.'

'We eat too early,' Leo said. 'Why do we always eat at six-thirty?'

His mother went back to the kitchen without replying but his sister Ruth, who had been looking through legal papers, said, 'You're always going on about it. Dad likes to eat early. So does Sidney.' She looked across at her husband as though daring him to deny it. 'Anyway, Stanley always eats early.'

Stanley was her six-year-old son, now sitting on the floor colouring in a picture book.

'One question and I get the complete lecture,' Leo said.

He had recently been re-reading *Hay Fever* and suddenly he saw his family in a Coward play.

We are in the drawing-room of the SILVER family's mansion flat in North London on a snowy March evening. The room is in need of redecoration, but has a faded, pre-war elegance. It lies in West Hampstead, on the wrong side of the Finchley Road, and is rent controlled. The owners have for many years been trying to get the SILVERS to leave, without success.

In the drawing-room we discover LEO SILVER, who is in his late twenties. He is dressed in black slacks, black polo-neck and black leather jacket. He wears black most of the time and is pretty damned presentable, if he says so himself.

His sister RUTH MARCUS, a solicitor, is eight years older. She is a large, heavy woman who favours long dresses

25

and ethnic jewellery. Her husband SIDNEY MARCUS, who has his own estate agency in Kentish Town, is plump, balding and, to LEO, something of a bore. Their son, STANLEY, is LEO's one and only nephew, of whom he is very fond.

From time to time LOTTIE SILVER, an untidy woman of sixty summers, puts her head round the door to tell them that dinner is ready. In the distance we can hear the tinkle of a keyboard. This is being played by the paterfamilias, MANFRED SILVER (original name SILBERBAUER) who is a pianoforte – his word – teacher and composer. We meet the family in their usual argumentative state.

Time, the present.

Enter MANFRED SILVER. He is short with a full head of silver-grey hair of which he is inordinately proud. To complement his artistic way of life he affects a small Van Dyke beard. As he enters he is drying his hands on a large paper napkin which he drops into a wastepaper basket already overflowing with similar used napkins.

He kisses RUTH and STANLEY. For a moment SIDNEY, the son-in-law, thinks that he, too, is about to be kissed and looks apprehensive. The moment passes . . .

'It's half past six,' Manfred said. Like his wife he still had a discernible Austrian accent. Both had come with their families as refugees just before the outbreak of war.

'Dinner's on the table,' Leo said.

'Has he . . . ?' Manfred said, looking at his grandson.

'Yes, father,' Ruth said.

'Me too,' Leo said. 'I've washed my hands, my feet, my ears. And so has Sidney and so has Ruth.'

'Don't be smart with me, Leo,' Manfred said.

Ruth glared at her brother, but Leo pretended not to notice.

'You want salmonella?' Manfred said. 'I'll visit you in hospital.'

'You ever heard Dardanella?' Sidney said to Leo as they took their places at the table. 'Marvellous.'

Mr Silver looked sharply at him and so did Ruth, but Sidney was devoid of sarcasm or guile. He found it difficult to discover a suitable personality for himself on these family evenings. Often he tried to work late, but Ruth would come to the office and drag him out. Leo had once described him to his father as a 'simple soul'. His father had replied that Sidney was a 'twat', a word Leo had never heard him use before.

Mrs Silver, on the other hand, put up with Sidney. He had, after all, married her rather plain daughter and given her the ultimate prize, a grandson. But now that she had one grandson she wanted more and Ruth was digging in her heels. She and Sidney worked hard and had bought their own house in a part of Kentish Town which Sidney described, in the only descriptive literature with which he was familiar, as 'lower Highgate'.

They were now paying off a huge mortgage and Ruth's income was vital. She worked for the firm of Bluestone, Koppel, Motzkin & Bloch in Camden Town, specialising in matrimonial upheavals.

They ate in silence for a while then Leo said, 'How's the symphony coming, Dad?'

'Better you don't ask,' Mrs Silver said. 'It gets bigger and bigger. Bigger than Mahler. Bigger than Bruckner. Bigger even than that man who died a few years ago. Havergal somebody.'

'Bryan,' her husband said.

'Brian Havergal? No, I don't think so.'

'Havergal Bryan, for God's sake! And it's not as big as his.'

'Full orchestra? Two choirs? Steer horn? Hour and a half? In this day and age who needs it? People want trios, quartets. Even a sextet is too expensive.'

'So now you're the expert,' Manfred said. 'Mrs Lottie Silver. Musical expert.'

'All right, Manfy, we all know you had a piece played.'

'A piece!' Manfred Silver said, helping himself to more fish. 'That's nice.'

In 1958 his 'Gog and Magog' for contralto, harp and tympani had been performed in the Wigmore Hall to an audience of twenty-four, all of whom had been friends or relatives. Its poor reception had been a seminal moment in his life. After that he had changed his style. He had rejected

27

Schoenberg (meretricious) and Alban Berg (unmusical) and turned back the clock. He had written a ballet 'The Happy Peasant' based on Brueghel's painting *Bauertanz* and set it to the music of Goldmark. He had used half a dozen Bach church cantatas to create an oratorio for four choirs and double organ. Neither of these had ever been performed. For the past five years he had been working on his great Falklands Symphony to celebrate Mrs Thatcher's naval assault on the islands of the same name.

'I think I'm getting a house in Reddington Road,' Sidney said, wiping his son's mouth.

'Reddington Road!' Lottie said. 'That's very posh. You start selling houses there and you'll be a millionaire in a few years.'

'It's not definite,' Sidney said hastily, in case he had given the wrong impression.

'Sidney says house prices are picking up again,' Ruth said.

'Apricots?' Lottie said, passing round the dish. 'You want cream or custard, darling?' she said to Stanley.

'Can I have both?'

They ate their puddings.

'Where's Zoe, tonight?' Lottie said, fixing her eye on Leo.

'Working.'

'She's always working late.'

'Not always. Sometimes.'

'It seems like it. She never comes to dinner any more.' Lottie brooded over this for a few moments and then said, 'When are you two going to get married?'

'Why? You want more grandchildren?' Leo said. 'We don't have to get married for that.'

'Don't get smart with your mother,' Manfred said.

'Anyway, who would marry a policeman?' Ruth said.

'People marry solicitors,' Leo said. 'Look at Sidney.'

'Anyway, he's not just a policeman,' his mother said.

'Yes, I am just a policeman.'

'You're a detective! That's not a policeman. And a sergeant.'

'Wow!' said Ruth.

'And one day you're going to be Commissioner.'

28

'If Leo gets to be Commissioner I'll eat . . . I don't know what I'll eat,' Ruth said.

The phone rang and Lottie, who was nearest, went to answer it. It was for Leo. 'It sounds like that Mr Macrae. That's always trouble. He's not a nice person, Leo. Can't you work for someone else? Get a transfer?'

'He looked like he was dirty to me,' Manfred said.

Leo pushed past her and took the phone in the hall. In a few moments he was back, pulling on his black leather jacket.

'Don't rush!' his mother said. 'How can you digest?'

'I'll digest in the car,' Leo said, kissing her.

'What is it?' Sidney said, his eyes suddenly shining. 'A murder?'

'Yes,' Leo said. 'A murder.'

Detective Superintendent George Macrae sat on the edge of his bed and replaced the phone in its cradle. He was naked and his large white back was turned to the woman on the bed.

'I've got to go,' he said.

She was naked too. She was in her early twenties and her name was Frenchy, although the nearest she had ever been to France was the seafront at Brighton. The name was not nationalistic but professional. She had been christened Sharon.

'That's a shame. We was only just getting going. I could do you a quickie if you liked.'

He bent down to look for his socks. The room was in a mess, but then it usually was. It smelled of whisky and tobacco smoke. She saw the long white ridge that travelled down his left arm and touched it lightly with her fingertips. She could feel him flinch as he moved his arm away. He never liked her touching the scar, which was why she did it.

'Some other time,' he said.

She leaned on one elbow and watched him dress. She was a large woman with large breasts and a bottom you could get your teeth into. Macrae liked them fleshy.

29

He stood up and felt slightly dizzy. Christ, he didn't want to go on a job in this state.

'Why don't you get us some coffee?' he said. 'Strong.'

'Sure.'

She got off the bed and, still naked, wandered downstairs to the kitchen.

He heard her voice from below and went to the bedroom door.

'What?' he said.

'I said you want to get this place cleaned up, George. There's dirty plates and old Chinese take-aways and I saw this bit of cheese in the fridge last summer. It's got fur on it.'

'I like it that way.'

He was putting on his jacket when she reappeared with the coffee. She was wearing his silk dressing-gown. The one Mandy had given him. Seeing her nipples against the soft silk he felt himself becoming aroused again but put the thought from his mind. There would be other times.

He drank the coffee and took some money from his wallet.

'No, George. You don't have to. You *never* have to.'

'I know that.' He took her face and kissed her on the lips in a surprisingly tender gesture. 'It's difficult enough to part a Scot and his money so take it while you can. Here.'

She looked irritated but took the five-pound notes. 'You don't like to be beholden, do you?'

'Lock up when you go. Put the key through the letter box. I'll ring you soon.'

He went out into the bitterly cold night trying to clear his head. Too many things could go wrong when it was a murder.

5

In London the snow had stopped but the wind off the Thames was bitter. The South Bank, including the Festival Hall and the National Theatre, with its walkways and stairways and underpasses and brutal concrete buttresses, was a deserted wilderness, its strings of coloured lights swaying in the wind.

Hungerford Bridge crosses the Thames at this point. It is really two bridges, a railway bridge and a footbridge. The footbridge has long been a place for dossers and meths drinkers and, in recent years, for street kids and teenage beggars.

A small crowd had gathered at one end. Here, there was a walkway. Above the walkway, among the concrete pillars and angular walls, was a hidden area the size of a small room.

It was lit now by the beams of two hand torches. One was held by Detective Superintendent Macrae of Cannon Row police station, the other by his assistant, Sergeant Leopold Silver.

The torch beams showed the area to be a kind of den or human lair, silent except for the noise of dripping water. There were two sleeping bags lying side by side, placed on newspapers and covered by polythene sheets, two candles in plastic bottles, and a small pile of magazines.

The torch beams moved along the walls illuminating festering patches of lime, which gave the place the appearance of some outbreak of concrete psoriasis. Water dripped into the area forming a pool on the floor. Next to the pool, its foot lying partly in the water, lay the body of a black man.

He lay on his back with his legs drawn up and both

31

hands covering his belly; the position of someone asleep on a grassy bank in the sun.

Macrae, who was just over six feet tall, was bent nearly double as he played his torch over the body.

'That leather jacket must be worth a couple of hundred,' he said to Silver. Then he looked at his watch. 'It's nine forty-three.' Silver made a note.

Macrae called down to the constable below him, 'Aren't those lights here yet?'

'Just coming, sir.'

In almost the same second, floodlights lit the walkway and the interior of the den.

Now the black man's face could be seen more clearly. The lips were open at the corners and the teeth were showing.

'I think that's what's called a rictus smile,' Leo Silver said.

'That's what you learned at the university, is it?' Macrae turned towards the lights. 'Any sign of the doctor?'

'No, sir,' came a disembodied voice. 'But Forensic's here.' He paused, then said, 'Screens are going up, sir. Do you want the footbridge closed?'

'What's the crowd like?'

'Nothing much. Too cold, sir.'

'Then the screens'll do.'

He turned back to the body and crouched next to it. Carefully he lifted the shirt. It had dark stains around what looked like a four-inch tear. The black stomach was exposed. Here the tear became a wound. Blood had caked and hardened and now only a light-coloured liquid oozed from it.

'Christ!' Silver said. 'That's what's-his-name . . . Foster. Henry Foster.'

'Who the hell's Henry Foster?'

'The TV journalist. He's on at breakfast time.'

'Never watch it. You sure?'

Silver leaned down and tried to visualise the face with the mouth closed. 'I'm sure, sir. Has his own interview programme called *Focus*.'

'Well, he won't be interviewing anyone any more.'

Just then a voice from below said, 'Doctor's here, sir.'

Macrae moved over against the wall and the police doctor

was helped up on to the concrete shelf that formed the floor of the shelter.

'Evening, G. D.' Macrae said.

'Oh, it's you, George. Evening, sergeant.'

The rota doctor, G. D. Kanwar, was an Indian in his mid forties, about Macrae's own age.

'I might have guessed it would be you. Every time a holiday comes up I say to myself there will be an air-traffic controllers' strike on the Continent and George Macrae will be mixed up in something nasty. Is it nasty?'

'Take a look.'

Dr Kanwar opened his bag and took out a stethoscope.

'The only thing you'll hear with that is the trains,' Macrae said.

Dr Kanwar ignored him. He listened briefly for a heartbeat and then began the examination proper. Macrae watched him broodingly. Silver watched them both. It was true, he thought, Macrae attracted crime like marmalade attracts wasps. Things always seemed to happen when he was on duty.

'I've found a new one,' Macrae said to Dr Kanwar.

'Oh, yes?'

'Hammersmith Broadway. The Red Hot Raja. Something like that.'

'Don't know it.'

'Proper tandoori. They've made a bloody great hole in the kitchen floor and stuck it in there.'

'What did you have? Madras? Or need I ask?' Dr Kanwar unbuttoned the corpse's shirt.

'Of course. Lamb. And stuffed parathas and onion bhajee. Mixed vegetables. Pilau.'

'Hot enough for you?'

'Well, you know me.'

'I suppose you asked for chilli sauce?'

'Just a little.'

Dr Kanwar began to examine eyes and ears. He said, 'My grandfather went through the curry cycle. Couldn't get it hot enough. Eventually he was eating pure chilli sauce with a little food on the side. There was a nasty noise one day when the capillaries in his abdomen burst.'

33

Silver felt his gorge rise. He had not seen too many murdered men – or women for that matter – and always had to steel himself. It wasn't the time for foodie jokes, he thought.

Dr Kanwar straightened up. Macrae said, 'How long do you think he's been dead?'

'Maybe two hours.'

After a few more minutes Macrae, Silver and Dr Kanwar dropped down from the area on to the walkway.

'All right,' Macrae said to a uniformed sergeant. 'Forensic can have him now.'

He looked past the screens to the small crowd standing in the icy wind. Some of them, with briefcases, would be late commuters, but the others were dossers and street kids.

He turned to the duty officer. 'I want the dossers and layabouts,' he said.

'All of them, sir?' There was surprise and distaste in his voice as he thought of them in the police station.

'The lot. Someone may have seen something. It's no good taking names and addresses because they haven't got any bloody addresses except cardboard boxes. If you don't grab 'em now you'll never find them again.' He turned to Silver. 'Come on, laddie, let's get to work.'

6

Terry had never been close to a horse before. Now, from his place in the straw above them, he could look down on the broad backs of six horses as they fed in their stalls.

It was a world remote from his experience and it both comforted him and made him nervous. It was a strange mixture. He was afraid of the horses. They were so big and so clearly *belonged* in this place. But at the same time he was comforted by the strong smell of manure and urine and hay which were mixed up together.

It reminded him of a small country circus to which his grandfather had once taken him. They had walked round the back of the big top and his grandfather had spoken to one of his friends who worked there and Terry had been able to get close to the animal cages.

He wasn't sure if this was the same smell as he had smelled then but it *reminded* him of that day with his grandfather. It had been a happy day.

The horses moved restlessly, stamping and whickering, as they fed. It had been this noise which had first drawn him to the stables.

After the park labourer had left him, Terry had wandered through the streets of Bayswater until he came to Paddington Station. By this time he was hungry. He had stood near the top of the stairs that come up from the tube station and had started begging.

'Excuse me, sir, can you spare some change for some food, please?'

That was the way Gail had done it and often she'd collected ten or eleven pounds in an afternoon.

Once, she had taken him on the underground trains and

35

had gone from coach to coach pretending he was her younger brother and that he needed a rail ticket to get home to Portsmouth. She'd made quite a bit of money that way. On the streets people could walk past and ignore you, but on the trains, if you stood in front of them and asked for money they would often give you a few coins just to get rid of you.

But he decided not to go on the tubes. What if he became trapped down there? What if someone saw him? How would he get out? No, better to beg in the streets. However, the people, on their way home on this cold March evening, did not want to part with their money and shoved past Terry angrily.

When he was with Gail he had seen one street kid, not much older than himself, go up to people at Waterloo Station and say, 'Gi' us some money. Come on. Gi' us some money.' And when they didn't he swore at them and gave them two fingers and once threw an empty beer can at an old man.

The boy's name was the Rat and he had carried two knives and a death star and said he'd once cut up a night watchman.

Anyway, Terry didn't get anything from begging. Instead, he was told by a policeman to move along. That had scared the wits out of him. He hadn't seen the cop at all. He'd come out of the dark roadway where the taxis emerge and had suddenly *been there*, right in front of him.

Terry had run across the road almost before the words were out of the cop's mouth. But just to show he wasn't afraid, not really afraid, he had grabbed a bunch of grapes from the street display of a Pakistani supermarket and had gone on running after he'd heard the owner shout: a hundred metres flat out and then floating across Sussex Gardens – just like Arthur Wint.

And that's how he had come to the mews where the stables were. The last thing Terry would ever have thought of was that there were stables in London. In fact if Gail, well, not Gail or his grandfather, but if anyone else had told him, he would have said bullshit.

He hadn't seen the stables, not at first. What had struck

him was that once he turned on to the cobbled surface of the mews, the sounds of London retreated and he could hear the thud-thud-thud of his trainers again.

The mews comprised facing rows of double-storeyed terraced houses which dated from the age when wealthy Londoners had carriages. The houses, where once the horses and the carriages had been kept, were now expensive *bijou* residences.

In summer their walls were covered in roses and clematis and most had pot plants at the front door. It was city-suburban, and Broadhurst Livery Stables (which hired out horses by the hour to be ridden in Hyde Park) did not seem out of place.

Terry had been able to read the name by the lights of the block of flats which towered above Broadhurst Mews. Then he had heard the stamping and the whickering and had smelled the smell of the circus.

In that instant he had decided to spend the night there. He had managed to reach a small window by standing on a tub of dead geraniums and in a matter of seconds had dropped down on to the other side and found himself among the horses.

Some jerked and stamped in alarm, turning wide apprehensive eyes in his direction. He stood in the semi-darkness for some moments. The stables were lit by a weak electric lamp and soon he could make out saddles and bridles and blankets, curry-combs and brushes, buckets and rags.

'Hello,' Terry said softly to the nearest horse, a sixteen-hand grey which was looking at him with mild interest. 'I'm Huntsman.'

Above the horses was a hayloft and Terry climbed up a wooden ladder. The hay had its own sweet smell, another he had never smelled before. He could look down on the horses now and see their flanks rise and fall as they breathed. He could hear the crunch of their teeth grinding the oats.

He had seen on TV how people had rubbed horses down and he thought he would like to do that. Not now, but some-time. He'd like to touch the warm skins and soft muzzles. But later, when they had got used to him.

37

He was glad he had decided to stay here for the night. It was warm out of the wind. He was snug in his track suit and his green beanie.

He finished the grapes. His hands were sticky. There was a tap below and he went down and washed them. He knew he was washing off the blood too, and suddenly he was hit by a quaking fear as he remembered what had happened. The blood spurting out. The groan. For that's all it had been. Just a groan. He took out the knife and washed it too. Don't think. Don't look.

Day . . . lee . . . Day . . . lee . . . It was a ritual incantation, a mantra, but Terry did not know that.

And then the stables, the smells, the horses, all seemed to occupy his mind, to calm him. He stood next to the grey for some minutes wondering if it had a name. He supposed horses had names but he had no idea what they might be. 'I'm going to call you Mr Garner,' he said softly, and put his hand gently on the grey's rump. Instantly, the skin twitched as though to reject a fly.

Terry stepped hurriedly back. 'I ain't going to do nothin' to you,' he said.

He climbed back up into the hayloft. The hay was in tied bales but behind the bales, over the years, straw had collected into a loose pile. Mice and rats lived here, but Terry gave them no thought as he burrowed down into the straw. He gave no thought to anything, and especially not to the following day.

For months and months, lying in his bunk bed and listening to his mother entertain her 'friends', either in her own room or the small lounge, he had tried to block out reality with thoughts of the decathlon.

Ten events in two days . . . that's what Daley Thompson had done and that's what he, Huntsman Collins, would do.

'Mon, you're small for the decat'lon,' his grandfather had said. 'But you'll grow.'

Anyway, what he did was take each discipline in turn, one a night, and thought about it just before he went to sleep. He loved that word *discipline*. His grandfather had never used it, he called them 'events', but on TV when they showed the athletics they always called them disciplines.

The discipline tonight was the long jump.

So, OK, Bob Beamon, Jesse Owens, Ter Ovanesian, (*that* was a name) and Huntsman Collins. Each with one jump left. Jumping at sea level and going for Beamon's Mexico City record. And Huntsman's left heel bruised and sore . . .

'You always going to have heel troubles, mon,' his grandfather had said. 'Every long jumper I evah heard of had heel troubles. All you can do is put in a rubber pad, 'cause you got to *bang* that heel down. You gotta *attack* that board. No use you just lolloping down that run-up. You gotta *hit* and then . . . up . . . into the hitch-kick and you flying . . . jest like a bird . . . ' That's where he knew his grandfather was old-fashioned. They didn't worry about the hitch-kick so much these days. Or the 'hang'. They ran so fast and jumped so far they didn't need anything else.

But that's how his grandfather had talked, and he loved it. In the high jump it was the 'western roll' and the 'eastern cut-off'. They sounded terrific names, Terry thought, even though no one jumped like that these days.

Anyway, it was Huntsman Collins to jump. His markers were red. If he hit each one he'd be on the board with a millimetre to spare . . . So get ready . . . The flag was up . . .

But somehow, tonight, here among the munching horses and the smell of urine and hay, the great competition at White City between him and the world's greatest, he could not quite get started. Gail's face kept coming between him and the long jump pit. It was as though she was standing there, looking along the run-up, a little smile on her face. And when he thought about her, he wanted to cry.

7

Maria was still in the small sitting-room. The fire had died and the TV was on but the sound was down. The flickering pictures were only there for company. She was trying to convince herself that one more drink would make no difference, would, in fact, help the sleeping pill to work, but she knew it was dangerous. She was listening to the house. She could hear the ticking of the long-case clock in the drawing-room. Richard had inherited it from his mother and when they had first come to Hampshire it used to strike the half hours and the hours. But when she was alone the strokes always startled, even frightened, her, especially the twelve strokes of midnight with their heavy symbolism. So she had begged him not to wind the striking mechanism and now the clock only ticked.

Suddenly, from her schooldays, she remembered a line, 'The clock that clicked behind the door.' Goldsmith. An example of onomatopoeia. God, that was a long time ago.

Other noises. The house timbers stretching arthritically. Rain water gurgling in the down pipes. The central heating boiler in the cellar switching itself on.

She had had a *vision* of coming to the country. It was a vision that would take them away from London. She no longer loved a London where their car had been broken into three times and the house twice, and where she no longer wanted to be alone on an underground train at night. Her mother had often told her what London had been like before she married Maria's father and went to live in West Berlin.

Then, it had been a series of villages. In the King's Road in Chelsea there had been real butchers, real fishmongers, real greengrocers. Hampstead was a village, so were Richmond and Chiswick and Greenwich. They had had their own characters.

Her vision had been a simple one, to leave the city and come to the country – something millions had done before her.

She had idealised their life: a baby (perhaps two), a dog, a cat, fields of ripening corn speckled with Flanders poppies. That was the summer. And, in the winter, long brisk walks, cosy evenings round a log fire, the dog stretched out on the hearthrug, the cat on her lap, Richard by her side. Like something out of a Victorian painting called *The End of a Perfect Day*.

Even at its best it would never, could never, have been like that. But that was the vision.

Instead, they had bought a grand but gloomy house, she had lost the baby, was living a life she hated and feared, and was now in the process of losing Richard.

Everything that could have gone wrong had gone wrong. Their kitten had died of cat 'flu. They'd gone to a dog rescue organisation and got Caesar: instant companion, instant protection. But no one had ever told the dog to be a companion, or trained it to be a protector. Later they learned it had been badly ill-treated.

She decided to compromise and have half a drink, so she poured herself a whisky and turned up the news. It was the story of an eighty-two-year-old woman who had been raped in her flat. Hastily, she turned it down again.

She put a Vivaldi flute concerto on the CD to cheer herself up. Richard had given it to her as one of her presents at Christmas.

She knew she was postponing going to bed because of the things she would have to do first. She would have to put Caesar out and sometimes he did not come back when she called. She wasn't going to go blundering about the garden tonight. If he didn't come back he could stay out.

And then she would have to check all the catches on the windows and the doors. She knew she had done them earlier but they needed checking again. Sometimes she checked three or four times.

She also had to find something to read. Something light but lasting, so that if she woke up at two or three she could read until dawn. And she was going to leave lots of lights on. Downstairs and upstairs. Everywhere.

At that moment the telephone rang.

Richard! This time it really would be him! He was phoning to tell her he was back! Or coming back tomorrow. She ran to the hall and picked up the receiver.

'Hello!'

The voice sounded far away, behind a barrage of other sounds.

'Hello?' she said again. 'Richard? Is that you?'

'Maria? It's Jack.'

'I can't hear very well.'

'Jack Benson.'

'Jack! God, I'm sorry, but it didn't sound like you. Where are you?'

'Bombay.'

'Oh.' She felt a sudden sense of disappointment. 'What on earth are you doing there?'

'Look, is Richard there? I need to talk to him.'

'No, he isn't.'

'You mean he's up at the house in London? I've just phoned there. No reply.'

'No, he isn't there either. He left for Lisbon this morning.'

'Oh, shit.'

'Why, is something wrong?'

'Will he be back tomorrow?'

'No. He's gone for the weekend.'

'The whole weekend? The *Easter* weekend?'

'On business. Yes, the whole weekend.'

She heard him laugh softly. 'Poor *liebchen*.'

Part of her was irritated by the soft laughter, but another part seemed to melt. He had called her *liebchen* years ago. It had been his pet name for her on those days when they had gone out to the Wannsee and lain in the sun and then, filled with summer warmth and golden Riesling, had gone back to his apartment behind the Kurfurstenstrasse to make love in the dusk. Her 'Berlin Days' as she thought of them now.

'Trust Richard,' he said.

'It's business,' she repeated, defensively.

'I never thought it was anything else. You on your own?'

'That's right. Is there anything I can do?'

'Well, now . . . ' He let the phrase hang there for a few moments and then said, 'Listen, I'm on my way home.'

'To Hong Kong?'

'Christ, no. London.'

'London!' Her heart gave a jerk. 'Why? What's happened?'

'I get in the day after tomorrow. Why don't we have dinner? I'll tell you about it then. I could come down to Hampshire. That's if you aren't booked up.'

'I'm not.'

'I'll have the day to get straight. We'll go out on the town, if there is a town to go out on down there.'

'There isn't. Not the sort of place you'd be interested in anyway. But . . . '

She paused.

'Are you there?' he said.

'Yes. I'm here.'

'Well, then, how about coming up to London? We could have dinner, do a show. You could stay at the house and I could drive you home the following day. How about that?'

'I don't think that would be a good idea.'

'Why not?'

'Well . . . Richard might phone or something.'

'And he might not. Look, you know Richard. He's a workaholic.'

'Yes, I know, but . . . '

'It's only for one night. You'll be back home the next day. I want to see you. It's important.'

'What is?'

'I'll tell you that, too.'

Other objections surfaced but she pushed them aside.

'*Liebchen*? Are you there?'

'OK.'

'OK what?'

'I'd love to.'

'Marvellous.'

'Why don't I meet you at the house round about six? I've still got my key if you're late.'

43

The house would be neutral ground, she thought. It was part office, part living space, and was often used by Richard's overseas agents when they came to London. Jack had used it several times in the past.

'All right,' she said. 'Six.'

'Oh, and *liebchen*, as far as you're concerned I'm still in Hong Kong. OK? Just in case anyone should ask.'

'Is there any . . . ? Jack?' But the line was dead.

She put down the phone and wandered slowly back to the sitting-room. Without thinking she poured herself a whisky and sat in front of the fire. She could feel her heart thumping away in her ribcage and she knew there was a flush on her cheeks because she could feel the warmth.

Of all the people to phone!

God, it was like a . . . what did they call it in English? A leading?

She tried to picture him. She had not seen him for some time. She conjured up his square good-looking face, with the cynical mouth and eyes.

'He uses people,' Richard had once said of him.

It was true, she thought. But people always used people. Who were they supposed to use? And now she was going to use Jack.

She felt flutterings of guilt and pushed them aside on the tide of another swallow of whisky. She hadn't suggested it, that was one thing. She had begun the sentence but hadn't finished it. Jack had suggested it. She had objected.

Anyway, what was she getting into such a fuss about? He was her husband's partner. His oldest friend. He was asking her to dinner. Helping to alleviate the loneliness of the Easter weekend.

That was all.

She shivered. No, it wasn't all. She knew exactly what she was planning to do. It was called adultery.

8

Cannon Row is one of the oldest police stations in London, and now, after the changes in the Metropolitan Police Force of the last fifteen years, it is probably the most important.

In its complex of new and old buildings it lies strategically near the Houses of Parliament, near New Scotland Yard – now no longer so much an investigative bureau as an administrative one – and its kingdom stretches from the River Thames in the south, to Harrow Road in the north, and takes in virtually the whole of central London.

It is part of the 'new' police force, the one that has replaced the Met of old. In the shake-up famous names like the Murder Squad have disappeared. Now, if you rape someone in Pimlico, beat someone half to death in Piccadilly, or plunge a knife into a black TV journalist's stomach in an underpass near the Thames, it isn't 'Superintendent Bloggs of the Yard' who is called in but 'Eight AMIP' – the Area Major Incident Pool.

London has been divided into eight crime districts; Cannon Row operates the one at the very centre of the very heart of the capital.

On this cold March night its charge room was full to overflowing with derelicts and vagrants, street kids, dossers, meths drinkers – much to the horror of the station officer.

All the interview rooms and many of the offices had been taken over to interrogate this flotsam. In one, Macrae and Silver were questioning a young white male of indeterminate age.

'What's your name, son?' Macrae said for the fourth time.

The boy did not reply. He was cleaning his fingernails with a matchstick.

'You'll tell us sooner or later.'

'Piss off,' the boy said, matter-of-factly, and Silver looked across at Macrae. Sometimes he reacted and sometimes he didn't. It just depended.

The boy was of medium height. Silver would have put his age anywhere between sixteen and eighteen. It was difficult to place him for he had a young–old face. Just looking at that face Silver knew it had seen more of life than he would ever see or ever want to see.

He was wearing a heavy, padded combat jacket in camouflage browns and greens, a pair of jeans and Nike trainers. His head was shaved and he wore two earrings in one ear. His skin was reddish from the winds of winter, his eyes were pale blue and the whites were flushed with red.

'You know what we do with little boys like you?' Macrae said.

'I bet you'll tell us.'

'Yes, I'll tell you,' Macrae said.

The room was sparsely furnished with a table and two chairs. The boy was sitting at the table. Macrae was looming over him, his foot on the other chair. Silver was standing with his back to the wall.

'We put you over our knees and give you a good spanking. That's what we do with little boys.'

'You like spanking boys? I usually charge a tenner for that.'

Macrae paused. Then, almost wearily, he turned his heavy, bull-like head towards Silver and said, 'You have him for a while, laddie.'

He went out and Silver sat down at the table. In contrast to Macrae, he was of medium height and slender. His dark hair sat closely on his skull and his brown eyes were set wide apart. He did not look like a policeman, that is if there is any stereotype of what policemen look like. He had a lithe, cat-like, movement. He might have been anything at all, a doctor, an actor, but his girl, Zoe, had always thought of him as a fencer; a foil to Macrae's blunt weapon.

'Gi' us a fag.'

'I don't smoke.'

'Scared of the Big C?' The boy had a heavy Scottish accent.

'That's right. I'll get you one if you like?'

The young man pursed his lips and blew Silver a kiss.
'You're the soft one, are you?'

'You've been seeing too many movies.'

'Ah, come on! He wants to put the boot in, you can
see that. You offer a fag. And isn't it usually a cup of tea
as well?'

'What's your name?' Silver said.

'What's *his*?'

'Detective Superintendent Macrae.'

'Macrae. I'm a Scot too.'

'I'd never have guessed.'

'Sarky!' And again he pursed his lips in a camp gesture.
'What's *your* name?'

'Sergeant Silver.'

'I knew a bloke called Silver once. Jewish. You Jewish?'

'That's right.'

'That makes us the same.'

'How's that?'

'Well, ethnic minorities. Jews are an ethnic minority. So're
Scots. Or they are in this bloody town. Anyway, I didna know
Jews became coppers.'

'They don't.'

'Why you, then?'

'It's a long story. But we'll have plenty of time to talk
about it.'

'How's that?'

'He'll keep you here.'

'But what for? I hav'na done anything.'

Macrae came back. He had a mug of tea in his hand
and sipped at it.

'Hey!' the boy said. 'You're a Scot. Me too.'

Macrae ignored him. 'Name's Rattray,' he said to Silver.
'Called the Rat for obvious reasons.'

'How long you going to keep me?' the boy said. 'You
got nothing to hold me on!'

'Go and get some tea, laddie,' Macrae said to Silver.
'And you can bring some for him.'

Now there was only Rattray and Macrae. Something

changed in the Rat's eyes. It wasn't much but it was significant and Macrae noticed.

Macrae sipped at his tea and said, 'Have we got it right? Is it Rattray?'

'Get lost!'

It was said with an attempt at bravado but just missed. It was as though his earlier behaviour had been supported by Silver's presence, as if it had been a performance for Silver's benefit.

Macrae put his tea down on the scarred table-top and said, 'There's only the two of us. No need to show off now.' And he hit him. He half rose and swung at the same time. He used the flat of his right hand and caught the Rat in the face, lifting him from the chair as it crashed over backwards. The boy landed halfway across the room.

Blood was pouring from his nose. Macrae sipped again at the hot tea, replaced it on the table, and crossed the room. He caught Rattray by the shirt and slammed him against the wall.

'The thing is I haven't time to play your silly games,' Macrae said. 'Time is money and we're running out of money. That's what they tell me. Oh, did you not know the police force is run by accountants these days? Well, it is. So we've got to be super-efficient. Now, in the name of efficiency I've used the flat of my hand on you. Super-efficiency means my fist. What's it to be?'

The blood was running down Rattray's face and dripping on to his shirt.

'Just you think about it, son. You're a rent boy. I know that. But if I take my fist to you it's going to be weeks before one of your clients'll look at you sideways. And you may *never* look as pretty as you do now.'

Macrae balled his fist and drew back his arm. The boy became a boy. He suddenly looked terrified.

Silver came in. Macrae ignored him. The blow was already shaped in his head. Silver managed to get the tea on to the table. 'For God's sake!' he said, and caught Macrae's arm.

'Tea,' Macrae said, shrugging Silver's hand away as though it had never touched him. 'Just the thing.'

Silver felt a familiar surge of anger and apprehension. 'What happened?' he said.

Macrae turned to look at him. After a moment he took the cup from Silver and placed it in front of Rattray.

'I told our young friend how pressed we were for time and he decided to cooperate. Isn't that so, son?' Rattray did not reply. 'They call you the Rat?'

Silver gave him his handkerchief and the boy began to clean his face. 'Yes?'

'What's your first name?'

The boy looked across at Silver. 'Can you get that fag?'

Macrae pulled out a packet of slim cigars and gave him one.

'First name?'

'James. Jamie.'

'Age?'

'Eighteen. Seventeen and a half.'

'All right, Jamie, they . . . ' He pointed vaguely in the direction of the charge room where the other derelicts were. 'They say there was a coloured kid and a girl dossing in that underpass. They say you knew them. Let's start with that.'

Detective Chief Superintendent Leslie Wilson was in his early fifties. He had a thin, sharp face, thinning grey hair and eyes that never rested on one place for more than a split second. When he was young he had been called 'Shifty' Wilson.

He was a neat man, vain about his clothes. At one time, before it was disbanded, he had been attached to the Murder Squad. When the pressure became heavy he had been known to go to his desk, take out polish and brushes and give his shoes a right going over.

He also had a tidy mind and the ability to file things away in his mental computer and recall them at will: arcane facts about suspects, ages of people he'd arrested in 1969, their middle names, hair colour, telephone numbers, car numbers.

In later years, he had been able to turn that talent towards administration, and now he was the boss of Cannon Row.

Forty-five minutes earlier he had been fetched from his home just as he was preparing for bed. He was not in the best of humours but he hid that now as he looked across his desk at George Macrae.

Of all the men in the Metropolitan Police, including Commanders, even Deputy Commissioners, Macrae was the one around whom Wilson trod most carefully. Like most people, he respected Macrae. He liked him and disliked him in about equal measures and was always somewhat apprehensive in his presence.

They had known each other for many years, had started together, come up through the ranks together, and survived together. That forged links. After a few drinks it was easy to grow sentimental, easy to forget the problems that Macrae posed.

Even though Wilson had known him for a long time, even though they had worked closely together on the Murder Squad, gone out together with their wives, spent Christmas at each other's houses, Wilson still did not know what Macrae would say or do at any given moment in any given situation.

Like his police work, his life was unorthodox. The word 'messy' had sometimes been used and Wilson knew that the top brass would have liked to see Macrae on the early retirement list. Wilson had always fought for him, for Macrae was what was known in the trade as a good thief-taker. His success rate made Wilson look good.

It wasn't something that either man was in doubt about. Macrae knew Wilson benefited from his expertise and his success; Wilson knew that Macrae benefited from his, Wilson's, ability to cover for him when his behaviour became just a little too unorthodox.

They knew each other's weaknesses and strengths; they knew they had to work out – and *had* worked out – a *raison d'être*. It was a symbiotic relationship – a word Macrae would have known, not Wilson. And lastly they both knew that if Macrae had toed the line over the years, he would now be sitting behind Wilson's desk, or indeed a somewhat grander desk with a grander title.

'This is a bugger, George,' Wilson said. 'Always happens before a holiday weekend.'

Macrae was standing with his back to the room, looking at the car park that glistened wetly under the sodium lights.

'How's the . . . um . . . the family?' Wilson said.

The word was used advisedly, for with two ex-wives and three children between them, picking out the different relationships and inquiring after the separate individuals, would have taken time.

'They're OK,' Macrae said. 'Beryl?' Beryl was Wilson's wife. She was small and plump and blonde and went to bed, so the word was, with creamed hands thrust into cotton gloves.

'Not best pleased,' Wilson said. 'She'd just got off to sleep. Anyway. What've you got?' He looked down at an early report. 'Have to tell you I've never heard of him, this TV chap.'

'Nor had I,' Macrae said. 'He's on at breakfast time.'

'Ah. Never watch the box then. It's a bloody bad place, Hungerford Bridge. For muggings, I mean.'

'I don't think it was a mugging.'

'Oh?' Wilson's eyebrows rose slowly making crease lines on his thin forehead. 'Man on his way to Waterloo Station on a bad night? Just the sort of time and place.'

'He wasn't on his way home. At least it doesn't seem like it. He lives in Sussex. Near Chichester. If he was taking a train he'd leave from Victoria.'

'For Christ's sake, George, you've got it down here. If it's not a mugging then what . . . ?'

'That's just the report they'll base the press release on. Gives me time.'

'George, he's a T-bloody-V personality! They're next to the royals. Anything happens to one of them and it's page one. You got to be extra specially careful on this one. And for God's sake you've got "black" here.' He tapped the sheet in front of him.

'Well, he is black.'

'So what? If he was white you wouldn't put white. Our masters are bloody paranoid about race at the moment. Every time some black brother complains about police harassment it's all over the papers, and questions in the House, and the

Commissioner has a gastric attack. The word is cool it. Don't make anything out of it. You don't need to call him black because people will see his pictures on TV and in the papers and they'll know . . . '

'I think he was stabbed by a black.'

'Oh, shit!'

Wilson opened the top drawer of his desk, scrabbled about, closed it, opened another. 'You got something to smoke?'

'I thought Beryl made you give it up?'

'Only at home.' He took a slim cigar from Macrae and drew on it heavily. 'What are you telling me, George? Black murders black. It's not a mugging. Are they family? Friends? It's not drugs, is it?' There was real apprehension in his voice now. Everyone knew about the crack wars in Washington and Los Angeles. Everyone expected something similar in London.

'Relax, Les. Not as far as we can tell.'

'What do you know about this Henry-bloody-Foster anyway?'

'Not a lot so far, but we're checking. He must have been pretty bright to get where he got.'

'And pushy,' Wilson said. 'You don't get anywhere just by being black and bright. All right, so he wasn't mugged. What was he doing there at that time of night? It's too late to be going to the Festival Hall or the National Theatre. I suppose he could have been coming back.'

'Only if he left at the interval.'

'Well, *whatever* he was doing there, someone stuck a knife into him on the bridge.'

'Not quite on the bridge, Les. A place underneath it. The sort of place dossers and street kids find. I suppose you could call it a shelter.'

'What about this other black? The one who stabbed him. You got a name?'

'Calls himself Huntsman. But that doesn't sound like a real name. He's a kid.'

'Got a description?'

'It's down there.'

'Oh, yes. Black and green track suit. A green bean? Oh, beanie. One of those woollen hats?'

'Right.'

'How old?'

'Mid teens. A year either way.'

'Jesus, they get younger all the time!'

'There's a girl too. He and the girl shared this doss. Called Gail.'

'Huntsman. Gail. They're getting pretty fancy. In my day it was Bert and Sally. Anyway, she shouldn't be too hard to pick up.'

'She could be anywhere by now.'

'Could be he was stabbed somewhere else and his body was hidden there.'

'G. D. did the examination. He doesn't think so. Anyway, this place is almost at head height. You'd need a couple of strong blokes to lift him.'

'What d'you think, George?'

'A couple of the dossers say Foster had come to the bridge and was asking for the kid.'

'Maybe he's his long-lost son.'

'Maybe.'

'What about Foster's family?'

'There's a wife in Sussex. She's being told tonight. I'll go down and see her.'

'If Silver can come up with the suspect's address that'll make a difference. We can't have this kid running around with a knife. What's he like, George?'

'Who, Silver? Why?'

'I dunno, you and Silver . . . It's just, well . . . he doesn't seem quite your cup of tea. I've always wondered about him. I mean a Jew. And with his education. He's over-educated, really. What the hell does he want in the Met?'

'To be Commissioner.'

'Oh.' Wilson smiled. Then frowned. 'You serious?'

'That's what his mother wants.'

Wilson was still bothered by the report in front of him. 'The media are going to be all over us on this. One of their own, et cetera.'

'Fuck the media.'

'For God's sake, George, be your age. And that reminds

53

me, there's something I've been meaning to mention.'

His eyes touched Macrae's face briefly then flitted away to the window, a chair, the desk.

'I think I know what's coming.'

'Seniority.'

'Thought so.'

'Look, I've got to write you up. You know as well as I do you could hold down a Chief Super's job but I've got to have something positive from you, George. You've got to show willing. That you want it.'

'But I don't want it. I don't want to be sat behind a desk pushing bloody papers.'

Wilson's face flushed. 'You think that's all there is to it? Let me tell you—'

'I'm a thief-taker. I want to be up and out and not in an office.'

'Two points. First, isn't it bloody better to give orders than receive them? I mean you've got the ability, no question about it. If you'd . . . if you'd just . . . you know what I mean. You'd be equal with me.'

Macrae smiled slightly and Wilson didn't miss it.

'But you've never given it a fair shot. You're not the most diplomatic of men, are you, George?'

'So?'

'I mean in relation to senior management.'

'Christ, there you go. Senior management! We're a bloody police force, not a paint factory.'

'Things have changed. This isn't the old days. The old days have gone, George. Disappeared. Vanished. You've got a new man at the top who—'

'Who costs everything. We're becoming a nine-to-five, five-days-a-week force. We should put up bloody notices.' He sketched out in the air with his fingers, 'To all criminals. To assist the police in their investigations please commit all crimes between Monday and Friday.'

'George . . .'

'It's true, isn't it, Les? They don't want us to work overtime. We have to have a budget for every job. See if it's *cost effective* to investigate. You know, there are thousands

54

out there who don't bother to phone us any longer. Car broken into? House burgled? Sorry, sir or madam, we're just too busy. Cost effectiveness! No wonder our clean-up rate is looking slightly better. We only investigate the ones we've got a chance with. That's not the way it used to be.'

'There's no point going down Memory Lane. Things *have* changed and we have to change with them. You're like a dinosaur, George. If you don't change you'll become extinct.'

'Dinosaurs had a bloody good time while they lasted.'

'And this driver you're always using. Twyford. You've got him tucked away clerking and every time *you* want him you pull him out. It's no go, George. We don't have personal drivers any more.'

'You leave Eddie out if it! This is my patch and—'

'George, don't you understand, we don't have "patches" any more, either? It's all been centralised and—'

'All we have is fucking sets of initials. AMIP! Send for AMIP! Jesus. It sounds like some Arab terrorist organisation. What was wrong with the Serious Crime Squad? And we never called it SCS! It's change for the sake of change, Les, that's all it is.'

'Christ, I don't know why I bother! It's just . . . '

'Second point?'

Wilson took a deep breath. 'Going out as a Chief would give you a better pension, you know.'

'I'll get by.'

'As long as you have us. Not quite what the song said, but you get my meaning. What the hell are you going to do outside the Met? You've said it yourself: you're a thief-taker. What're you going to do, go into security? Private practice? You think you'll be happy? You're a copper, George. At the sharp end. Give you a nice grisly murder and you're as happy as a sandboy. I've been with you. I know.'

Macrae was becoming angry. 'Let's cut the lecture. You brought it up. You write what you like.'

Wilson breathed out. Shrugged. Looked down at his desk once more. Macrae began to move to the door.

There was a knock and Silver came in. 'Foster had a flat in town,' he said.

'Well done, laddie. Where?'

'Fulham. I've got the address. And there were keys on the body.'

'Let's go and look, then,' Macrae said.

'What about the Press?' Wilson said. 'They'll be waiting.'

'You deal with them, Les, you're better at that sort of thing than me.'

A look of relief crossed Wilson's face. Except for one or two reporters, Macrae's relationship with the Press was diabolical.

'OK, George, if that's how you want it.'

Among the bales of straw and the rich farm smell of the Broadhurst Mews stables, Terry Collins slept. He dreamed of his grandfather.

In her bed in the dripping Hampshire countryside Maria Dunlap lay awake, staring at the ceiling – too excited, too afraid of what she was getting into, to sleep.

9

Dawn, a grey, sleety dawn with a wind puckering the surface of the Thames, was more than half an hour old, when
Leo Silver let himself into his house in Pimlico. It was one
of a thousand similar terraced houses that lay between the
Buckingham Palace Road and the river. Most had two pillars
and a portico, most had been refurbished over the past few
years and were now expensive properties. At this time in the
morning, except for an occasional car, Pimlico was devoid of
movement.

Silver's was a four-storeyed house which had been con-
verted into flats in the sixties. He and Zoe Bertram occupied
the top two floors, which had been turned into a maisonette.

It sounded grand, Silver thought, as he mounted the inner
staircase, until you realised that the house was narrow and that
the apartment consisted of only three rooms. The top floor
had been knocked into an open-plan area which contained
living-room, dining-room, and kitchenette. On the floor
below there were two bedrooms and a bathroom.

He came to the door of his flat. He was bone-weary, so
tired that he leaned against the wall for a moment before
pulling from his pocket a ring with several keys on it. He
began unlocking the first of the three deadlocks on the
heavily reinforced door. It sounded, he always thought, like
Bluebeard unlocking the room in which the bodies of his
wives hung.

He had never said that to Zoe, not even as a joke. Not
joking about anything that might frighten her was part of
the price they had to pay for what had happened.

He entered the apartment, relocked the door, and put
up a solid security chain. Their bedroom door was closed

57

and he opened it gently. She lay on her back, with her arms above her head and her mouth slightly open. The room was shadowy but he could see a note pinned to his pillow. He took off his shoes and tiptoed silently across the room.

She looked like a child, her face innocent and unlined. He leaned over her, smelling the talc from her bath the previous night, and carefully lifted the note. It said: 'What have you done with Dr Millmoss?'

He smiled. She had introduced him to James Thurber. She was something of an expert on his cartoons and short pieces, and Leo had become so infected and infatuated that he had not only read everything possible that Thurber had written, but also several biographies of the great man. He took out his pen and wrote, 'He's with the owl in the attic,' and placed the note softly on her chest.

He decided to make some breakfast, see her off to work, and then go to bed. He went up into the open-plan floor above and put on the kettle, standing in the window as he did so and staring out at the cold, wet street. His view took in the houses opposite and ended with the tall chimneys of the old Battersea Power Station. Not much of a view but better than some.

The feature about the apartment which had caused them to borrow more than they could afford was that it had a flat roof and a skylight that led up to it. In the spring they would start to make a roof garden. Ruth said that Sidney had said that they would have to strengthen the roof first. What the hell would Sidney know about such things? He was like Leo's father. He couldn't change a light bulb.

Silver had brought with him a pile of morning papers and now glanced at their front pages. They were all calling the death a mugging.

He made himself coffee and sank into one of the old easy chairs which they had bought at a junk market and had had re-covered. On the coffee table in front of him was one of Zoe's work folders. She was a copy writer at Runcorn, Friar and De Groote and often brought work home.

On top of the folder was another note to him. 'We need

a jingle for a new line in canned beans. Get to it – but no farts, please.'

He thought for a moment and wrote, quoting Remarque, 'Every little bean must be heard as well as seen.'

He sipped at his coffee and felt the warmth go down into the pit of his stomach and spread out from there. He knew if he went round the house there would be other notes. It was her way, he thought, of occupying her time when he was working late, keeping herself amused, banishing thoughts. Underneath the surface, under the layers of humour and sophistication, of sudden aggression and equally sudden contrition, underneath all that, he knew she was still raw.

How long had it been? He worked backwards. Last September. Six months.

There had been a time in the weeks after it had happened that they spoke about it every day. For Zoe it had been a compulsion. It was as though by talking she could exorcise the ghosts of memory. But for some months now it had not been mentioned.

For a while he had thought she might be over it but he had done his reading and he knew that sometimes the trauma was so great that some women never got over it.

Recently he had read of a new school of psychiatric thinking which had emerged in Israel from work with Holocaust survivors. Its thesis was that if you could bury traumatic memories deeply enough you lived a happier, less psychologically disturbed existence. This stood Freud on his head. He wondered if that was what Zoe was doing now – burying it.

He sat there, in the grey light of early morning, sipping at his coffee and gradually the pattern of events shaped itself in his thoughts.

It had been such a lovely day. One of those golden mid-September days. It was his nephew Stanley's sixth birthday and Leo had promised to take him for a pizza in Hampstead. Ruth had taken the day off and Leo, Ruth and Stanley had decided to walk on Hampstead Heath through the Vale of Health up to the Whitestone Pond and then back to the Pizza Express.

Each held one of Stanley's hands as they walked down

the deserted road that led to the Vale of Health. It is a strange place, an enclosed village within the Heath itself, cut off by trees and undergrowth from the surrounding houses, as though a dozen brownstones from upper Manhattan had been uprooted and plonked down in the wilder part of Central Park.

It is an expensive part of London. Very quiet. Few cars come and go. It lives its own secluded and élite existence, and on this midweek day in September there was hardly a soul about.

'Why is it called health?' Stanley said. He was a plump child and had excruciatingly bad eating habits. He liked almost nothing except junk food but Leo had a soft spot for him.

They came abreast of the first of the red-brick houses.

'Because it's healthy,' Ruth said.

She was wearing her hair short, had on heavy spectacles, a long dress and old-fashioned open-toed sandals.

'Once upon a time,' Silver began and Stanley swung his head towards his uncle, eyes shining. 'Once upon a time there was a terrible sickness in London called the plague and people were dying in their thousands and—'

'We don't talk about misery,' Ruth hissed at him, shaking her head sharply.

'Why not? It's part of life.'

'Maybe your life. Maybe that's all you see. I should have thought . . . '

'And all the people died . . . ' Stanley said. 'Go on.'

'Well, those that lived here didn't,' Silver said. 'That's why it's called the Vale of Health.'

'Why didn't they?'

'I don't know why you had to bring it up,' Ruth said. 'It's his birthday. We don't want to talk about that.'

'You're right, it's too nice a day.'

'Why didn't the people die?' Stanley said, yanking at his arm.

'You see?' Ruth said.

'I'll tell you later,' Silver said. 'On your seventh birthday.'

'No.' He yanked at Silver's arm again. 'Now.'

'Sssh . . . ' Silver said. 'What's that?'

They stopped in the narrow little road, listening. Silence. Then a strange noise. It sounded as though someone was gargling. Abruptly it was cut off. Then there was a kind of long drawn-out moan.

The sounds were coming from behind one of the houses on their left. A small lane wound round the back.

'What the hell . . . ?' Silver said.

'You're not on duty,' Ruth said.

'What is it, Uncle Leo?'

'I don't know.'

'Leo!'

But he had dropped Stanley's hand. 'Take him over there,' he said, pointing to a pub about fifty yards away.

'Leo, for God's sake, whatever it is you—'

He went quickly down the lane. He wasn't frightened yet. In his mind was some kind of animal situation. A dog tied up. Cruelty of a sort. He could feel the adrenalin streaking through his muscles. He felt light. He had nothing on him, no gun. He saw, on the ground just inside the fence, the handle of a spade from which the head had broken off. It was heavy and solid and he picked it up. If it was a dog it might be aggressive.

The sounds were louder now and seemed to be coming from a small shed at the end of the overgrown garden.

Even now six months later he could not manage a complete picture. The scene flashed on his inner eye fractured into psychedelic images as though by a strobe light . . . Her body, half naked, on an old potting table . . . a track-suit top . . . trainers on her feet . . . the black V of her pubic hair and the thin red line above it . . . the pearls of blood oozing into tiny rivulets . . . her face suffused . . . rags stuffed into her mouth . . . the man holding a knife in one hand, his penis in the other . . .

That's when everything froze in Silver's mind. It was like a photograph in a pornographic magazine; a picture carefully staged for the SM trade.

Silver only had an impression of the man, a thin face with long hair, jeans and an anorak. About thirty.

As the man opened his mouth and said, 'Noooooo . . . '
Silver hit him with the handle of the spade. He felt and heard
the crunch of the wood as it met his cheekbone and stove it
in. Then he hit him again . . . and again . . . He was lucky he
hadn't killed him.

He got up restlessly and went to the window again staring
out but seeing nothing. Thinking about it shredded his nerves,
yet he found he could not bury it. Just when he thought it had
gone, here it was popping up to ambush him.

They had gone over it so many times at first because
her counsellor had said it would be of benefit to her. The
first time had been in the hospital when he had gone to see
her. He had taken her flowers. She'd looked tiny in the bed.
Her black hair was spread on the pillow, her damaged hands,
where she had grabbed for the knife, heavily bandaged.

'I brought you these,' he had said, looking round for
somewhere to put them.

'Thank you,' she said, not meaning the flowers. 'Thank
you . . . ' Then she began to cry.

Crying had also been part of her therapy. He'd come
to see her several times in hospital and she had cried each
time.

After she'd left hospital she went to stay with her father
in Surrey. Silver went down to visit her and took her to
dinner in Guildford. She began to talk about it then, rapidly
and compulsively, and before she had even started her food
she had begun to cry.

After a few weeks the crying stopped. She still went on
talking about it though: the lovely day, the decision to jog
on Hampstead Heath. The man working in the garden as
she had run past. Asking her for the time. Grabbing her as
she paused to look at her watch.

Then the 'if onlys'. If only she hadn't gone jogging, if
only the day had been cold and wet, if only she had taken
a different route, if only . . .

That had taken a week or so. It coincided with a growing
dependence on him. She would phone him from Surrey and
ask his advice about the simplest things: she was changing her

bank, which did he recommend? Which did he use? She was going to buy her father a present, what would he suggest? The calls rained down on him.

Then one day they stopped. He didn't hear from her for a week or more. He began to miss her. He phoned her and got her father. She'd gone back to work. She was sharing a flat with three other young women in Wandsworth.

Silver thought about her for two days. He couldn't get her out of his mind. Wherever he went he saw her: small, dark, high cheekbones, wide-set brown eyes. He always thought she looked Spanish and should be wearing one of those figure-hugging dancer's dresses. And he wasn't far wrong because her mother was half Spanish.

He'd phoned her. She sounded brisk, in control. 'I've made a fool of myself,' she said.

'How's that?'

'The way I've been harassing you, making your life a misery.'

'That's not true.'

'Yes it is. But I want you to know how grateful I am. And I want you to know that I'm over it, thank God.'

'When can I see you?' he said.

'Leo, I don't think that's a good idea. When I say I'm over it I mean I'm halfway over it. I've got a new job, new flat, new environment. I think it might be a mistake.'

'You mean seeing me might . . . '

'Just start things up again in my mind.'

'Yes. I understand. But I miss you. Miss, hell. I think I'm in love with you. No, not think. I'm sure.'

She said something then which he only half heard, but the word 'miss' was quite clear. Then the phone went dead.

Two days later, about six o'clock on a December evening shortly before Christmas, the duty officer at Cannon Row called him away from his desk saying there was someone to see him in the waiting room. She was sitting on an old wooden bench warmed mostly by criminal bottoms. She was wearing a black suit with a red blouse and a double strand of black beads at her throat. For a moment she took his breath away.

'I was passing,' she said.

'Passing?'

'On my way home. I always go the long way round. It makes life so much more interesting.'

'Would you like a drink?'

'Try me.'

'Where? The West End?'

'No, somewhere we can talk. Somewhere quiet.'

They walked along Whitehall, crossed Parliament Square into Petty France, entered the first pub they saw and found a corner table. He fetched two glasses of white wine from the bar.

They chatted on a superficial level, circling each other verbally. She told him about her flat, the women she shared it with, her new job. They had a couple more drinks and then she said, 'I should be getting back.'

'I'll take you.'

'Why don't I buy a bottle?' She went to the bar and came back with two bottles of red Rioja. 'Just in case.'

'Are you inviting me to dinner?'

He could see she was nervous. In the car she was very bright and brittle, waving her hands around. Her flat-mates had gone for the weekend and they had the place to themselves. She drank rapidly and talked as quickly.

He sat beside her on the sofa and instantly she got up and crossed the room and sat in one of the black leather and chrome chairs with which the place was furnished.

She kept on topping up her glass and he said, 'Should I go out and get something? There must be a take-away around here.'

She found some peanuts and put them in a dish. 'First course,' she said, holding them out to him.

She sat down, but got up almost instantly. 'I think there are some crisps in the kitchen.'

'Don't worry.'

She went out. Came back. 'Sorry.' She held out the peanuts again and he took her wrist.

'Sit,' he said. 'You're making me jumpy.'

She tried to smile but her face had become frozen.

'Excuse me for a moment,' she said.

When she came back she was wearing only a short silky kimono. She sat next to him on the sofa and took his hand and put in on her breast. It was small and firm. 'Do you get the impression I'm trying to tell you something?' she said, forcing brightness into her tone.

'I get the impression this is a kind of experiment,' he said.

She held his hand and took him in to her bedroom. 'Let me undress you,' she said. Her speech was thick and slightly fuzzy.

He felt her fingers on the buttons and zips of his clothes. He wanted her but not like this.

They lay down on the bed. He put his arms around her. She felt cold. It was like embracing dead flesh.

The knife cut was a thin white line against the smooth brown of her stomach skin. He bent and kissed it and felt her stiffen even more. One of her hands came down to cover it. He picked up the hand and kissed that too.

'Now,' she said.

'I can't.'

'Please.'

'I'm sorry.'

'Tell me what you like.'

He felt her lips travel down his stomach and rolled away.

'I'm frightened, Leo.'

'It'll take time. You're like someone who's been in a car accident. You think you've got to get back into a car.'

'Leo, I want you to know something. He never . . . He didn't have time . . . '

'Is that what's worrying you?'

'I wanted you to know.'

He propped himself up on his elbow and looked down at her. 'I love you,' he said. 'I'm not going away. I'm here. Let's just take it step by step. We've got all the time in the world.'

'What's the first step?'

'Why don't we try kissing each other?'

That's how it had been. Slow. Cautious. Mostly in the beginning it didn't work for either of them. But they let their love for each other dictate the pace and finally they became physical lovers as well. She no longer had to get drunk.

Silver, standing lost in thought at the window of his apartment, heard a noise and turned. She had come up the stairs from the bedroom. She was dressed in the same see-through kimono with nothing on underneath. Her eyes were filled with sleep. She crossed the room without speaking and put her arms round his waist. Her head came up to his shoulder.

In a thick, muffled voice, she said, 'Where the hell have you been, Silver?'

They had a second cup of coffee and, as she gradually grew into wakefulness, he told her.

10

Less than two miles away, on the opposite side of the river in Battersea, Macrae was letting himself into his house. It was a small Victorian villa, two up and two down, in a street of exactly similar terraced villas. On one was chiselled WOODBURY COTTAGES 1889. Each had a little patch of garden in front, each had a bow window, each a recessed front door. At one time they had been the homes of respectable clerks and office workers. Then they would have had lace curtains and aspidistras in the front parlour. The gardens would have been filled with early bulbs and primroses.

Now the houses looked out on dereliction. The street was dotted with the dead carcasses of stripped and rusting cars; the gardens had been covered in concrete. Where once flowers had grown, weeds sprouted, and each garden was separated from its neighbour by spindly hedges of variegated privet, their leaves, in the grey morning light, looking diseased and dirty.

Macrae hardly noticed the street any longer. For him it was no man's land, a place to get through into his own territory. And that territory, in the jargon of the brutal school of architecture, was called, not a home, not a house, not a dwelling, but 'defensible space'.

The house was dark and permeated by the smell of frying, but the wreck he had left had been cleaned up. The kitchen was tidy, the crockery washed up and put away, the piece of cheese which had so offended Frenchy, thrown out.

He made himself a mug of coffee, put in three sugars, and went to the sitting-room. The purple curtains – a legacy of his second wife – were closed and he left them as they were. He found a whisky bottle on the floor next to the sofa where he and Frenchy had been watching TV, poured himself a dram and threw it into the back of his throat.

She wasn't a bad sort, Frenchy. At least she'd earned her money. She was one of those women who can't abide untidiness, or not for long anyway. Like his mother. She'd fought a war on dirt and lost a battle each day.

He poured himself another shot of whisky and took it at one gulp. It was the way his father had always taken it, as though it was medicine, hating the taste but wanting the effect. Macrae had seen other alcoholics drink like that. They would order a drink and leave it on the bar-top, and look at it for a long time and then pick it up and, with a shudder, drain the lot.

Well, he wasn't an alcoholic, Macrae told himself. He enjoyed the taste as well as the effect. He wasn't going to be like his father. Not now. Not ever. No matter what happened to him.

When he was a boy his father had been head keeper on the Morile Estate in Inverness-shire. It had been a wild place of hill and heather and river. The laird ran a few sheep but it was mainly a sporting estate. In summer the river was let for salmon fishing and from 12 August the moors were let for grouse shooting. In November there were the hinds to shoot and later on the stags. Hamish Macrae ran all this with great efficiency. Often he would take George with him to help.

It was then that George began to see the two sides of his father. It was all yes sir and no sir and three bags full sir to the wealthy clients who came to fish and shoot. Often, watching them order his father about, George had felt ashamed. He had wished his father would act like a man, tell them to go to hell, or at least have the dignity of some of the other keepers he knew.

But he wasn't like that. He bowed and scraped to people George wouldn't have given the time of day to – wealthy factory owners from Birmingham and Leicester who spoke in adenoidal tones and shot with expensive Purdeys. The real gentry were almost never to be seen.

But when Hamish Macrae came down off the hill in the evenings he became a tyrant. He'd bring in mud on his

68

great hobnailed boots, just when his wife had cleaned. He'd rant and rave about people he'd just touched his forelock to, and take out his humiliation on his wife and son.

It was at these times that George would avoid him. His mother could not. They fought all the time, often over George.

He was doing well at school, was the brightest in his class. When he won a scholarship to the Academy in Aberdeen his mother was overjoyed. His father said no. What was the use of education? How did that tell you when a grouse had thread-worm or how to cast a fly to tempt a running fish? He wanted George to start earning a living as soon as he could. And that was that.

After half a bottle of whisky he wasn't easier to live with but worse. Once he beat his wife so badly he broke her arm. It took her a long time to recover, not so much from the physical hurt but from the psychological.

The next time he beat her – not just the slaps and blows which punctuated their daily lives, but really badly – she was found floating in the Home Pool by one of the tenants who'd gone down to catch a trout before breakfast.

The jury at the inquest brought in a verdict of accidental death even though everyone knew she'd drowned herself.

Six months later Hamish Macrae was felling a huge old rowan tree when it unexpectedly crashed the wrong way and killed him.

By that time George had begun lessons in boxing. He had a fantasy that one day he would fight his father and knock him to the ground. The rowan tree saved him from that and the boxing relieved him of a pent-up aggression he sometimes thought would blow the top of his head off.

Now, sitting on the sofa in his darkened living-room he decided, in memory of his father, not to have another drink but instead went upstairs to bed.

He lay for a while staring at the ceiling. Part of him wanted Frenchy beside him. Or, if not Frenchy, someone, a warm body. He just wanted to touch the flesh with his fingertips to know that he was alive.

Instead, he began to think about the dead man and how

he had got where he'd been found and who would want to kill him. His mind began to go through the case step by step until finally sleep came. But just before he dozed off another thought came into his mind. It was something Wilson had said and Macrae knew he was right. Living like this without the Met to give him a background would turn him into a replica of his father – and that would be the end.

11

Terry woke early. Light entered the stables through dusty windows. He looked down from his nest in the straw. Two of the horses were lying down, the others were standing as though asleep. He searched for a word in his limited vocabulary to describe what he was feeling about them. All he could think of was 'kind'. They were asleep and quiet but mainly they seemed kind.

He wished Gail could see them, perhaps even stroke them as he had done.

He lay curled up in the straw, his arms around his knees because it was cold. He knew he would have to leave this place but did not know where to go. Soon people would come and do whatever they had to do to horses in the morning, feed them perhaps, give them water. They might need the straw that was sheltering him. He wanted to be away from there by the time someone arrived.

He thought of the arcades where he had spent the last week playing video games. He couldn't go there. He thought of the army surplus stores and the tourist shops where he and Gail had nicked clothes and sweets. Those would be too dangerous now. He couldn't go back to Hungerford Bridge and he couldn't go to the steps in Piccadilly and he couldn't sit on a Circle Line tube all day. London, which he knew to be a vast and sprawling city, seemed to have become small and dangerous.

Suddenly he saw the man's face and he was filled with terror again.

Day . . . lee . . Day . . . lee . . .

OK, so, it's Daley Thompson and Jürgen Hingsen and Huntsman Collins. First day of the decathlon over, and only thirty points separating them. Now, the first event of the second day – 'the aristocrat event', as his grandfather had called it – the one-hundred-and-ten-metre hurdles.

But the magic wasn't working any longer. Huntsman Collins and the world record no longer seemed able to close his mind to what was happening to Terry Collins. Gail was the key. She would know what to do. The only trouble with Gail was that she might be zonked out.

Once Terry had been caught sniffing glue in the toilets at school. The teacher had taken him home. His mother wasn't there so she'd told his grandfather. She said if it happened again they'd report him to the police.

Terry had been fearful of how his grandfather would react. He wasn't afraid of violence. He was simply afraid of the look in the old man's eyes.

Garner Maitland had nodded and smiled and made no trouble and said he would take care of things and it would never happen again. Finally, the teacher had left.

The old man, still without saying anything, had gone into Terry's cupboard and pulled out his spikes, thrown them to him and said, 'C'mon.'

They had gone to the park. It was abandoned now by mothers and children because the swings and roundabouts had been vandalised and there had been several gang rapes. Parts of it were used as a dumping ground for old bedsteads and car tyres.

In one corner of the park there was a sandpit where once children had played. Garner Maitland had marked a run-up and already Terry had used it so often that it had become worn.

'Now I going to teach you the hitch-kick.'

They spent the next two hours by themselves in the far corner of the park and Terry tried and tried to learn the hitch-kick but somehow his legs would not follow his brain until his grandfather said, 'See it in your head, mon, before you start.'

Terry had made a picture in his head of what he wanted to do. This time it worked – running down, taking off, the legs bicycling in the air.

'That's it, mon! You got it!'

On the way home, through the mean streets, his grandfather mentioned drugs for the first and only time. 'We doesn't need drugs, Terry. We better than that.'

Terry had never been sure what he had meant by that. Were black people better? That couldn't be right, not from what he had seen on his own housing estate. Or athletes? And that didn't sound right either; not with steroids. Maybe he meant that Terry and himself were better than that.

Gail took anything: speed, smack, angel dust, acid, crack. Anything that was going. And sometimes a cocktail. He hated her then. But when she was off the drugs it was just the other way round. He wasn't sure what love was. There was a special feeling he had had for his grandfather. He had the same feeling for Gail, only slightly different.

He had met her through the Rat. It was his first night on the streets and he'd gone to Centrepoint, the night shelter for homeless young people in Soho. There had been several street kids hanging about the entrance. The Rat had come up to him and been friendly. He'd offered him a drink from his can of Heineken. Terry had been vulnerable then. He'd been scared, even though he was putting a brave face on it. He'd never slept rough before and didn't know how to go about it. But he'd heard of Centrepoint, so he'd gone there.

'You're never sixteen,' the Rat had said. 'You've got to be sixteen before they'll take you. Otherwise they go to the police.'

That was the last thing Terry wanted, especially after what he'd done to the classroom.

'I can get you money,' the Rat had said.

'How?'

'You see that punter over there?' He pointed to a well-dressed City type holding a brief-case, standing near the doorway to Centrepoint looking at his watch and pretending he was waiting for someone. 'He'll give you a tenner.'

'What for?'

'Doing what he wants.'

Terry paused. He had heard of this, of course. You couldn't

73

grow up as he had without knowing. But he didn't like the idea. On the other hand he wanted the money.

'I could probably get you fifteen. A coupla punters a day, maybe three, and you'd be rolling in it.'

'Fifteen?' He felt nervous but didn't show it. The whole point was never to show it.

But what would his grandfather have said? He couldn't even imagine. Yes, he could. But his grandfather was gone. He felt a kind of confused anger. He was gone and Terry was here. Left on his own. For he did not count his family. It would teach his grandfather a lesson. Teach them all a lesson.

And then Gail had come up to them and held out a can of beer to Terry. 'I haven't seen you here before,' she said.

'I haven't been here before.'

He took a mouthful from the can. He didn't really like the taste of beer but this wasn't the time to go into that.

'I'm just telling him how to make it,' the Rat said.

Gail was short and thin with cropped brown hair. She wore, as they all seemed to, a track suit and trainers. Her face was spotted by acne but her smile was open and warm.

'Make it? Like you? You're bloody positive!' She turned to Terry. 'He's positive. Been on the game since he was twelve.'

He hadn't understood her then, but later he came to understand that 'positive' meant HIV-positive and he had washed his mouth and lips from contact with the Rat's beer can.

'I got a fiver on the trains,' she said. 'You want something to eat?'

Terry was hungry. 'I don't mind,' he said.

Afterwards she asked him where he was going to doss and when he said he didn't know she said, 'You'll die out there. You better come with me.'

She took him away from the West End to the dark empty streets of Westminster near the Tate Gallery. There, in the basement area of a block of old mansion flats which were being demolished, she showed him a small den where the refuse bins had once been stored.

He hardly slept that night. Each time he woke he sensed

74

that Gail was awake too. Once or twice he turned and looked at her. Each time she was watching him.

The following day they hung around together. It was assumed, without any discussion, that this would be the pattern. She took him to the right shops to nick things and soon he was wearing a brand new track suit and trainers. He was warm for the first time since leaving home.

She had also taken him to a camping store and they had stolen a sleeping bag and a plastic groundsheet and she had brought him back with her to her lair under Hungerford Bridge.

It was comfortable, much more comfortable than the dustbin room. He was warm. He was also excited. He was in the middle of things. It was better than home, that is until she popped a handful of pills and was out for nearly sixteen hours.

When she woke she taught him how to beg on the trains and in the underground stations and in narrow passageways linking the various lines where it was difficult for people not to notice them.

He wasn't sure at the beginning why Gail had taken him back with her. Later he realised she wanted someone she could trust while she was zonked out. Someone who would watch her gear. There had been someone before him, a girl from the north, but she'd gone home.

He needed Gail now. She would know where he could hide, where he'd be safe.

He came down from his nest and said goodbye to the horses, then he climbed up to the window, pushed it open and swung himself through. It was still early and there was no one about.

He was walking towards the end of the mews in the direction of Paddington Station when he saw the police car. It was parked on the opposite side of the street.

He panicked. He turned and ran back to the stables, hoisted himself up and was through the window in a flash. The horses jerked in their stalls, turning wide eyes towards him. He shot up the ladder and flung himself down in the straw.

He had only been back a few minutes when he heard locks being turned and chains lifted and the big stable doors were swung open. A young girl, not much older than himself, took a fork down from the rack and began to muck out each stall in turn. As she did so she spoke softly to the horses.

Soon she would want more straw, he thought. Soon she would come up the ladder. He pushed himself further and further into the old straw until finally he was against the wall between the stable and the adjoining house. He moved along the wall, silently working himself as far from the top of the stairs as possible. He was now almost buried by straw and hidden by bales and pieces of old tack which had been thrown up there over the years.

His hand touched something. He moved the straw away. He saw a small door, no larger than a trapdoor. It was held by a bolt and padlock. But neither had been used for many years and the woodwork was rotten. He waited until the girl went out into the mews to empty a bucket of water then he gave the padlock a wrench. The screws came away easily. He opened the little door and wriggled through. He found himself in the roofspace of the house next door. He pulled the trapdoor closed behind him.

12

The telephone shattered Silver's dream. He came bursting through into wakefulness like a missile leaving a silo. There was a faint memory of a languorous, golden moment but it was sucked away by the blast.

Its very urgency caused him to sit up in bed, heart racing, stomach twisting.

'Is that you, laddie?'

'Yes.'

'Did I wake you?'

Silver looked at the wall-clock. It was 10.45. He'd had three hours' sleep. 'Yes,' he said.

'Missing Persons have come up with a candidate. Eddie'll pick you up in forty-five minutes.' The phone went dead.

Slowly Silver lowered himself back on to the pillow. The cold light of mid-morning seeped in through the yellow curtains. The whole apartment was yellow and orange: fitted carpets, sofa and chair coverings. They had had to go to the limit of their credit ratings. 'In London you're on the inside looking out,' Zoe had said. 'The inside's got to be good.'

Forty-five minutes. He didn't have to rush. Shower, change, and another cup of coffee. Easy.

A line of Thomson's suddenly flashed into his mind: 'A pleasing land of drowsy-head it was . . . ' It had had something to do with his dream.

Was it about Zoe? He often dreamed about her. Sometimes he dreamed they were making love and he would wake and find her next to him and they would do it for real. And afterwards, if the sun was coming through the yellow curtains, the moments would be golden and languorous.

Earlier, they had done a turnabout. He had got undressed

and into bed and she had gone to work. He had lain in bed watching her dress. Her breasts were small and firm and high and she had no need for a bra. She sat on the bed to put on her tights and he had cupped his hand round one of her breasts and stroked it.

'Like lemons,' he had said. 'Those big luscious Italian lemons.'

She had removed his hand and crossed to the built-in wardrobe. 'Don't handle the fruit if you're not going to buy.'

'You want to try me?'

'You're very brave when you know you're safe. Let's save it for tonight.'

'If there is a tonight. Christ knows what Macrae's got up his sleeve.'

She shrugged into a blouse and began to button it.

'He's a bastard,' Silver said.

'So?' Her voice lost some of its playfulness.

'We had a kid in for questioning. He sent me out to get him a cup of tea. When I came back there was blood all over the kid's face. It's not the first time either.'

She didn't react. It was as though she did not want to hear criticism of Macrae or the police in general, he thought. She was absolutely one hundred per cent certain that criminals deserved all they got and if people were a bit roughed up in the process that was just too bad. The police were angels and she was on the side of the angels.

It wasn't hard to understand why but it had the effect of making Silver's own attitude ambivalent and he didn't want to be surrounded by doubt. His family, with the exception of his mother, were dead against the police. Especially Ruth.

My daughter Ruth, the lawyer. My son Leo, the police sergeant.

Not quite the same ring, he thought.

He wanted to defend the police, not find fault, yet Zoe in a sense turned him against himself.

'You told me once you had to cut corners. If you didn't you'd never get anything done.'

'That's not me. That's Macrae. He's got it tattooed on his forehead.'

78

'No, it's what you said. I remember.'

She moved round the room busily and then went into the bathroom to put on her face. When she came out she said, 'If you don't like him why don't you do something about it?' She kissed him lightly on the forehead. 'You thinking of an orgy tonight?'

'I hope so.'

He heard the chain being lifted and the locks turning and the door closing, then being relocked. This was what the holding cells at Cannon Row sounded like when they had a batch of prisoners.

At eleven twenty-five Silver finished dressing and finished his cup of coffee. He looked at himself in the long mirror in the bedroom. He saw a slender man of just over medium height dressed all in black. It was part of a style he had begun to develop at university. Black rollneck sweater, black leather jacket, black needlecord slacks and black loafers.

He locked the apartment and went out on to the cold, blustery pavement. At precisely eleven-thirty an unmarked Ford Granada drew up beside him. Eddie Twyford was at the wheel. Macrae sat beside him. Silver got into the back. They grunted at each other. The car took off into the traffic.

'Caesar! Caesar! Where are you?'

Maria walked down the drive between the hedges of laurel, calling the dog. The snow and sleet of the previous night had given way to racing clouds and a blustery wind and she was wearing a heavy sheepskin coat.

'Caesar!'

She was angry with the dog, yet, at the same time, she knew that she was only using him as a focal point. She was angry at herself; also frightened and guilt-ridden, and this was exacerbated by the hangover she felt from the mixture of sleeping pills and alcohol.

She had slept badly then finally heavily and had woken up an hour ago to discover it was past ten o'clock.

'Good boy!' She tried to make her voice cajoling.

She went down to the end of the drive where it joined a

small road. Other drives to other houses began here and at the bottom of each drive were a couple of dustbins set out for collection later that day. Caesar was investigating some further up the road.

'Here you are,' she called.

The phrase penetrated the dog's mind because it was often used in conjunction with food. He came back in a fawning manner and took a dog biscuit from her hand while she slipped the catch of the lead on to his collar. As she did so she noticed a man at the end of the road. He had been looking towards her, now he turned and walked quickly away and got into a small white car.

She felt better with Caesar on the lead. He was a big dog. If someone didn't know how cowardly he was she supposed he might act as a deterrent.

She walked back to the house and put Caesar into the kitchen. She was going out to do some shopping before everything closed up for the weekend. Suddenly she thought: *I don't have to meet Jack!* All she needed to do was phone the house around six o'clock and tell him.

On the other hand she wanted to do *some*thing. She did not want to sit at home. She went to her bedroom and picked up her bag.

Or she could spend the Easter weekend in a hotel. But she thought of the faded country hotels around her. More like homes for the aged than lively establishments. Nothing would be more depressing than sitting at one end of a dining-room with the muzak turned low and half a dozen spinsters/divorcees/widows alone at their personal tables with their personal tomato ketchup bottles and their personal napkin rings.

To hell with that.

She locked the door and drove to the shops. The little white car was there but no sign of the man.

In the police car crossing London, Macrae and the driver Eddie Twyford were arguing about the route as usual.

Eddie was saying, ' . . . along the Euston Road, then the Caledonian Road, and into Holloway Road . . . '

He was touchy about his knowledge of routes. He'd been a police driver in the old days and had worked for Macrae for the past few years, much to Wilson's irritation. When Macrae talked of him, he would say, 'There're two things Eddie Twyford knows, cars and routes. That's why I want him.'

But, Silver thought, there was a third. Houseplants. Eddie and his wife lived in Tooting in a small council flat and you practically needed a machete to get into the living-room. Silver had been there several times. The foliage of spider plants, rubber plants, ficuses, ferns, Swiss cheese plants, hanging baskets of pelargoniums, was so luxurious that he would not have been surprised to see monkeys in the foliage or hear the distant beat of drums.

Eddie was thin and bald and had a greying moustache. He had joined the police at the same time as Macrae but had never been promising material. Except as a driver. He could find his way anywhere in London better than most taxi drivers and was proud of it. Twice Macrae had saved him from being made redundant. The result was that for most of the time Eddie would have walked on hot coals for him. But not when he argued about routes.

'The best way is through Regent's Park, then along Camden Road,' Macrae said.

'Camden Road was jammed solid last time we went anywhere near it, guv'nor.'

'That was because of a burst water-main.'

Eddie swung the wheel savagely and they sped up Baker Street towards the Park. Almost immediately they were checked by traffic. Macrae scowled through the window.

'What do you want me to do, guv'nor?' Eddie said, angrily.

'Go any way you like.'

This is how it always ended, Silver thought, and again he wondered why Macrae bothered.

Eddie usually kept up a running commentary about other people's driving. 'That's right, don't signal . . . ' or 'What d'you think your brakes are for . . . ?'

Most of the time neither Macrae nor Silver took any notice.

Now Eddie said, 'Look at that bastard!' pointing to a black

man on a bicycle who was weaving in and out of the cars. 'All the way from Trinidad to cause a bloody traffic jam in London.'

'You just keep your eyes on the road,' Macrae said, as Eddie turned to shout at the cyclist.

Silver switched off. Something was troubling him. Zoe? No. His family? They always troubled him, but not any more than usual at this moment. Then he remembered. It was the dead man's apartment.

It was at the far end of the Fulham Road, one of a block of post-war flats, comprising sitting-room, bedroom, small kitchen and bathroom.

A police constable had been on duty outside the door when they arrived sometime after midnight. To Macrae's inquiry the PC said that Forensic hadn't been yet.

The two of them had gone in. Macrae had taken out his pen and used it to switch on the lights.

'There's something bothering me about Foster's flat,' Silver said to Macrae.

'Oh?'

'It was too neat.'

'How d'you mean?'

'Well, I thought of what it would have been like if it'd been mine.'

'And?'

'It wouldn't have been neat.'

Both Macrae and Silver were thinking the same thought. They were thinking of Macrae's house. Silver was remembering the last time he had been there. Macrae had been so drunk he could hardly stand and Silver had had to put him to bed. This was not a rare occurrence and Silver had hated each occasion. He hated seeing Macrae – the good thief-taker – so paralysed he couldn't find his way to his own room.

The first time Silver had seen the interior of the house he had gagged at the unwashed dishes in the kitchen.

'Well, go on,' Macrae said.

Silver thought of Foster's living-room with the severe office furniture, the word processor, the photo-copying machine, the bookcase containing fifty or sixty video cassettes. Then the

82

bedroom. A double-bed. Cheval mirror. Built-in cupboards. The bed neatly made, everything in its place.

'It just doesn't seem . . .'

'You don't murder someone because he's neat.'

'Come on! Come on!' Eddie said to the driver in front.

Macrae had turned to listen to Silver and now he waited for him to continue. Macrae took thieves because he had good contacts. The psychology of crime held little interest for him. When a crime was committed he would get on the telephone. The word would go out. He'd meet someone in a pub near King's Cross and be halfway to solving it.

But for the past two years he'd watched Silver at work. It was a different method from his own, but that didn't mean it wouldn't work. Just that it wouldn't work most of the time.

'It wasn't only the neatness,' Silver said. 'I'll have another look at it.'

13

The estate was called the Douglas Garden Estate, which was a bitter irony. It lay in North London just beyond the borders of fashionable Islington. It had been created at the end of the nineteenth century by the wealthy philanthropist, Sir Gavin Douglas, for the new breed of factory workers drawn into London from the poverty-ridden countryside.

Sir Gavin had visualised the kind of village – with vegetable gardens and roses round the doors – which they were used to, or which he thought they were used to, instead of the slums of Shoreditch and Whitechapel.

His dream lasted until the 1960s when the town planners ripped it down and put in its place a series of high- and low-rise apartment blocks surrounded by lawns and trees, with concrete walkways and concrete playgrounds.

On paper it had looked terrific. Now, less than thirty years later, it was suffering from neglect, vandalism, blight and the result of cheap-jack system building.

Silver had never been to the Douglas Garden Estate and, as Eddie Twyford drove slowly into the grounds, he looked about him with a rising sense of disgust.

At first, it seemed as though the place might have been the scene of some World War I battle. Trees were stripped of their branches, the grass was churned into mud, the grey walls of one apartment block were stained by smoke, and many of the windows were boarded up with corrugated iron sheets.

'Nice, isn't it?' Macrae said.

'It looks like a bomb hit it,' Silver said.

'It did in a way,' Eddie said. He turned to Macrae. 'Remember 1986?'

84

Silver knew that it had been the scene of a riot that had ended in a battle between the local youth and the police in which a policeman had been killed.

The car moved slowly up one of the concrete roads which linked the apartment blocks.

'You're looking at a no-go area, laddie. We tell everybody there aren't any in London. Well, this is one. The postmen don't call here any longer. The milkmen won't deliver. Nor will anyone else. And if you have a heart attack say your prayers because ambulances won't come without police protection.'

As Silver looked around, he could not see a living soul.

Macrae read his mind. 'They're watching us all right. Don't you mistake it.' He waved at the grey concrete towers. 'Every window's like an eye. More crack's sold here than anywhere else in London.'

'What's the name? Thack-something?' Eddie said.

'Thackeray.'

The blocks had been named after famous authors: Thackeray House, Trollope House, Eliot House, Austen House and Dickens House. Silver doubted whether many books got read on the Douglas Garden Estate.

'Here you are guv'nor,' Eddie said, coming to a stop. 'Thackeray House.'

Macrae and Silver got out. Nothing moved. The cold wind blew scraps of paper on to a chain-link fence.

'It's like a bloody graveyard,' Macrae said.

And as he spoke something landed behind them with a terrible crash.

Not more than a few feet away was a block of concrete about the size of a brick. It had smashed on landing and parts had struck the car. Eddie leaped out. 'Jesus Christ!'

Silver was already racing into the front of the building. The lift had an Out of Order notice on the open doors and he took the stairs three at a time.

In the TV movies this was the time to whip out the old police special but the only thing Silver had to point was his finger.

The block was four storeys high with a fixed ladder leading

to the roof. Silver looked about for some implement. The landing stank of solvent and there were empty glue tubes everywhere. But nothing he could use as a weapon. He mounted the stairs and pushed open the door to the roof.

It was flat, surrounded by a parapet. The roof too, was littered with empty tubes and plastic bags and there were several needles. Apart from that it was empty. But on the parapet were three more pieces of concrete all the same size as the first one. Ready and waiting. *Boy scouts be prepared.* No wonder no one came near the place, he thought.

He went down and reported to Macrae. 'Well, there's not much we can do about it. What's her number?'

'Twenty-eight. It's on the second floor.'

The door to Number 28 was like all the other doors in the block. It opened on to a long exposed corridor that ran the length of the building. The mauve paintwork was cracked and peeling, one window had been broken and was boarded up, the second was heavily re-inforced with wire mesh.

Macrae pressed the bell but that was broken too. He tried to rattle the letterbox flap but it had been blocked. He banged on the door for several seconds and then put his ear to it. 'There's someone there all right. I can hear voices. Come on! Open up!'

He rattled the door handle and banged again. After what seemed like an age Silver heard a lock turning. The door opened a fraction on a heavy chain.

At first Silver could not see anything, then he let his eyes travel downwards. A little girl was looking at them through the crack.

'Is your mother in?' Macrae said.

'Are you a new friend?' the little girl said. Silver thought she might have been seven or eight.

'We're from the police.'

The little girl stared at them.

Silver went down on his haunches. 'What's your name?' he said.

'Sharlene.'

'That's a lovely name. We want to see your mummy. Will you let us in?'

'I'm not allowed.'

Behind her, Silver could hear voices, then music. He realised it was the TV.

'We're new friends,' Macrae said. 'Your mummy will want to see us.'

Sharlene closed the door and slipped the chain. As Macrae opened it she ran back to the sitting-room. She picked up an old teddy bear and sat in a torn chair in front of the screen.

'Leave her be,' Macrae said, closing the lounge door.

There were two bedrooms. They looked into the first. It contained two bunks with cheap duvets crumpled on them. The floor was a mass of dirty clothes and broken toys. They moved to the other bedroom. Macrae knocked on the door and opened it. The smell was almost solid; a mixture of stale perfume and marijuana.

The walls were painted black and the closed curtains were dark red. Paper mobiles hung from the ceiling and when Macrae switched on the light Silver saw that its shade was a Japanese lantern.

On the floor on the far side of the room was a double mattress. Someone was asleep on it. Macrae went over and shook the sleeper by the shoulder.

'Wake up.'

Silver found himself standing in the centre of the room unwilling to touch anything in case whatever made up the patina on the furniture came off on his fingers.

'Are you Mrs Collins?'

This time Macrae was rougher. The woman groaned and turned. Macrae said, 'Open the curtains, laddie.'

The hard grey light of March rushed into the room.

'What you want?' The voice was a subterranean croak.

'To talk to you,' Macrae said.

This took some moments to sink in. 'Can't you see I'm sleeping?'

'Mrs Collins? Mrs Delilah Collins?'

'What?'

Macrae took out his warrant card and held it in front of her.

'Police? How you get in?'

'Your daughter let us in.'

'Shit! I tell her no one!'

'We're new friends,' Macrae said, drily.

'To hell.'

Mrs Collins got to her knees, wrapping a blanket round herself and then rose slowly. She was a light-skinned coloured woman with a skin tone like beech leaves in winter. Her black hair came down to her shoulders. She heaved herself up and in doing so the blanket slipped and Silver saw that she was naked. She had large breasts that were beginning to sag, but her body was still quite good.

They had checked on her before leaving Cannon Row. Twenty-seven years old, with a history of petty crime. Married to a lorry driver called Wayne.

'What you want?'

'It's about Terence.'

'Who? Oh, Terry. Listen I . . . ' She rubbed her face with her hands as though trying to clear it – and clear her mind at the same time.

'Maybe she'd like to get dressed,' Silver said. 'We could wait in the sitting-room.'

'You want to get dressed, Mrs Collins?'

'What the time?'

'About noon.'

'You find Terry?'

'You get dressed,' Silver said.

They went through to the sitting-room. Sharlene was sitting about three feet from a huge TV set. The teddy bear was on her lap and she was sucking her thumb. She was watching an old black-and-white programme about World War II in France. She was staring at it like a zombie and Silver realised she was not absorbing anything. After a few moments Mrs Collins came into the room. She was dressed in mock leopard-skin pants and a white see-through blouse.

'Go to the bedroom,' she said to Sharlene.

Instantly the child slipped out of the room carrying her teddy.

'Now, what you want to aks me?'

'How many children have you got, Mrs Collins?' Silver said.

'What you want to know that for? You aks me about Terry, nothing else.'

She had recovered, and all her inherent distrust and hatred of the police was written on her wide face. Silver had wondered first of all if she was a dealer, but she looked too dim for that. He had met her type several times before. Caught in a poverty trap, abandoned by her husband, probably only semi-literate, almost certainly innumerate, she would not have been able to cope with even the modest complexities of drug dealing.

It was much more likely that she was a tart and that the 'new friends' which Sharlene let in and out were clients.

'Where's Terry? Where's my boy? You've had more than a week.'

She padded round the room, found a pack of cigarettes and lit one.

'Tell us about Terry,' Macrae said.

'What can I tell you?' The anger was near the surface now. 'He's fourteen years old. He run away. What more is there?'

'Photographs?' Silver said. 'You got any?'

'No . . . Yes.' She rummaged in the drawer of a scarred bureau and finally found a creased photograph. It showed a boy in running vest and shorts holding a small silver cup. Beside him was a coloured man in his sixties, his arm about Terry's shoulders.

'He's an athlete,' she said.

'Who's the man with him?' Macrae said.

'His grandfather. He was teaching him.'

'When did Terry leave home, Mrs Collins?'

'A week ago. I said so!'

'It's nearly two weeks ago,' Macrae said. 'You couldn't have seen much of him.'

'That's my business how much I see of people.'

'What was he wearing the last time you saw him?' Silver said.

'Shirt . . . brown jersey . . . jeans . . .'

'What about a hat?' Silver said.

'Hat?'

'Hasn't he got a green woollen hat?'

89

'Oh, that. Yeah. His grandfather give it to him.'

'Why would he run away?' Silver said.

'Yes, why?' she snapped back. 'He has a good home here. Everything. TV. You aks why he run away? You find out, you tell me. I'm going to lather him when I find him.'

'You lather him often?' Silver said.

'What you want to know for? What business is it of yours?'

'Watch your mouth!' Macrae said. 'I know all about you. I know the sort of person you are. I know what you do for a living. I know how you spend your days and nights. You start getting cheeky with us and I'm going to start asking questions about Sharlene. Why she's not at school. Why she's being brought up in an unwholesome atmosphere.'

'Unwholesome!' Her voice rose.

'For Christ's sake!' Macrae said. 'Just answer the questions.'

'What d'you mean teaching him?' Silver said. 'You said his grandfather was teaching him. What? Reading? Writing?'

'No. Not that. Running. Jumping. They were always in the park.'

'Was your father an athlete?'

'He done some in Jamaica. He always telling people. Talking big.' She spat it out and Silver registered that her anger had switched from them to her father.

'Where is your father?'

'He's dead.'

'When?'

'Two months ago.'

'Did he live here?'

'He slep' there, on the couch.'

'All right, Mrs Collins,' Macrae said. 'Let's get back to Terry. Why d'you think he ran away?'

'Maybe the school business.'

'What business was that?'

'You don't know?'

'You tell us.'

'He try to burn it down.'

'What, the whole school?'

'His classroom.'

'Why?'

'How can I know? You aks me questions I tell you, but no one knows what going on in that boy's head.'

'Where's his school?' Macrae said. She told him. 'All right, we'll do some checking and we'll get back.'

'Here?'

'That's right. And when we come back I don't want to see Sharlene here. I want to hear that she's at school. You understand me?'

She did not reply, but stood with her hands on her hips, staring at him.

'You better do it,' he said.

14

Terry was in the house. He was safe. It was a piece of cake. That's what his grandfather always used to say when he meant something was easy. *Piece of cake.*

When gas had been brought into these houses late in the nineteenth century, the pipes had been laid in the roof spaces and had run the length of the mews. All the houses were the same height, all looked the same.

When Terry had come through the party wall from the stables he had entered the roof space of the house next door. He had wriggled along the narrow planks and the sound of the horses vanished and the smell vanished and he lay in the loft, which was lit only by a dusty skylight, and tried to work out what to do.

He was afraid, and for those early moments the enclosed space helped. It was a kind of cave, a shelter, a den – like they'd had under Hungerford Bridge. If Gail had been there he would have been all right.

He knew he was over the rooms in a house because there were small holes in the ceiling and he could look down on to floors and a bed and a bath. But he did not know if the house was inhabited.

He lay quite still for a long time. If he remained like that no one would ever find him. He would die there. He had seen corpses and skeletons in horror movies, the kind his mother and her friends sometimes watched. That's what they'd find up here one day. And when they touched him everything would turn to dust and no one would know who he was.

He had little idea how long he remained in this confined and chilly place but eventually he began to try and stretch his limbs and make a plan for the future. Not the future that other people planned for, but the next few minutes.

He had listened and listened but heard nothing from below. Now as he moved about he found a couple of old dusty suitcases and a canvas golf bag with half a dozen ancient clubs behind a galvanised water tank. He also came upon a short ladder.

If someone had stored suitcases and there was a ladder then there must be a way up and a way down. He was 'thinking'. 'Use your brains, mon,' his grandfather had always told him. 'Think.'

But he couldn't see how the ladder could go anywhere until he realised that it was itself fixed to a trapdoor. He pushed on the ladder. Slowly the trapdoor swung down and the ladder gave access to the top of the house.

He lay in the loft for a while listening and looking. He could see two doors leading off a tiny landing. Everything was tiny in this house. There was blue wall-to-wall carpeting and the paintwork was white. The place had a chilly look.

He climbed down the ladder. Each step was an exploration in itself. He looked into the top-floor rooms and recognised the double-bed in one as the bed he had seen through the hole in the ceiling. He looked into the bathroom. There was no sign of it having been recently used.

Slowly he went down the stairs and found that he was holding the knife in his hand. Hastily he put it away.

The rooms were suffused by a soft grey light coming through the venetian blinds that covered each window. There were two rooms on the ground floor. One had a sofa, chairs, a filing cabinet and a desk. Off it was a small kitchen. He noticed there was a layer of fine dust over everything and the musty smell of a house which has not been opened for some time.

He stood in the centre of the room, his ears like hydrophones searching for the slightest noise. Suddenly there was a sound behind him. He whirled. He was looking into the kitchen. But it was empty. He realised that the fridge had switched itself on. In his hand was the knife. The blade was extended. He had no idea how it had got there.

He opened the fridge door. There was nothing in it except icetrays. He opened a long food cupboard. There were dozens of tins and packets. He knew now that the house had not been used for some time. He smiled. He felt almost arrogant. He had a house in London. He had food. He opened a tin of baked beans and ate it with a spoon, then opened a pot of apricot jam and ate that. His hunger was stilled for the moment.

He went into the sitting-room, opened drawers and cupboards. There was nothing that interested him. On a low coffee table there was a carved wooden box containing cigarettes. They were stale and brittle but he lit one and smoked it.

For the first time in many hours he felt safe.

'They go like that,' Howard Smith said. 'Call it puberty, bad company, modern society – call it what you like. One week they're young boys. Biddable. Even sweet. The next they're bloody monsters.'

Macrae and Silver were in a small ante-room at the Edward VII Comprehensive School in North London. It was part red-brick, part 1960s 'modular' with an asphalt playground and a perimeter fence that would have looked more natural, Silver thought, at Auschwitz. Apart from the buildings there was some exhausted grass squeezed in between a plastics factory and a British Rail goods depot.

When they drove up to it Macrae had said, 'No wonder they turn out knife artists.'

'I went to a place like that,' Eddie Twyford said, pulling up at the kerb.

Silver had thought of his own school. Also Victorian red-brick but a world away from this.

Howard Smith was – or had been, it depended how you looked at it – Terry Collins's form teacher. He was in his mid twenties, with a pudgy face, thinning hair, and heavy-framed glasses which gave him the look of a technocrat. Which was what he was going to be.

He had told them, in almost his opening sentence, that he was getting out of teaching. 'You've seen how grim it looks,' he said, waving his hand to encompass the school, 'and they expect us to come here day after day and teach for a pittance. How would you like to earn—'

'We're not here to listen to a speech about teachers' pay,' Macrae said, still angry about Sharlene. 'We're talking about a boy.'

Smith flushed. 'I know that. You don't have to take that tone with me. I'm just telling you why I'm leaving the profession. Why I'm going into industry. And from that you should be able to build a picture of part of the reason why Terry is like he is, why he did what he did. Oh, I'm not excusing the little bastard. You think I shouldn't talk like that about the country's young? Well let me tell you about the country's young. They're—'

'He ever call himself Huntsman? Or a name like that?' Macrae said, cutting brutally across Smith's rising inflection.

'What?'

'Huntsman.'

'Not that I ever heard. His name was Terence. Terry.'

'You ever see him carry a knife?' Silver said.

'Not that I can remember. But he came from the Douglas Garden Estate. Nothing would surprise me.'

Macrae said, 'Tell us about the fire.'

'It was about two weeks ago. He'd just finished a project. It was his idea. He'd built an athletics stadium. The stands were made out of *papier mâché*, the grass was green plastic matting and the running track some sort of rubber which he'd painted light brown and then marked with lanes. That's all he thought about. Athletics.'

'Well, it's different, isn't it?' Silver said. 'Who coached him? You?'

'Me? Heavens, no!' He threw up his hands. 'I don't know the first thing about running. Even if I did it would be a non-starter. Not with what we're paid. They want us to teach? We'll teach. They want us to oversee games, they pay us to oversee games.'

For a second Silver caught an old-maidish tone and he looked at Smith more closely.

95

'Who coached him? I've seen a picture of him holding a cup.'

'I don't know anything about a cup but, if he was coached at all, it would be by the P. E. teacher. All I know is he'd been in trouble before. Sniffing glue. But they all do that. I had a talk with him. Didn't get anywhere. So I spoke to Social Services and they sent someone round to his home. Then one of his relatives died. An uncle or a grandfather. I remember that because he stopped work on his project. It was nearly finished and he just stopped. I kept on at him about it and finally I told him if he didn't finish it I'd withhold his marks and he'd fail his year.'

'And?'

'And so he burnt it. And the classroom went up. And the books and desks. It's a miracle the school didn't burn down.'

'And?'

'He disappeared. We told Social Services and they went to see his mother. Something of a case, I hear. And that's that.'

'What d'you mean, that's that?' Silver said.

'I mean that's it. Finished. As far as I'm concerned anyway.'

'When do you leave?'

'Tomorrow. Thank God! One thing: I didn't realise the police spent as much time as this on a missing person. I thought you just wrote it down in a book and that was that.'

'Everything's pretty much that's that with you, isn't it, sir?' Macrae said. The 'sir' was like an expletive. 'Well, now you know. You better give me your private address.'

'Whatever for?'

'In case we need to interview you again.'

By the time they got back to Cannon Row the weather was beginning to clear. It was still cold but there was blue sky over London and the old brick glowed.

Macrae stuck his head into the Incident Room. Because of the victim's high profile it and several other rooms were full of detectives manning the phones, interviewing members of the public who thought they had vital pieces of evidence, and writing reports. All the media pressure, and it was considerable, was handled by the press room in Scotland Yard. Detective Sergeant Laker, who was in charge, came to the door.

'How's it going, Harry?' Macrae said.

'Like bloody Bedlam, guv'nor.'

'All right, fill me in.'

Macrae went to his own office, followed by Laker. There was a pile of official message sheets on his desk and he began to leaf through them as Laker talked.

'He's been sighted all over the place,' Laker said. 'We've had calls from bloody Scotland. Even Ireland. 'Course, everybody wears a green hat there, or so they tell me.'

'Always happens when we release details to the media.'

'There's some punter in Liverpool says he's caught him and locked him in his garage. But we've checked with the local lads and they say he's round the bend.'

'Forensic?'

'Should be there, guv'nor,' Laker said, pointing to the message sheets. 'There it is. Anyway, they found nothing but Foster's prints.'

'Anything else?'

'The Coroner's office has been on. PM's tomorrow afternoon.'

Macrae was looking at a sheet of ordinary paper with a personal message. It had not been logged and read simply: 'Mrs Macrae phoned. Says will you phone her back?'

Laker said, 'And the Chief wants to see you, guv'nor.'

'I haven't had my bloody lunch yet. See if you can find Silver. Tell him to eat something now. We're not going to have too much time.'

Macrae stood alone in his office for a few moments. He always cut an old-fashioned figure next to Silver. In fact, he did so next to most officers. The bomber jacket was very much the style among the young DCs and sergeants, but Macrae tended to wear more formal dress. He was wearing a heavy black and grey tweed overcoat with the collar turned up. It made him seem even bigger. He got an outside line and dialled his ex-wife's number.

15

Terry stood at the bedroom window staring down at the mews. By adjusting the venetian blinds he could look out without being seen. He had never been in a mews until the night before. He thought it looked pretty. It was cobbled and each little house was painted a different colour, most were pale pink or pale green. Many still had garages on the ground floor with notices asking people not to park in front of them.

There were several cars in the mews. They looked expensive and well-kept. On the opposite side, a few doors away, a man was working on a large Toyota station wagon. The bonnet was up and he was leaning into the engine.

Suddenly, Terry was back on the Douglas Garden Estate, looking down from the apartment window, watching his grandfather work on his car.

In his inner ear he could hear his mother come up behind him and say, 'I'm expectin' company. Go down and help your grampa.'

That's how he had first come to know what she was doing. That and the rows between her and his grandfather. They were extensions of the rows his mother and father used to have.

He couldn't remember his father clearly. He had left some years before. If the truth were known, Terry hadn't cared much one way or the other. His father was a long-distance truck driver and most of the time he was on the road. Sometimes, late at night or early in the morning, the door would open and he would come in. And it seemed to Terry that almost from the moment he set foot in the flat the rows would start.

And then one week he simply hadn't come home and they never saw nor heard from him again. Instead, Garner Maitland had come to occupy the sofa in the sitting-room and Terry's life had changed.

The rows went on, but unlike those between his parents these did not carry a sense of danger. They just went on and on in a low-key, hopeless kind of way.

They argued about everything, money, food, TV, the children's upbringing, until finally Garner Maitland seemed to give up and accept the status quo.

What Terry had never been able to understand was how a man like his grandfather, a famous four-hundred-metre runner, a man who had just missed selection for the Jamaican relay team in the 1948 Olympics – the strongest team in the world – how a man like that could have worked for the London Underground.

Terry had seen black people in the underground stations and they always seemed to be doing menial work, cleaning and sweeping.

One day he had asked his grandfather and the old man had paused while he gave the question some thought and had then said softly, 'We all has to work somewheres. I likes trains.'

Then he had retired and his pension was small and that was another subject on which he and his daughter would argue. He wasn't giving her enough for his board and lodging, she said. She accused him of spending more on his old car than he gave her.

It was true, he did lavish money on the car. He loved that car. It was a little Morris Minor. He had owned it since before they became collectors' items. He worked on it every day, cleaning and polishing, and tuning the engine. It had furry seat covers and special mats and extra lights in the rear window that came on when you braked. It had a steering wheel cover and a special aerial and a host of other knick-knacks.

Terry had never seen a car that shone like it. Even the outside of the tyres was blackened so that they looked new.

Because of the dangers of leaving it outside, the old man

used part of his pension to rent garage space. One night the garage was broken into, the car was stolen and the police found it across the river in Rotherhithe. There was almost nothing left of it except the chassis. The wheels were gone, the body panels had been removed, the radio had been ripped out and even the engine had been stolen. That was the end of Garner Maitland's life as a car owner.

But they still had to keep out of the flat so they started to go to the park. At the beginning it had just been a place to go to. And then one day the old man had tied a piece of string to a tree and held the other end and said to Terry, 'See if you can jump over it, mon.'

And that's how Terry became the world's greatest athlete. Well, second greatest athlete. Only Daley was better.

He became tired of watching the man in the mews work on the car and lay down on the bed and looked up at the ceiling. He stared up for a long time thinking of Gail, wondering where she was, what she was doing. He wished she was with him. This is what they had always wanted, what they had talked about.

But the man had come between them. The man and the knife. He felt tears come to his eyes then. He hadn't wanted to *harm* him. It wasn't his fault. And yet, who would believe him? Finally exhaustion overtook him and he slept.

'One lamb tikka,' Macrae said to the waiter. 'One beef Madras. Two pilau rice. Two chappatis.' He looked across at his former wife. 'Poppadums?'

'All right.'

'Two poppadums. Onion bhajee. Mixed vegetables. And some mango chutney and lime pickle and—'

'I am bringing you all the condiments, sir,' the waiter said.

He ordered a glass of white wine for Linda and a lager with a whisky on the side for himself and then, as the waiter was turning away, he said, 'Oh, and bring me a little bowl of chilli sauce as well.'

Linda Macrae had watched this with the slight feeling of nervousness she always felt when George took her out to a restaurant. He was such a big man and he was so firm that the waiters were usually in awe of him. He didn't mean anything by it, it was just his way. But she was always relieved when the waiter smiled and went off to the kitchen.

'Well . . . ' she said, looking down at her hands and wishing she had her glass of wine to fiddle with.

Macrae lit a thin panatella and drew in the smoke hungrily. 'How long has it been?' he said.

'You mean since we saw each other or had a meal together?'

'I don't know. Either.'

'We haven't seen each other for a year and we haven't had a meal together since God knows when.'

They were in a small Indian restaurant on the borders of Battersea. She had recently bought a flat in Clapham. 'So we're neighbours,' she said. 'I never thought I'd live as close in to the West End again.'

She and her daughter had been living out at Tooting, but since Susan had left home to stay with her boyfriend, Linda had become restless.

'You're better off in a smaller place,' he said.

'That wasn't why I bought it.'

She looked very good, he thought. Like some of those women you see in the West End coming out of offices about six o'clock in the evening. Well-dressed. Well-groomed. Smart. Christ, who'd have thought that Linda would have turned into this?

'You've put on weight,' she said. He opened his mouth and she stopped him. 'Oh, I know. So have I.'

'It suits you.'

'Thank you, but I'd be happier if I shed ten pounds.' It did suit her, he thought. She had been thin when they'd married. And then put on weight when she was pregnant. He recalled her face then. Not quite plump, but smoothly radiant. And then she'd lost it again. Especially over the period of the divorce. Then she had become quite haggard. Now, she was just about right.

She was of medium height with light brown hair and a face that had once been soft and pretty and which was still attractive, but not soft any more. It was a lived-in face. Her breasts, he had noted when he helped her off with her

101

coat, were fuller than he remembered and her legs were still good. He had to tell himself that she was forty-three and not thirty-three and that she had a daughter of twenty-one.

'Why did you?' he said.

'What?'

'Buy a new flat if the other place wasn't too big?'

'I thought I needed a change.' He looked surprised. 'Well, Susan's gone.' She smiled tightly at him. 'Flown the nest.'

The waiter brought the drinks and she took up her glass of wine. She wouldn't have known what a glass of wine was when they were married, Macrae thought. She had a glass of sherry at Christmas and that was about it. God, the times he'd taken her to office parties and she'd just sat there sipping an orange juice and lemonade while the young PCs tried to look up her skirt. It was something to smile about: Macrae the tough thief-taker and his innocent little wife. Now here she was drinking dry white wine.

He had noted her clothes. She was wearing a skirt and blouse. The blouse looked like silk and the skirt one of those you saw in the windows of Simpsons in Piccadilly. She was probably earning bloody good money, he thought. He'd heard that managing directors' PAs were well looked after. He wondered if she let the boss get his leg over and felt a momentary pang of . . . what? Envy? Jealousy?

'You said on the phone you wanted to talk about Susan,' he said. 'Bad news?'

'No. Not really. You want to talk about it now?'

'Let's eat first.'

'Anyway, that's why I bought the new place. New life. New phase of it anyway. It's like a face-lift.'

'You're going to miss her.'

'I do. You think that when you have the place to yourself, when you don't have to wash their dirty dishes and pick up their dirty clothes, you think life will get a little easier. But then, after a while, you start missing it. Now the place is squeaky clean.'

'You always kept a clean and tidy house,' Macrae said. 'You were the world's number one nest builder.'

The food came and they helped themselves and he spooned

102

some of the chilli sauce over his rice. Within a minute or two he started to sweat below the eyes. He ordered another round of drinks and gave his attention to the food. He ate quickly. The chilli sauce poured on to his stomach lining like Greek fire.

'I don't know how you can eat that stuff,' she said.

'I'm supposed to be near the end of something called the curry cycle. Next time I explode.'

She smiled. He didn't often make jokes.

He finished long before she did and sat looking broodingly at his empty plate. To make conversation she said, 'What are you on?'

'A murder.'

'Not the TV one?'

He nodded.

'I might have guessed. You were always working on holiday weekends. And Christmas. You remember that Christmas when the three of us were going to the Holiday Inn? Where was it? I can't remember.'

'Portsmouth.'

'That's right. And we'd packed our suitcases. Susan and I were just about to get the train. You were meeting us down there. And then you phoned that something had come up.'

He drew hard on the cigar and inhaled the smoke. He remembered very well. He'd been on the Flying Squad then. They'd had a tip that some villains were going to tunnel through a dry cleaning shop near King's Cross Station into the bank next door. They'd had the dry cleaners under surveillance for more than forty-eight hours. The villains were supposed to go in on the evening of Christmas Eve. So he'd phoned Linda and told her. Then, almost immediately, their informant was on the blower to say the job had been called off.

They'd gone back to Scotland Yard and had a few drinks and it had turned into a Christmas party and he and Mandy had ended up in a hotel that night. He'd gone home the following day about noon.

'Yes, I remember,' he said.

He ordered coffee and asked her if she wanted another drink and she shook her head. He ordered a large brandy

103

for himself then said, 'Come on. Have a liqueur. It isn't every night we go out to dinner.'

'That's true. I'll have a Calvados.'

His heavy eyebrows shot up. He looked at the waiter. 'You have Calvados?'

'Yes, sir.'

When the waiter had gone he said, 'Since when did you start drinking Calvados?'

'There's a lot you don't know about me, George.'

'I can see that.'

'I suppose in a way we'll always be little Linda Brown and big George Macrae to each other. I've never told you this, but I never liked you at school.'

'You hardly knew me. I was a couple of years ahead of you.'

'We still talked about you. You were known as the bruiser, because you boxed. Some of the girls didn't like boxing much.'

'Some did.'

'Boxing was all part of it, wasn't it?'

'Part of what?'

'What you had to get out of yourself.'

'I suppose so.'

They both knew what she was talking about.

'It certainly came out of me the night you found me,' he said. 'Not the way it was supposed to either.'

By that time he had left school and he was boxing for a club. Some said he might be the next light heavyweight champion of England. He'd won a narrow points decision against the champion of a club in Hackney and some of the local lads didn't fancy George, or the decision, and they'd beaten him up and dumped him on the pavement near his own house. That's where Linda had found him.

'I nearly didn't take you in that night,' she said. 'I hardly recognised you your face was so swollen.'

'I learned a lot of things that night.'

'Such as?'

'When you fight, you fight to win. Doesn't matter if it's clean or not. Your father wouldn't have liked that, would he? I mean, me saying it.'

104

She sipped the Calvados. He wasn't ageing well, she thought. There was a kind of seediness about him, a quality she had recognised in other men without women. Half the police force seemed to have been divorced.

'No. He wouldn't.'

She'd been living with her father then. He had recently been invalided out of the police. By the time George met him he was dying. White hair and white beard and looking like an Old Testament prophet. He'd seen something in George and George had found something to respond to in him that he'd never found in his own father. He was only a sergeant. He'd never wanted to go further. Sergeant Joseph Brown. He'd been the one who had influenced Macrae into going into the police.

Several times he had said, 'You only need to remember two words. Self-discipline and self-respect. Remember them and you'll not go far wrong.'

In those days Macrae was working in a bank and he used to come round to see Linda and her father in the evenings. They would talk about the police. The old man liked to reminisce. Linda would always be doing something: mending for her two brothers, preparing meals, washing up. Then there had been all the added work when her father became bedridden.

Self-discipline. Self-respect. Both had been abandoned with all the other luggage of his life, Macrae thought.

'You know George, I've never told you this but when you le— When we split up . . . I thought my life was over . . . '

He shifted uneasily in his chair and swallowed a mouthful of brandy.

'I went completely numb. For a long time I didn't know what day of the week it was. If I hadn't had Susan to look after I think I would've . . . well, I don't know what I'd have done. You see, I'd always looked after someone. After mother died I looked after my brothers, then my father. So it was natural to transfer everything to you. I suppose I transferred the father–daughter relationship too. That's what probably made it more difficult for you.

'But I've never been as happy as when we had that police

105

house in Norwood. The one with the damp in the sitting-room. I didn't really mind when you went on night duty or different shifts or had to work over holidays. I knew you'd always come back. You're right. It *was* nest building. So when you . . . When we broke up, it almost finished me.'

'Why are you telling me this?'

'Because you think you know me and you don't. You look surprised that I drink white wine. Surprised I know what Calvados is. I've seen you looking at my clothes. At me. I'm not the same Linda Brown you knew. Or even the same Linda Macrae.' She paused and then said, 'I hated you George, really hated you.'

'For God's sake!'

'No, no, that's over. Now I'm grateful to you. For two years I just sat watching Susan grow up and feeling sorry for myself. I had no skills, you see. I never learned anything. Except to look after people. And Susan was at school and you'd gone, so there wasn't anyone to look after a lot of the time.

'I remember thinking things would get better in the future. And then one day Susan had gone to school and the house was empty and I was having a cup of coffee and I think it was raining and I suddenly realised this *was* the future. Nothing was going to get better unless I made it get better. That's when I took shorthand and typing and accountancy and word processing. And I did really well.'

'You were always clever at school.'

'That's when little Linda changed. Now I've got a very good job. I know what good clothes are and I know what Calvados is. And I've been abroad and I've done a lot of reading. You once said I should read *Great Expectations*. Well, I've read it and half a dozen other Dickens'. And I know lots of things I didn't know before. And the thing is I've got you to thank for it, George.'

He wanted to say something but there was nothing to say. When he'd begun his affair with Mandy, Linda had forgiven him. Forgive was not strong enough, he thought. She'd become a bloody martyr. He'd felt stifled and more guilt-ridden as a result. It had been like sinking gently into a thick soup, drowning in love and sentiment and forgiveness

106

when all he wanted was to get out of the house and take Mandy to bed.

She finished her liqueur and put the glass down firmly on the table. He sensed her change of mood.

'Susan?' he said.

It was quickly told. Susan and her boyfriend wanted to do what many young people were doing – to wander through South-East Asia and Australia. They wanted to fly to Singapore then, using local transport and coasters, island-hop to Perth.

Linda outlined the plan as matter-of-factly as possible. Macrae listened, his head dropping slightly forward like a bull's.

'And?' he said, when she'd finished.

'She'll need money, George.'

'That's what I thought it was about. How much?'

'They've worked it out and they think they should have three thousand each.'

'Three thousand!'

'It's not a lot these days, George. Not if you take fares into account.'

'How long are they supposed to be away?'

'As long as the money lasts.'

'Three thousand!' He shook his head slowly. 'You might as well ask for ten thousand or a hundred thousand. Every penny I have goes on Bobbie and Margaret.'

Her face hardened. 'Susan was your first child, George. You owe her just as much responsibility.'

'I've discharged that. She's twenty-one. She's got a job. She doesn't *have* to got to South-East bloody Asia. Bobbie and Margaret are still kids and—'

'I don't want to talk about them!' Linda broke in. 'I don't want to hear either their names or their mother's.'

'Listen to me,' George said, dropping his voice in the hope that she would take the hint. 'It's not only them. I'm still paying off the house.'

'That has nothing to do with Susan. You know, George, from the moment I started earning I didn't take a penny from you. So your other family has me to thank for extra

107

maintenance. The only money you paid us was to help Susan. And that wasn't a lot. We never badgered you. We've always wanted to be independent.'

'I know that.'

'Well, now your daughter wants to do something that's important to her. She's in love with a young man and she wants to be with him. I think it's up to you to give her the opportunity, because it'll never happen again.'

'What about the boyfriend? If he loves her so much why doesn't he pay for her?'

'For God's sake, he's still a student. I'm sure he would if he could.'

'So where's he getting his money?'

'From his father.'

'He's probably a bloody sight richer than I am. What's his name anyway? What's he do?'

'Her boyfriend's called Peter. Peter Kerman.'

'Kerman . . . I knew a Kerman once. Ronnie Kerman. He was the fence for that Hatton Garden diamond robbery. Remember?'

'He's the same man.'

'Christ, he got four years!'

'I know. Peter told Susan.'

'But I put him away!'

'I know that.'

'Do they?'

'No.'

'Jesus . . . and you want me to give her three thousand pounds to go—'

'Keep your voice down,' she said. 'It's not his fault. He was just a baby when it happened. You can't blame him for something his father did.'

'There's a rotten streak in families.'

'That's simply nonsense. I've met Peter and he's a sweet boy. Anyway, he's the one Susan wants. You don't have to see him or talk to him or do anything at all.'

'Except cough up the money.'

'That's right.'

'How the hell did she get mixed up with people like that?'

'With people like *what*? She hasn't got mixed up with the father. She's got mixed up, as you put it, with a very nice boy who's taking engineering at London University. Look, George, it's got nothing to do with either of us. She's twenty-one, it's her life. And she doesn't want you to give her the money, she wants to borrow it.'

'It makes no bloody difference one way or the other. A, I haven't got it and B, she probably couldn't repay it.'

'If you'd given any thought to us and your – your other responsibilities you'd have done something about it by now.'

'Like what?'

'Like got yourself promoted. You could have been a Commander by now. Everybody said so. And then you'd have had more money.'

'Money! Money! I'm sick to death of the word.'

'Well, you should have thought of that before you started an extended family and took on a couple of wives. George, I don't want to spoil this evening by getting into an argument with you. I've told you what the problem is and now it's up to you.'

He drove her home to Clapham and stopped in a street of Victorian terraced villas. They had been built at much the same time as his street. But this one was neat, with neatly parked cars and neatly tended gardens. It was middle class. A world away from the dereliction of his own street.

He half expected her to ask him in for a coffee. Instead, she leaned over and kissed him on the cheek and said, 'Thanks very much, George. I enjoyed that.'

'I'll ring you,' he said.

'Yes, do that.'

He watched her go up the steps to her front door. She walked confidently. He thought what a nice pair of legs she had. Then he turned the car and drove back to Cannon Row.

16

Leo Silver was so tired he could hardly see straight. In the past thirty-six hours he had only had about four hours' sleep. He and Macrae were in the Goodwood Sporting Club in an alley between the Strand and the river. It was nearly midnight and the club was full. Macrae was at the bar ordering drinks.

It was what was called in the trade a spieler, a club whose membership was almost totally made up of villains but of which a few coppers were honorary members.

It was a big room with a small bar at one corner. The decor was almost exclusively the Turf. There were pictures of Derby winners on the wall and a life-sized wooden carving of a jockey at the door.

It existed for gambling as much as drinking and at this time of night it was full, with half a dozen *kalooki* tables on the go and a small crowd standing round each one watching the play. Silver, who had been to the Goodwood several times with Macrae, found the game reminiscent of the gin-rummy he had played with his family when he was younger.

The first time he had visited the club, he had been surprised by the amount of money wagered on the cards. Players seemed to flaunt their 'wedges'. Some had them in metal clips, some in loose piles on the table-top. Each wedge contained hundreds, perhaps thousands of pounds.

There was a distinct social stratification among the villains. There were the heavies, the robbery-with-violence merchants, flash in silk shirts, silk ties and cashmere suits, and adorned with gold chains and gold bracelets, all smoking Upmanns or Romeo y Julietas.

Then there were the lesser fry, the con artists and hoisters. Silver, in spite of his exhaustion, was interested to see how both sets reacted to Macrae. They all greeted him, but it was in the quality of the greeting that they differed. The robbers nodded briefly. They tolerated his presence without welcoming him. The others kept sliding up to him and greeting him by name, always the formal 'Mr' before it. Macrae himself nodded briefly to them all. He was the biggest man in the room and although not by yards the best dressed, easily the most impressive, Silver thought.

'A dram and a pint,' Macrae said, putting down a pint of bitter and a double shot of whisky in front of Silver. 'And a dram and a pint for me.'

The room was filled with smoke and very warm and Macrae's face was red and sweaty. Silver had been waiting for him in the Incident Room at Cannon Row, thinking of Zoe and knowing that the evening was wrecked. Macrae had arrived, reeking of curry, to check the messages on his desk.

Silver had said, 'We're still getting sightings from everywhere. Green hats are the flavour of the week.'

Macrae grunted. 'I need a drink. Come on.'

They had driven up Whitehall into the Strand and parked outside the Goodwood. Now Macrae threw the whisky back into his throat and drank nearly a third of the pint of bitter.

'Well?' he said. 'What d'you think about Mrs Rose-Mary-bloody-Foster?'

The post-mortem had been brought forward at Macrae's request and afterwards they had gone down to interview the bereaved wife.

Silver said, 'I think I'd have had a flat in London if I was married to her.'

Macrae nodded slowly. 'She's a female Svengali.' He drained another third of his pint mug and rose. 'Bloody chilli sauce,' he said, and made for the door.

At first he had surprised Silver with his literary allusions. He had been equally surprised when he had seen the bookshelves in his house. There were modern novels but also Dickens and Trollope and Sir Walter Scott. It had taken Silver a little time to work out that Macrae deliberately gave the impression of being less clever than he was. In the case of Mrs Henry Foster, he was absolutely right.

111

They had left London in the early afternoon to drive to Sussex and the holiday traffic was building up. This meant that Eddie Twyford was in his element. Macrae had told him to get a move on and Eddie's way of fulfilling his guv'nor's wish was to abuse other motorists, and gun the car down quiet suburban streets to the terror of young mothers pushing prams. In this way he soon had them out in the open country.

Macrae sat in the back, enveloped in an overcoat and his own thoughts. Silver was in front with Eddie, who was never really happy outside London. 'Too effing draughty down here,' he said. 'Look at them cows. Freeze their balls off, this weather.' It was his proud boast that he had only ever been abroad once, on a day trip to Boulogne, and had not been near the seaside since he was a child.

The countryside was still in the grip of winter. Iron grey clouds were rushing over brown ploughed fields. Occasionally there was a splash of green where winter wheat made a brave showing, but spring was still a long way away.

Eddie drove fast. He had done his homework and as they entered Sussex he left the main roads and shot through tiny villages, deserted and forbidding.

Ninety minutes after leaving London they reached the Fosters' house. It lay in the folds of the South Downs west of Chichester and stood among beech trees at the end of a muddy lane. Silver had been expecting something cottagey, hung with red tiles. But the house was starkly modern, built of timber and grey brick.

Mrs Rose-Mary Foster met them at the door and took them into the sitting-room. The fire was laid but not lit and the air in the room had the chill of a crypt. The furnishing and colour tones, pale greys and greens, seemed to make it colder.

'I'm sorry to make you come all this way,' Mrs Foster said, 'but as I told your staff, one of my sons is ill and I can't leave him.'

She was in her late forties, with short cropped greying hair, and was wearing a dark grey sweater over a white blouse,

112

a dark blue skirt, dark claret-coloured woollen stockings and flat-heeled black brogues. She wore rimless glasses and her plain, sallow face was devoid of make-up.

'I'm sure you'd like some tea. Gerald!' she called into the silent house. They heard the pad of feet coming down the wooden staircase.

A boy of about eleven appeared. He was in pyjamas and a dressing-gown and his ancestry showed in his dark yellow skin.

'My son has had chicken-pox,' she said, 'but he is no longer infectious. Gerald, would you please put the kettle on.'

The boy had a serious, wide-eyed face. 'Yes, mother.' Silver's first impression of the house and its inhabitants was of a lack of emotional as well as physical warmth. There was no sound of music or TV coming from upstairs as there might have been in the sick-room of a child in an ordinary house.

For a moment he saw, in his mind's eye, the council flat on the Douglas Garden Estate, with Sharlene watching the TV hour after hour. He had a momentary pang of gratitude for his own family. Infuriating, opinionated, aggressive – at least they throbbed with life.

'Now, how can I help you?' Mrs Foster said.

'I'm sorry we have to intrude,' Macrae began. 'I realise what—'

She cut him off. 'Yes, thank you, Superintendent, let us assume the niceties.'

She was dry-eyed, Silver noted, and there was no evidence that she had been weeping. 'I'll do whatever I can to help you,' she said. 'My main preoccupation now is trying to keep life on an even keel for the sake of my two boys. But I also very much want whoever killed Henry to be brought to justice. So . . . what do you wish to know?'

'We want to know what sort of man your husband was, Mrs Foster,' Macrae said. 'We want a picture of him. We're interviewing his colleagues, of course, but they will only know his professional side.'

'What you're really asking is how did someone like myself meet and marry a coloured man, isn't that it?'

113

'I wouldn't—'

'Superintendent, I'm a member of the West Sussex County Council and I sit on the Social Services Committee. I know exactly what the police think of coloured people. And what they do to them. I know you must be wondering how a white English woman . . .'

'Why you married him is your business,' Macrae said, his heavy head falling slightly forward. 'It is our business to find out what he was doing under Hungerford Bridge with knife wounds to the stomach.' It was brutally phrased and Silver saw her flinch.

Gerald brought in a tea tray. 'Thank you,' his mother said. 'Go back to bed now.'

'Can I put the TV on?'

She hesitated. Silver thought she was about to refuse, but their presence must have made her change her mind. 'All right. But only for half an hour.'

She waited in silence until the boy had gone upstairs, then she said, as though they were old friends and neighbours, 'How do you like your tea?'

Silver watched her pour. There was something about her that made him uncomfortable. She reminded him of his sister, Ruth. When he was little he used to call her bossy-boots and regularly got a slap in the face. That's what this woman was, a bossy-boots, and given her head she would grind them into the pale grey Wilton carpet.

But Macrae was not going to give her her head.

'Do you want to expand on that?' she said.

'Not at the moment,' Macrae said.

It was like watching two fencers, except that Macrae didn't go to war with a foil but with a battle-axe.

She switched to attack again, 'Have you arrested anyone?'

'Not yet. If it's all right with you, Mrs Foster, I'll ask the questions.'

'I'm sorry,' she said, stiffly. 'I have certain rights.'

Macrae put his cup down. His face was slightly flushed. 'Of course you have. Now let's start at the beginning.'

Mrs Foster must have realised that her time had not come.

She retreated into a chilly dignity which exactly matched the room.

She spoke in short sentences without emotion. Henry Foster had been the son of a black solicitor whose practice was in an outer London suburb. Unlike most blacks in Britain, Henry had gone to a small private school and emerged with ambitions to become an actor. He had worked with amateur groups and then with a small repertory company, but after a year without a part had taken a job as a trainee TV announcer. From there he had moved over to TV journalism and gone into the provinces. It was while he was working for Hampshire Television that Rose-Mary had met him.

She had been working for one of the big London TV companies as producer/interviewer, making short community programmes about battered wives, child abuse, the chronically ill.

'We were recording a studio discussion in Winchester,' she said. 'When we finished he came in to do a short piece for their own local news about widow's pensions, which interested me. I asked him to have lunch so we could talk about it. Eventually it turned into another in my series.

'The first thing I registered about Henry was that he had a good relaxed manner. It's not easy to communicate to a camera but there are some people who can. Henry was one.

'He was far too good for provincial journalism so I saw the right people in London and two months later he was taken on by the BBC. He worked there for five years.

'We married and had two children which meant me giving up my job in London because I had *always* considered that the bringing up of children was the most important function a woman could perform. In any case, I'd become disenchanted with television. It's hit and miss. You try to change the social fabric but it's never possible to quantify your result. Coming to live down here and getting on to the County Council I could push forward my plans and see them come into being.'

Silver stifled a yawn and Macrae broke in before she could continue. 'You were telling us about your husband.'

She looked at him sharply then said, 'After Henry had

been five years with the BBC I was able to pull some strings and get him on to Channel Four. They gave him a slot at breakfast time where he could pursue some of the social problems that I . . . that we both felt needed pursuing. One of which, I may say, is to get more people from ethnic communities into broadcasting. I want to see more blacks and Indians and Pakistanis and . . . '

'And Jews?' Silver said.

She gave a short mirthless laugh and said, 'Oh, I think Jews can look after themselves, don't you?'

'Were you older than your husband?' Silver said.

'Why do you ask?'

'Please,' Macrae said, wearily.

'Yes. Henry would have been forty-one next month.'

'And you are?'

'I'm forty-nine, since you ask. But it made no difference to us. That's so much rubbish. Anyway, we were linked by common interests.'

'What about the apartment in Fulham?' Silver said. 'How long had Mr Foster had that?'

'I bought it three or four years ago. It seemed nonsense for Henry to get up at four in the morning to drive to London. Anyway, it disrupted the family.'

'Did you often go up and stay in the flat?' Silver said.

'Never. I simply do not have the time to go jaunting these days.'

'Mrs Foster,' Macrae began. 'I must ask you some rather personal questions. I wouldn't if I didn't think the answers might help us.'

She drew her lips into a thin line.

'Was your marriage a happy one?'

'I . . . yes, it was. I told you we had common interests – in social change, in the caring side of humanity, such as it is. We had our children. A love of the country. Walking. Henry had recently taken to bird watching.' She indicated a number of bird books on the coffee table.

'Was there . . . had there ever been problems with other women?' Macrae said.

'I hope I do not understand you.'

116

'Had Mr Foster, to your knowledge, ever had affairs? Was he that sort of person?'

'Certainly not, and I find the suggestion offensive.'

Macrae looked down at his big square hands. 'Mrs Foster, let me repeat. A man has been killed in London. There are many motives for murder but the three most likely are money, women or drugs.'

'Have you thought of a simple mugging?' she said sarcastically.

'That's the first thing we thought of. It's unlikely in this case.'

'Did he have any other interests?' Silver said. 'You mentioned bird watching. Anything else he could have pursued in London?'

'Such as?'

'People collect stamps or medals or coins. Something that would have brought him into contact with a group of people with common interests.'

'No. Nothing like that. He worked on his programme. Either at the flat in Fulham or at the studios.'

'Did he have a secretary?'

'Only for correspondence at the studios. And that's where the researchers were, in case you're wondering about them as well. Mostly he worked by himself. Did you see his programme?'

'No.'

'I should have thought that would have been the first thing to do. The format was simple. I thought of it for him. A variation on the talking head. Henry would do an interview but he himself would largely be edited out, except for topping and tailing. That made it appear that the interviewee was talking straight to camera. It produced a natural "live" feel. The programme went out five mornings a week. At weekends he and I would go over the names of possible future subjects.'

'Did you always agree?'

She looked surprised. 'Yes. We talked things through. In the end we always agreed.'

'What were the ratings?' Silver said.

'You don't expect a programme like that to make an impact on the ratings. I would have been horrified if it had. That would have meant we'd gone for the cheap option.'

They questioned her for another half an hour and then left.

In the car going back to London Macrae said, 'What'd you think of Mrs Foster?'

'Grey.'

'What's that supposed to mean?'

'Word association. You say, "Mrs Foster" and I say, "Grey". That's what comes to mind. Greyness and neatness.'

'You've got neatness on the brain.'

'I've never seen such neat places as his flat and his house. Can you imagine living like that, guv'nor?'

Macrae ignored him. 'I tell you what,' he said. 'I thought he must be bloody pushy to get where he got. You've got to have something extra if you're black. Like a woman. I mean to get on. But now I've seen her my guess is that's where the push comes from. I wonder if he'd been having it off. Living most of the week in London and married to a bitch like that. I know I would.'

At the Goodwood, Macrae put a bottle of whisky down on the table in front of Silver. 'Save us going backwards and forwards,' he said.

Silver looked at it. It was going to be one of those nights. It sometimes happened on a Friday, or before a public holiday. Macrae never wanted to go home.

'Evening, George,' a voice said above them.

No one in a spieler ever called Macrae 'George' and he lifted his head now and glared at the speaker. Then his expression changed.

'Hello, Tommy.'

Silver looked up to see a tall, thin man, older than Macrae. His hair was grey and there were deeply incised lines on his face. He was leaning forward on a stick.

Macrae introduced Silver and then said, 'Have a drink?'

'Can't, George. I'm on pills.'

They stood talking for a few moments and then Macrae

said, 'You ever hear anything about a fence called Kerman these days?'

'Ronnie Kerman? The one we put away after the Hatton Garden job? Not a thing. I think he's clean nowadays. Why?'

'Just wondered.'

When they were alone again, Macrae said, 'That was Tommy Ballard. He was my guv'nor at West End Central until he stopped a bullet. Smashed his thigh joint. But he likes to keep his hand in. Come on, drink up, laddie. You're not a girl.'

17

When Terry woke he was frightened. He lay in the dark for a long moment unable to comprehend where he was. Then memory flooded back and, like an animal that is beginning to form a territory, fear was replaced by a tenuous feeling of safety. This was *his* house, he told himself. *He* had found it. He felt like one of those children in the fairy stories his grandfather had told him; children who were lost in the forests and mountains of Jamaica and came upon sugar-cane cutters' houses made of beaten out kerosene tins. (When he got to school they laughed at him. Children got lost in northern forests. There were no cane cutters. And the houses were made of gingerbread.)

But, in the fairy stories, something horrible always happened to the children before they were saved. The horrible thing had already happened to him. Now he wanted someone to save him.

His grandfather had told him there was a God who watched over everyone and who knew everyone's secrets. And he remembered that his grandfather sometimes bargained with God, offering to do things in exchange for favours. Terry wanted to bargain himself, but what could he offer in exchange?

He got up, straightened the counterpane and went down to the kitchen. He could not put on any lights, of course, but enough streamed through the venetian blinds to see by. He went to the window and looked along the mews. It was deserted. Most of the cars were gone, except for the Toyota. The man was working now by the light of a torch.

He opened another tin of beans and ate them with a spoon. Then he smoked another stale cigarette. What was the point

120

of having your own house, he thought, with a larder full of food . . . if you were all by yourself?

When he had lain next to Gail in the den under Hungerford Bridge and when she wasn't zonked out they would talk in soft voices and the trains would rumble over them. He had felt safe then. She would tell him about herself and where she had come from and what had happened to her and he would tell her about his grandfather and his athletics. She was the only person he ever told. Indeed, she was the only person, with the exception of Garner Maitland, that he had ever really talked to. It was just sad about the drugs.

Then he thought of something brilliant. If she came to live in the house with him she wouldn't be able to get any drugs. There was enough food to last them a few weeks. There was a television set they could carry upstairs, maybe put it on the little landing where there were no windows. They might be able to watch it there. He was certain that all sorts of things could be done to make them safe.

Then there was the secret door to the stables, no one knew about that. No one had used it for years and years. And during the day he could go out and find some food and bring it back. And they could talk.

And so, in the cold black night, Terry went through the stables and stroked the horse called Mr Garner and slipped out of the window into the mews and set off in search of Gail.

Almost immediately he started to run. He crossed the Bayswater Road. The park was locked up tight for the night and he ran the long way round it. Running he became a different person.

Kutz . . . Landy . . . Zatopek . . . left right, left right. Day . . . lee . . . Day . . . lee . . . Except Daley was no distance runner. He always struggled. Even in the 1500 metres, the last event – no, not event, the last 'discipline' – of the decathlon.

Terry wasn't alone. Half a dozen late exercise-takers, all dressed much the same as himself, were jogging along the wide pavement.

Marble Arch and down Park Lane. Crossing the pain barrier now and getting his second wind. Zatopek leading

121

in that funny head–on–one–side–this–is–my–last–agonised–step style of running. Then Kutz. Then Huntsman Collins.

'In those days there wasn't no black distance runners,' his grandfather had said. 'We was sprinters. Blacks have special thigh bones. Longer than whites. Always remember that. But then our brothers from Africa come along. They run the distance, we run the sprints. Between us, mon, we takes everything.'

Kipchonge Keino . . . Mike Boit . . .

Lapping at sixty-eight . . . Don't get boxed . . . Eyes in the back of your head . . . Who's going to make the break . . . ? Who's going to cut you up . . . ? Bumping . . . Elbowing . . . Watch out for spikes . . . ! Here's the bell . . . Who's got the legs . . . the finish . . . ?

Keeping to the shadows now, the dark places, the alleys. Coming into the real London. Dossers in their cardboard boxes. Past midnight and not much traffic on the streets.

Tomorrow is Easter Friday, but Terry doesn't know that.

When he stopped he was less than three hundred metres from the Goodwood Sporting Club where Macrae was telling Silver to drink up. He was standing in the small garden that runs along the Embankment near the Savoy Hotel. He was hidden by a laurel bush that grew well above head height. From there he could look directly at the end of Hungerford Bridge. What he saw made him realise that Gail would not be there.

A uniformed cop walked slowly up and down. Terry watched him for nearly twenty minutes. He would walk thirty or forty metres one way and then thirty, forty, maybe a hundred metres the next and Terry would think he was going on along the Embankment and would soon disappear. Then he would turn and walk slowly back. Time after time. Sometimes he would stand still and beat his freezing hands together and Terry would feel his own icy fingers. But there was no gainsaying it, he was there, an implacable presence.

Terry wasn't surprised but he'd had to make sure. He felt a bitter sadness, for now he knew he'd lost her.

He had decided that the policeman was never going to go away, so he left the garden, crossed the Strand, and made for

Leicester Square. Usually at this time of night it was jumping, the amusement arcades going, the fast food places going, the meths drinkers on the benches going. Now everything was closed and barred and freezing. Where could she be? Where could he look?

Then he remembered the first time they had met. She had taken him to the place below a derelict block of flats. But could he ever find it again?

Orienteering now. Running and looking and looking and running. No maps. But the mind of a city kid. Drop him down anywhere in London and like a dog he could return home.

Find the place she'd taken him to eat. That was his starting point. It had been somewhere on the edges of Soho. Theatres around. He knew he couldn't be far. Casting like a hound. First one way and then the next, running for a block, looking, another block, looking. Until, abruptly, he came out on Shaftesbury Avenue and *there* were the theatres. And *there* was the pizza place Gail had taken him to.

He began to move in a south-westerly direction.

Running again. The marathon now. The London marathon. And Abebe Bikila leading. And Huntsman Collins just behind. Three kilometres to go and the crowds thick. All he could see were Bikila's thin legs pumping ahead of him, the thin legs that carried him over the hills and dales of Ethiopia.

Terry had never run a marathon before. He was nearly at the end of his stamina. But the roar of the crowd lifted him, put new energy into his muscles.

And there it was. In a deserted street. The old block of half-demolished flats and all around it paper blowing on the cold north-east wind.

No neon in this part of London. No cars. Empty streets lined by bleak red-brick buildings some of which were occupied some not. He was behind the Tate Gallery now, not that that would have made much impact for he had never heard of it.

Somewhere away to his left were the Houses of Parliament. He knew them because he'd taken a bearing on them, and they must have lain within his subconscious. He must have seen them when Gail was taking him along the same route.

He paused under the orange sodium lights. Where had they entered this no man's land of rubble and brick? A pathway led round to the rear of the building and he took it. Here were the old garages. There was something familiar about the area. He had spent a night of his life there.

Down steps into cold concrete caverns. Some smelling of petrol and oil, some of nameless things. Moving from one roofless cavern to the next. More stairs. Underground parking corrupted by water and stained by lime, everything rusted and smashed. Nothing of value left. This was more like it.

Then he heard a noise, a scrabbling, scratching noise, and thought of rats as big as cats. Where had that come from? A nursery rhyme? His grandfather?

Dark and dingy now and there was no way Daley could help. And yet he knew he was in the right place.

The noise again. Coming out of the dark. Then a kind of moan, a human sound. Gail?

He pressed forward silently on rubber soles. The orange light penetrated these caverns through broken roofs. He entered a small room and saw the dented dustbins and knew he was there. He picked his way across rubble, turned the corner of a broken arch and saw the dark flapping wings of a giant crow tearing at a corpse. Not a crow. A dark figure. Crouching over something. He saw feet. They had stolen the trainers together. Above her, pulling at her clothing, her pockets, her things, the black bird of prey. He turned and Terry saw it was the Rat.

He launched himself before he thought. The knife lay unremembered in his pocket. Arms flailing he beat at the Rat and pulled him away from her. They fell. His hand closed on a piece of broken masonry. He smashed it against his shoulder, his neck, the side of his head. The Rat broke away. Running footsteps receded. Terry was left with Gail.

She lay on a mattress of cardboard and newspapers. The sleeping bag had been pulled from her. The light fell on her face, softening it. Saliva had come from her lips and

124

shone on her cheek. The track suit was open where hands had rummaged for money or drugs.

He knelt beside her and took her hand. It was cold but then so were his. He tried to warm it. But the chill was permanent although it took him a long time to realise it.

He sat with her, trying to bring her to life, knowing that what she had said would happen had happened. 'One day I'll OD,' she had said. 'And who'll care?'

He cared. It was as though the other light, the proper light in his life, had gone out, and he was left with only this orange light, a half light and a half life.

He sat with her for more than an hour. Not crying. Trying to warm a hand that would not be warmed.

Then he buttoned up her clothes and put her back in her sleeping bag and zipped it all the way up. It had a kind of hood and he put that over her head and zipped that up too. She wasn't very big and she fitted into the sleeping bag easily. That was the best he could do. That was her burial.

He returned to street-level. It seemed colder than it was before. He began to run.

Day . . . lee . . . Day . . . lee . . .

Left . . . right . . . left . . . right . . .

But the ghosts of the past did not run with him, no Arthur Wint, no McDonald Bailey, no Harrison Dillard, no Garner Maitland . . . not even Huntsman Collins. There was only Terry, running all the way back to the house he thought of now as home.

18

It was just before two o'clock in the morning when Macrae and Silver left the Goodwood. They had been talking about the case and Macrae had reached a somewhat drunken conclusion.

'The deed was done by a person or persons unknown, one of whom was wearing a green hat. Not hat. Woollen cap. He used a sharp instrument, probably a knife. Motive? Unknown.'

'Anyway, we've got a suspect,' Silver said, the whisky swimming in his brain.

'Oh, yes, a fourteen-year-old who burns down classrooms. Who's been seen everywhere from Land's End to John o' Groats.'

Macrae stopped at his car and fumbled for his keys.

'Remember Hockley, guv'nor?'

Macrae paused. Over the years dozens of London cops had managed to get out of drunken driving offences. But recently an edict had come down from the top that there was to be no, repeat *no*, drinking and driving. The next day a Sergeant Hockley of the CID chased a wanted robber half way across London at speeds of over eighty and killed a mother and child on a pedestrian crossing.

When they tested Hockley they found twice the permitted limit of alcohol in his blood and this time no one had tried to save him and he was now serving two years for manslaughter.

'Don't be bloody silly,' Macrae said. 'Course I can drive.'

But at that moment a taxi turned up towards Charing Cross and Silver stopped it.

'You're like a bloody woman,' Macrae said, but got in without any fuss.

126

He had the whisky bottle in his coat pocket and Silver knew what would happen when they reached Battersea: Macrae would insist on them having one last drink, and then another, and finally he'd end up by putting Macrae to bed. It had happened before and it would happen again. It was the holidays that did it. He could understand that. Easter was a special time, like Christmas, times when families got together and when you didn't have a family to get together with you felt bloody awful.

Sometimes, when Silver complained about him, Zoe would say, 'Well, ask for a transfer, then.'

But a transfer to where? The point about Macrae was that things always seemed to happen around him and he had the best informants in London. And if you wanted to get on you started off by hanging on to his coat tails and finally leapt upwards from his shoulders. That's how Silver had written the scenario. Except that he wasn't certain now whether Macrae was worth hanging on to. The top brass didn't like him, which meant that some of that dislike might rub off on Silver. He'd have to be careful.

In a way, Silver had been surprised when Macrae had got into the cab so meekly. He'd fully expected him to argue. Was he going soft in his old age?

There was a no smoking sign in the cab but Macrae ignored it and lit a slim panatella as though challenging the driver.

'Well, what's next?' he said thickly, not expecting an answer, simply thinking out loud. 'What's after Mrs Rose-Mary-bloody-Foster? Christ, what a bitch! You see the way she treated that kid? She only let him watch the TV because we were there. It's tough enough in this world being a half-caste without having a mother like her. Poor wee sod.'

'There's the physical education teacher,' Silver said.

'Right. The physical jerks bloke. We'll have a word with him.'

The taxi crossed Albert Bridge with the river glittering coldly in the moonlight. The traffic was down to a trickle, the city was dead to the world. Soon they entered a little enclave of mean streets and warehouses and old Victorian factory buildings now grime-covered and boarded up, waiting for the developers to raze them and make up their minds what sort of London the citizens were going to be landed with for the next few hundred years.

The cab stopped outside Macrae's house. Silver was paying when they heard a car door slam only a few feet away. A woman's voice said, 'Macrae, you bastard! Where were you?'

Macrae was leaning against his garden wall. He turned. 'Who the hell's that?'

'Who d'you think it is?'

Silver saw a woman come across the street towards them. She was in her mid thirties and her coat, opening as she moved, showed a heavy, earthy body. Her face was plump and her breasts large. Once she might have been described as Junoesque.

'You said—'

'Oh, it's you,' Macrae said.

'Mandy!' A voice called from the car and a second door slammed as a man came after her. 'Mandy, you said you wouldn't—'

'Oh, fuck off, Joe!'

Silver stepped to one side as the second Mrs Macrae, now Mrs Joe Parrish, stormed on to the pavement.

'You promised! You said you'd be there with the money!'

'For Christ's sake!' Macrae said, as lights began to come on in neighbouring houses.

'Sorry about this, George,' Joe Parrish said. He was slightly shorter than his wife and although about her age was already bald. 'She said she was only going to—'

'Shut up!' his wife said, turning on him. Then she turned back to Macrae. 'You promised you'd have the money last week. Then at the weekend. Then you said tonight, for sure. Well, I'm not putting up with this. You've got two kids to maintain and maintain them you will or I'll go to your DI and you'll be up to your neck in it!'

Macrae moved away from the taxi. The driver, who had been watching the scene in some alarm, now put his foot down, causing Joe Parrish to jump for the pavement.

128

'Where the hell are you going?' Mandy said, trying to hold Macrae by his coat.

He shook her off and stood in the gutter some little distance away, being sick.

'God, what a pig you are!'

Silver planted himself in front of her. Of all the things cops hated most, 'domestics' – rows between husband and wife – were the worst.

'Take it easy!' Silver said.

She turned towards him. She had long dark hair and a heavy, sensual face. He had first known her just before the divorce. At that time she was going over the side with anything in pants. She'd tried it on with Silver himself but failed.

'Still trouble-shooting for him, Leo?' The sounds from up the street were distressing. 'Listen to him. You think he's worth it?'

'Would fifty pounds do? I could give you a cheque.'

'Be your age! Fifty quid!'

'Mandy, you said—' Joe Parrish began.

'I can't make it any more.'

She thought about it for a moment. 'All right. If you think you can get it back from him. But you tell him I want the lot by next week or I'll put the boot in. And then he can forget promotion. That's if it was ever on.'

In the bitter wind Silver wrote her a cheque. She took it, folded it, and put it in her pocket. Then she looked at him more closely. 'I wouldn't expect any favours, if I was you, Leo. He's a genuine bastard. One hundred per cent kosher. You remember that. Come on, Joe.'

They got back in the car and as they were driving off she called from the window, 'And I want my curtains, George! You hear me!'

Macrae had come back to his house and was leaning against the front door, his big head hanging forward as though his neck was unable to support it.

He opened his mouth to ask Silver in for a drink, changed his mind, and said harshly, 'Pick me up at ten.' Abruptly he went in and Silver was left on the icy pavement. He stood looking at the house for some seconds then he turned up his collar and walked up to Battersea Park Road where he picked up a lonely cab on its way back to the West End from Wandsworth.

As usual the door to their apartment was locked and barred and Silver started his own version of what, in the Tower of London, is called the Ceremony of the Keys. Only this time something was wrong. He opened the lock at the base of the door but couldn't get his key into the one in the middle. It was jammed. Then he realised that the key had been left in the lock on the other side. He'd have to go back into the street, ring the bell and hope it woke Zoe and then she could let him in. He looked at his watch, it was a little after three.

He heard a faint noise, so faint he wasn't sure what it was. Then it came again. 'Leo? Is that you?'

'Of course it's me.'

There was a rattling of keys and the door swung open. Zoe was sitting just inside the door wrapped in a duvet.

'What the hell's going on?' Silver said. He was tired, cold, irritable and had a headache from lack of food and too much drink.

She rose. 'Where the hell have you been?'

'I told you on the phone.'

'Oh yes, the phone. Everything's OK if you use the phone.'

'It's the mark of civilised man,' he said, hoping to head off what he knew was coming.

He bent and kissed her. 'You reek,' she said.

'I was with Macrae.'

'That's your answer to everything!'

She turned and went back into the bedroom, threw herself down on the bed and pulled the duvet up.

'What's with the locking?'

'Never mind!'

'OK, never mind.' He began to take off his clothes.

'We were supposed to have the evening together, remember?'

'And something came up. I phoned you about it. Remember?'

'I've been sitting here for hours waiting while you've been toping with Macrae.'

'Toping. I like that. You must use it sometime in one of your ads. Tope a glass of Guinness a day.'

'Leo! You arsehole!'

'So now it's flattery.' He tried to keep his voice light. She sat up. 'You bastard!'

'Everybody keeps calling everybody that tonight. OK, you're angry with me. I can understand that. So just to punish me you decided to stay awake, sit in the cold hall and put the key in the lock.'

'Don't you understand *any*thing?'

He paused and looked at her. She seemed so small in the big bed. 'Again?' he said.

She nodded.

'When?'

'It must have been just after midnight.'

'Where?'

'At the door.'

'What did you hear?'

'Footsteps.'

'Could have been the Chalmers.' They had the apartment below.

'They were out. I heard them come back about one.' He sat on the bed and took her hand. 'Oh God, Leo, I was frightened!'

'Footsteps. And?'

'I went to the door. I thought it might be you.'

'And?'

'Well, I thought I heard breathing. As though someone was standing with his head to the door.'

'And?'

'And, so I put the key in the lock and sat there waiting for you.'

Noises in the street. Someone on the roof. On the stairs. At the windows. She heard them all. He understood.

'How many locks are there on the door?'

'Three. Three deadlocks.'

'And a chain. And two bolts. You think anyone could get in?'

'They take the doors off these days!'

'Not if there're steel plates. They can't if there're steel plates.'

'Leo, are you sure?'

It was the same question he answered each time and it wasn't about the efficacy of steel reinforcing plates on the door. It was about the man in the garden. The man who had cut the thin line on her belly. And the question meant, was he still locked up? Was she safe?

'Yes, I'm sure.'

She let him take her in his arms then. She was frozen and shivering. This happened once every few weeks. The intervals between the incidents were growing longer.

'Had you been asleep?' he said.

'Yes. I was waiting for you. I dozed off.'

'Did you dream?'

'I can't remember.'

He thought she probably had. Then she'd woken up and been frightened.

'Can't you get days?' she said. Each time she became frightened she asked him this.

He said, 'People get murdered at night. They get raped at night. And mugged and robbed. It's not a nine-to-five business.'

She nodded bleakly, then said, 'Would you like some coffee? I bought some de-caf.'

'OK. You stay here. I'll get it.'

When he came back with two steaming mugs he saw her nightdress on the floor. She was leaning back against the bedhead with the duvet up to her waist. Her two sharp little upturned breasts were aiming their hard little nipples directly at his face. He put the coffee down on the bedside table and her thin arms twined round him like vines.

At these times her need for him, for his protection and the security he offered, manifested itself in a voracious sexual

132

hunger. She gave herself to him with an abandon that always shook him. She was all over him like a monkey. Her muscles were like bowstrings and he felt that if he pulled one it would twang.

She fumbled at his trousers and roughly undid the top, then unzipped them. She took out his penis and began to fondle it. As it hardened she moved on top of him, pushing it into herself and grinding down on his pelvis. It had nothing to do with gentleness or marriage, love or children. It was a physical act like wrestling. His face was wet from her saliva. It was as though she wanted to eat his lips and swallow his tongue.

And then in a series of jerks she came to a violent climax and slowly her body softened and she grew calmer.

He felt her muscles slacken. She turned from a bundle of stringy, fibrous tendons, to a soft dough. Then she slipped off and lay in the cradle of his right arm.

After a while he said, lying, 'That was marvellous. And you?' She did not reply. She was asleep.

She could do that. Go out instantly like a candle. He wished he could do the same. He lay there on his back in the darkness with a tight band round his forehead, his mind racing like the fast-forward on a video.

It had been an incredibly long day. He thought of Mrs Collins and Sharlene and the grotty teacher in the grotty school. He thought of the house lost in the South Downs and the little boy with the wide serious eyes. He thought of Macrae in the Goodwood and Mandy and what she had said about Macrae.

A genuine bastard. One hundred per cent kosher.

Kosher.

His mind flipped. 'Hey! Kosher!'

It was a childhood memory. No one had called him that for years. But the picture in his brain was suddenly sharp. He could see himself in the young boy walking along the leafy avenues of Finchley with a little blue suitcase in his hand.

The nickname had been earned when he started taking

133

his own food to school. That had been his father's idea. It was because of dirt.

'So where have their hands been? You tell me?' he had said to Lottie.

'Whose hands?'

'The luncheon ladies.'

'Dinner ladies,' she had corrected him.

Leo's father had meant the women in the school canteen. The women who made the school lunches and served them. They weren't clean enough for Leo so he had to take his own food.

Ever since he could remember, his father had been washing his hands. Before every pupil and after every pupil. He had a washbasin in the music room and used to wash his hands like a doctor.

'Don't touch it!' His father would say, meaning the Bosendorfer that still stood in the corner of the music room. And the boy or girl would start back nervously.

'That pianoforte comes all the way from Vienna. Those keys are faced with ivory coming all the way from Africa. And you want to touch it with dirty fingernails!'

Washing hands, Leo knew, was supposed to be a symptom of Freudian guilt but if his father ever felt guilty about anything he never showed it.

'You think dinner ladies are dirty?' his mother had said. 'I tell you who is dirty. Men are dirty. They stand in urinals. Then they put their feet on the chairs!'

'Not ur-eye-nals. Learn to speak English.'

Neither spoke it brilliantly. Even after all these years in London they both still had strong accents and every now and then, especially under stress – which, it seemed to Leo, happened a lot more than just now and then – they inverted phrases, fractured sentences and mispronounced words.

This question of the purity of speech was only one of many areas which Lottie and Manfred Silver found to be filled with fertile soil for argument.

There was the question of their backgrounds. Manfred always described his early life as, 'When I was a boy in Vienna,' which Lottie would instantly challenge.

'Not Vienna! Mödling is *not* Vienna!'

Mödling is a small town on the road between Vienna and Baden. Manfred did not like being pinned to small-town Austria.

'Tell me, where are the Vienna woods? Near Mödling, yes?'

'I don't care where are the woods.' Sometimes in her heated state she would pronounce it 'voods'. 'Vienna it is not.'

Lottie was unassailable in this. Her father had been an abdominal physician with his offices just off the Graben and they had lived in the leafy suburb of Sievering. She was Viennese to the core and from a professional family.

This could not be said of Manfred. He always described his father as a publisher and, if Lottie was in a good mood, she might let him get away with it. But, if she was irritated with him for some reason (and, God knew, Leo thought, there were many reasons, for his father was not an easy man to live with) then she would say, 'Not publisher, translator.'

Which was true enough.

And then there was Manfred's obvious lack of success as a composer. The fact that he was a brilliant teacher, that his pupils not only comprised young girls and boys but also students from Goldsmith's College and the Royal College who came to him for master classes, and sometimes even performing pianists who needed to listen to Bach or Schubert with Manfred's ears, all this made no difference to Lottie. He described himself as a composer and she judged him by his own self-delusions. If he was a composer, she would say, then he should compose and have his music played and be paid for it like Mozart, who had lived in Vienna, not Mödling.

Over the business of the school meals Manfred, as usual, got his way and Leo was made to take the little blue suitcase.

He had sat with it on his lap in the school dining-room and while the others were having beefburgers and chips, or sausage and chips, or something and chips, he would delve surreptitiously into it and pull out a piece of cold chicken or a Marmite sandwich.

One day, soon after he had gone to the school, one of the supervising teachers saw him at his special lunch and, frowning, asked him if it had any religious significance. Was it kosher?

Christ, Leo thought, it was like tying a label round his neck. It had stuck. And for all the time he was at his junior school they had called him 'Kosher'. He supposed it was better than Yid or Jewboy. Anyway, it wasn't that kind of school. There were plenty of Jews in North London. But the other Jewish boys at his school hadn't taken kindly to him either. His exposure made them feel threatened.

A boy called Myron Sapperstein had opened his suitcase and thrown the contents on the ground and then hit him in the face. Leo hadn't understood the reasons then, but he did now. It was what he thought of as the 'camouflage syndrome' and it applied not only to Jewish boys but to all boys: don't stand out in a crowd.

Sapperstein's aggressiveness had two beneficial effects on Leo. First, he realised he didn't have to eat the food in the suitcase. On the day Sapperstein had thrown it on the ground Leo had simply eaten what he could get in the canteen. The following day he threw away his home-cooked food before he ever got to school.

The second was that it made him realise he couldn't run to his mother if something happened in the school playground. He had to sort it out himself. But he was small for his age, so instead of using his muscles he used his brain.

Zoe stirred and came slowly awake.

'I dreamed you hadn't come home,' she said, turning to him and throwing an arm over his stomach. 'What's the time?' He turned to look at the clock but she said, 'It doesn't matter. It's Good Friday.' She was silent for some moments and then said, sleepily, 'Leo?'

'Right here.'

'I love you.'

'That's what they all say.'

Pause.

'Leo?'

'Still here.'

'Why don't we get married?'

'Why don't we get some sleep first?'

136

19

'Tea, sir? Coffee?'

Jack Benson woke with a start. 'Coffee, please.'

The air hostess poured him a plastic cup of black coffee.

'Milk, sir? Sugar?'

'Just sugar. Sweet and hot.'

She had heard the phrase a thousand times but smiled gamely and moved on to the next row of seats. Benson watched her as she bent across to a passenger on the other side of the aisle. Her briefs were outlined against the tight skirt. Good legs, he thought. Good bottom. He'd often had success with air hostesses. They lived strange insomniac lives and were grateful for dates who would stay awake with them into the small hours as they tried to adjust their internal time clocks. Especially the ones who had never been to Hong Kong before. He'd been able to show them a really good time before carting them off to his flat in Stanley.

The Far Eastern Airlines jumbo was half empty. He'd picked up the flight in Karachi. It seemed he had been travelling for weeks instead of days. He had criss-crossed the Far East and the Pacific, flying from Perth to Sydney, from Sydney to New Guinea, from New Guinea to India and finally to Karachi. He'd never left the transit lounges of the airports and had bought his next-stage ticket at the last possible moment. Perhaps it wasn't perfect but he couldn't think of any better way and he was pretty sure he was not being followed.

He drank his coffee and lit a cigarette. The man in the middle aisle looked at him disapprovingly. To hell with him, Benson thought, he was perfectly within his rights.

He checked the suitcase at his feet. It had never left

his side from the moment he had taken it from his office. Some of the money was gone, of course, for air travel was expensive, but there was so much left it was hardly possible to see that some was missing. He'd bought clothing in India for himself and a silk sari length for Maria. She had always loved exotic prints. He tried to imagine her wearing it and it made a pleasant picture.

He was not as tired as he might have been. Fortunately, he was a good traveller. Put him down anywhere and he could drop off in a minute. What he wanted was a bath, a decent breakfast, a sleep, an hour or so in an outfitters in Regent Street – and then he'd be ready for her.

Good old *liebchen*, he thought. Wonderful days. He remembered she'd called them her Berlin Days. But the trouble with *liebchen* was that she always became serious. And that complicated things. Keep it light had always been his motto. Never get into the heavy stuff. But with Maria it had been talk of the future. And nothing scared the boys off faster than that. He'd never promised her a thing. He'd shown her a good time in Berlin and taken her on holiday to France. And she seemed to have got the wrong impression.

When someone says, 'When we have a place of our own,' or something like that and you've just made love, or are just about to, you don't say, 'Look, *liebchen*, we aren't going to have a place of our own.' You just nod and give her another kiss – and then it's the old one-two.

He regarded the long legs of the air hostess with renewed interest. Maybe, if he played his cards right . . . He could always phone *liebchen* and tell her he'd picked up a bug. People were always picking up bugs in aircraft.

But then, he thought, why bother? Not too long ago he'd met a young hostess in Hong Kong and she'd laughed at him and called him sugar daddy. That hadn't been nice. He wasn't *all* that old. No, Maria was a known quantity and, if she was feeling the way her voice suggested she was feeling, then she must be hungry.

And disenchanted with Richard. Well, he had it coming. You didn't leave a good-looking woman like Maria for an

Easter weekend and expect her to be tucked up in bed with a book when you got back. Or maybe Richard did.

Breakfast came but Benson waved it away. There were the usual queues at the loos. Then the plane began its descent.

He had planned exactly what he was going to do. He had a British passport so he had no problem at Immigration. Then he took the Green Exit through Customs. As far as he knew there was no law which said he couldn't bring a large amount of mixed currencies into Britain but that was only as far as he knew.

By the time he reached the Green hall he realised that something was up. Instead of passengers flowing through, many were being asked to open their baggage. Two young Pakistani men were wheeling their trolley just behind him. He slowed, they moved ahead. There was only one Customs officer free. He looked quickly from Benson to the Pakistanis. For a second there was indecisiveness in his eyes, then he said to the two men, 'Have you read the notice?' He pointed to the wall.

Benson ambled past and reached the arrivals hall. Only then did he realise what a fool he'd been to take a plane from Pakistan. It was the major heroin route into Britain.

He decided on a cab and sank gratefully on to the seat. As they drove off to join the motorway into London he looked out of the window to the grey flocky sky, the blue smoke of car exhausts, the dirty snow still lying by the roadside. It wasn't Hong Kong. It wasn't where he particularly wanted to spend any time. But it had one immeasurable asset. There was no Mr Shao.

'Caesar! Come, boy!'

Maria stood in the hall waiting for Caesar to appear from the kitchen. She had closed up the house, double and triple checked each windowlock and each tap. It was only 9 a.m. and she was not due to meet Jack until the evening but she knew if she waited any longer she wouldn't go.

'Caesar!' She went to the kitchen. The dog was in his basket eyeing her apprehensively. 'Come, we're going to your lovely kennels.'

Normal dogs bounced about with joy when they saw the lead, but not Caesar. She slipped the hook on to his collar and dragged him from his basket.

She had put her overnight bag into the car and now let Caesar on to the back seat. She did one final check of the house, set the burglar alarm, closed and locked the front door and drove down the drive. She felt wound up as tight as a violin string. The past twenty-four hours had been a nightmare. Ten times she had decided not to go. Ten times she had reversed that decision.

As she turned out of her drive on to the street she noticed the little white car again. They really should have a Neighbourhood Watch scheme, she thought. If they had she would report this car. She stopped and wrote down its number. The man in the car was wearing a trilby and she could not see his face clearly but she stared aggressively at him just to show she was marking him down. She drove off telling herself she was being socially responsible.

The kennels were about four miles away on what had once been a farm but which had now 'diversified'. Barns had been turned into apartments, there was a trout lake, and the kennels. It was a seedy-looking place but was reasonably clean.

She was greeted by the owner, Mrs Gore, a heavy woman with hands like coarse sandpaper, who walked amid a flock of yapping Yorkshire terriers so small and mobile they gave the impression of leaves being stirred by her feet.

'Going off for a break, dear?' she said as she gave Maria a receipt for the dog.

'Just to London for the night.'

'That's nice. Nothing like a break, dear.'

She took Caesar's lead. He seemed quite pleased with the transfer.

'Anything special?'

'Our wedding anniversary,' she said, to put a stop to the conversation.

'That's lovely. Mr Gore and I used to go to Birmingham. His mother lived there. You know Birmingham?'

'No.'

'Horrible place.'

Maria drove out of the farmyard. There was no putting it off now. The motorway beckoned. London beckoned. Jack beckoned. Her stomach felt tight and she had a tension headache at the back of her neck.

Wedding anniversary.

She shouldn't have said that. It was like pretending someone was ill. She didn't like lying about personal things. She always had the feeling that the Fates would intervene – and not in a nice way.

She drove across country and picked up the motorway. She hardly saw a car. This, she thought, was how England might look after an atomic holocaust. Just herself, if she was unlucky enough to survive, and a few others.

Don't be morbid, she told herself. You're on your way to your lover, be excited, be happy. But the business about the wedding anniversary sat like a stone in her stomach.

She wasn't really superstitious. She touched wood and didn't walk under ladders, but that was about all. Except for lying about things like illness. And her wedding anniversary. Just at this moment it seemed such an important date. She tried to excise it from her mind but she couldn't. In another six weeks she and Richard would have been married for eight years. So the seven-year itch was over, or should be. If only she'd had the baby. She wouldn't be driving along a grey, deserted motorway, that was certain. She would be at home now, probably giving him? her? breakfast. And she wouldn't have Caesar. She'd have a dog to amuse her and give her companionship.

So it wouldn't matter so much that Richard was working over the holidays. She would have had her own family within the family. And later there would be other babies. Three or four. It was what she had always really wanted.

Instead, after she and Richard were married, she had put her inheritance into a kitchen shop in Maida Vale. It had done well. So, she had bought a second. It did well too, which was fortunate because Richard's business had not done brilliantly at first. But then it had picked up and for a time they had been well-off. Smart cars. Holidays in Alaska and Central Asia, a trip through South America. And still there

141

was plenty of money in the bank. It all seemed a dream come true.

She'd worked damned hard and so had Richard. The time was right to start a family. And then – crash. Everything seemed to go wrong. She lost the baby. Richard's business went into a nosedive – at least the Far East part of it did – so finally she had this big old house in the country which they couldn't sell, and a smelly dog for company.

Now came the final touch: the other woman! It wasn't unusual, she supposed. She knew a dozen couples the same ages as themselves who were having problems. Especially if the wife worked as well. Then the couple inhabited different spheres and in those spheres met other people who were also occupying different spheres. No wonder the divorce rate was so high.

The thought of Richard in bed with someone else brought a flush of anger to her cheeks. Bugger him, she thought. If he was having it off – then why couldn't she?

20

Zoe was still asleep when Silver let himself out of the apartment. London was dead and Pimlico as silent as the grave. The curtains were drawn in every window and there was not a living soul to be seen except the milkman. And it wasn't going to get much better, he thought. He drove through Sloane Square and into the King's Road. It no longer had the reputation it once had when London was supposed to be the swinging capital of the world, but even so there were one or two groups of Japanese tourists with their cameras.

He had had a restless and disturbed night, kept awake by a mixture of things. There was something still nagging him about Foster's flat, and there was Macrae and the second Mrs Macrae; he had come in on the tail end of that marriage and very nasty it had been.

And then, of course, he had begun to think about Zoe. She was talking about marriage more frequently and there would come a point where his light prevarications would no longer be accepted.

On the surface things were good between them. He loved her, he was sure of that, and she loved him, or at least she said so often enough. The sexual chemistry was usually marvellous. But there were the dark times, like last night, which had to be endured.

What worried him was *why* Zoe wanted to marry him. He couldn't simply accept that it was a need that came from love and affection. There was too much of the past in the present for that.

He thought it might be the other way round: love and affection produced by a need; a need for security, a need for someone to lock the locks and bolt the doors, for someone

143

with whom she could feel safe, whose job itself was a symbol of security.

He didn't want that. He didn't want marriage because of his job. He wanted marriage because of who he was, everything about him.

He turned up Sydney Street and into the Fulham Road and drove past a rash of wine bars and boutiques. What if he had been a solicitor, like Ruth? Or a piano teacher, like his father? Would she still have wanted to marry him? But he wasn't. He was a policeman, whatever his mother said. And this was something they all found it hard to believe. Why would a bright Jewish boy become a policeman?

What if he really told them? Would they be able to take it? He couldn't come out with a logical set of phrases. But what if he told them of the hazy and obscure forces which had combined to place him where he was? They would be hurt, of course. But would they understand?

It had started on his thirteenth birthday. He was at his senior school then, a good one. How good and how expensive he had only found out later.

His mother gave him a party. The guests consisted of boys from his school. They were the sons of businessmen, architects, doctors and barristers. They could not fit Silver's family into any known category, but even that might have been all right if it had not been for his father.

Manfred had declined to register that a party was to take place even though Lottie had told him the date three times. This was normal behaviour. Things he did not like he did not contemplate. So that on the day of the party he expressed surprise mixed with horror.

'What for?' he said.

'What do you mean what for?' Lottie had said. 'Everybody gives parties. They don't ask what for. A party is a party. It's for pleasure.'

'Whose pleasure?'

'The people who come, of course. Maybe they didn't give parties in Mödling. But in Vienna we gave parties. In London people give parties.'

'And what about me?'

'You're not coming to the party.'

'Oh?'

'It's not for us it's for Leo's friends.'

'Young boys are savages.'

'Manfred!' When she called him that things were serious.

'What must I do, sit in the lavatory?'

'You must go out.'

'Out! You want to send me from my own home?'

'Go to the movies. Go to the chess club. Go anywhere. But don't come back before eleven.'

With much cajoling and finally with threats she had at last succeeded in getting him out of the flat.

'Don't let them in the music room,' he had said on the doorstep. 'For God's sake lock it.'

It had been an ordinary party. Several of the boys had brought beer mixed with cider in soft drink cans and three boys had been sick.

Manfred had managed to stay out until ten-thirty. When he returned he found Lottie sitting quietly in the bedroom, and a dozen young guests in the music room. There were empty drink cans ringing the top of the Bosendorfer and one boy was vamping tunes on the keyboard.

It was like the arrival of Attila the Hun. Manfred had instantly stopped the party, made them wash their hands, and then sent them, against Lottie's violent appeals, to wait on the pavement until their parents came to fetch them.

That had finished Leo as far as his school friends were concerned and it had made him briefly hate, then be embarrassed by, his parents.

Suddenly, he found their Austrian accents ludicrous, and their habit of arguing in front of strangers shaming. He hated the way his mother called his father Manfy. He hated the fact that his father was a kind of semi-Bohemian instead of being a doctor or a lawyer.

It was a bad period for him.

And it was during this period that he took some money. He liked to use the word 'took' but steal was more correct.

He had taken it to use as a bribe. He had seen Rosenberg stuff it in his anorak pocket then take his anorak off to play

145

soccer. He took a total of five pounds. He'd bought chocolate and Cokes and dispensed them to his group in a desperate effort to buy friendship. The police had been called and Leo had been taken to the headmaster's room to be interviewed by a detective from the local station. He'd confessed instantly, there seemed little point in denying it.

The detective had written it all down and then closed his notebook with a snap and said, 'You're Jewish. My mother's Jewish. That makes me half Jewish. And I'm going to tell you something, sonny. Jews don't steal.' He'd gone to the headmaster and suggested he drop the case, which he had. Then he'd seen Silver once more. 'Don't forget what I said, sonny. And God help you if you ever do anything like it again.'

He never had and he had never forgotten.

That was the first part of the equation.

The second was a combination of things, but mainly his parents' lifestyle. To their eccentric ways was added the hazard of always being on the point of bankruptcy.

'We're poor Jews,' his father often said, cheerfully. 'That makes us special.' Being an artist he despised the commercial life.

So, it was not unnatural, when Leo left university and found that his degree meant nothing and that he was just one more in a total of three million unemployed, that he should want a job and security. Only the police were recruiting.

His family had been against his joining from the start, especially his father and Ruth. She was just qualifying then and thought the Metropolitan Police were a bunch of corrupt thieves and robbers. It was the fact that they didn't want him to join that made it even more imperative.

Now, it all seemed a long time ago.

He reached Foster's apartment block. There was no porter or carpeted foyer, just an entrance hall with a couple of lifts. A constable was still on duty outside Foster's door. He looked bored and tired and Silver chatted with him for a few moments then went into the flat by himself.

It was an odd feeling, he thought, going into someone else's home, being among someone else's possessions when

146

the owner wasn't there. In the grey morning light, the apartment was sombre and filled with muted tones. His first impression of neatness and order was intensified.

Forensic had been over the apartment and found nothing except the usual smudge of prints. The only clear ones belonged to Foster himself.

He looked at the desk. He'd been through the drawers and found nothing unexpected. But still he felt there was something, an aura, an atmosphere that wasn't right.

He went into the bedroom. That's what it was precisely, a bedroom. Again, the overwhelming sense of neatness. But, as Macrae had said, you don't murder a man because he's neat.

He opened the wardrobe and looked at the clothes. The shoes, all in shoe trees, stood in neat rows. They'd be like that in the Sussex house too, he thought.

A sudden picture of Foster in bed with his wife came into his mind. He thought of how restrained and cool their sex must have been in producing their two sons.

He went into the bathroom. This was the one room that seemed to have been remodelled recently, for it had an opulent look about it. The overall colour was rose, magnified and multiplied a hundred times by the mirror tiles around the bath. The bath itself was bigger than most.

He poked about in the bathroom cupboards. Nothing heinous there. Towels hung neatly on the rail. A shower bracket high up on the wall, but the shower itself had been removed, probably because the trailing pipe made it look untidy.

He ambled back into the kitchen. It looked as though it might have come from a catalogue. He pressed the foot pedal of the rubbish container under the sink. It was empty and a new plastic bin liner had been put in place. He wondered if a cleaner had been in just before Foster had left. She might have been the last one to see Foster alive. He made a note to check.

Back in the living-room he stared at the row of tapes all marked, 'Name of programme: *Focus*.' Then the times and dates.

147

He had a strong desire to get to know the man whose corpse had been found at Hungerford Bridge. He switched on the video and TV set. The little green light on the video lit up to show there was a tape in it. Part had already run through so he reversed it and pressed play.

There were one or two ads and then the single word *Focus*. He switched up the sound as Henry Foster's head and shoulders replaced the title.

'As everyone in London knows,' Foster said to his early morning audience, 'getting to work is becoming more and more difficult. Traffic jams and transport strikes are now everyday occurrences. A recent study states that cars are now moving at an average speed of eight miles an hour in Greater London – the same speed as horse-drawn carriages a hundred years ago. What can we do about it? I have with me in the studio Professor—'

Silver ran the tape back and started at the beginning again. The face that spoke the words was solemn and serious and earnest. Foster was neatly dressed in a dark suit, tie and white shirt. He wore a pair of heavy horn-rimmed glasses and his hair was going grey at the temples. His voice was a rich baritone.

Silver ran the tape several times, but Foster's face was like the apartment, it gave nothing away. That was the point, he thought, there was not one tiny thing that was out of character. At least, not in Foster's life – but there sure as hell was in his death.

He locked up and took the stairs down to the yard at the back. There was no rubbish chute and the bins were lined up. There were eight apartments, so eight bins. But when he counted there were only seven. They were numbered. One, two, three, four, five, six, eight. Seven was missing. Foster's apartment was number seven. He began to search and soon found it. It had become separated from the others, probably when the refuse collectors had returned it. Now it stood behind a staircase.

He had, for a moment, felt the old adrenalin, but when he opened the bin he was disappointed. Here too all was as neat as a rubbish bin could be. The rubbish itself was in plastic liners. He poked through them turning over damp tea bags and brown banana skins. It was all just kitchen rubbish except for one which contained broken china – as though someone had dropped a tea-tray.

He replaced the lid, walked to his car and set off to pick up Macrae. It hadn't been much to get out of bed for.

London may have been dead on this cold Good Friday morning, but not Cannon Row police station. Easter, like Christmas, brought out the sadness in some and the violence in others, just as it brought out the goodness in many more. But the Met wasn't concerned with goodness. In Central London there had been a dozen suicide attempts. Some had used razors, some ropes, one woman had set light to herself. There were several young coppers in Cannon Row now who were sick to the stomach at what they had seen.

A dosser had died under the arches near Charing Cross; there had been several muggings in the South Bank complex; the window of a gift shop in the Vauxhall Bridge Road had been smashed and its contents looted. An elderly man who weighed nearly three hundred pounds had become stuck in his bath and had died of a heart attack as the police were breaking down his door; there had been several late-night and early-morning accidents and the result of one, blood-stained and shaking, was in the charge-room now, giving his account. And there had been four rapes, one in a churchyard off Piccadilly.

But the big one was still Henry Foster.

Macrae was with his boss, Detective Chief Superintendent Wilson. He showed no signs of the previous night's drinking but his stomach was still reacting badly to the chilli sauce.

'It's beginning to hit the fan, George, and that's a bloody fact,' Wilson said, his eyes darting from one side of the room to the other. 'And I'm in it up to here.' He touched the top of his head. 'The DI's catching it from upstairs and he's coming down on me and—'

'You're coming down on me.'

'Of course I am. Specially after the TV stuff.'

'What TV stuff?'

'Didn't you see her on the news last night?'

'See who?'

'His bloody wife, George. The one you and Silver went to interview. Christ, you never look at TV, never read the bloody papers! Listen, she said the police were dragging their feet. Said they'd have had someone by now if her husband hadn't been black.'

'Oh, Christ.'

'She as bloody good as said you and Silver were a pair of racists who treated her like a piece of shit because she'd married a black.'

'That's a lie!'

'You don't have to convince me, George. I'm telling you what's being said. And they don't like it upstairs. I mean this guy isn't some scrote pushing crack in Brixton, he was on the bloody box.'

'I know.'

'Well . . . I mean, what the hell's going on, George? You say you're looking for some little half-caste you think may have been responsible, well, where is he? Jesus, he's running around London in a bright green hat and he's bloody invisible!'

'He's gone to ground somewhere. We'll winkle him out.'

'You better.'

'There's an "or" in there somewhere, isn't there?'

Wilson paused. 'You got a cigarette?'

'Only these.' He gave Wilson a thin panatella.

'There's no "or" in it. Well, yes, I suppose there is. This is high profile, George. You're under the microscope.'

'I told you they can stuff promotion.'

'I know you did. But people change. Even you, George. Even the Great Thief-taker. Money, George, money. It makes the world go round. And, speaking of which, there was a new duty sergeant yesterday afternoon. He logged six calls from Mandy. You've got to do something about her.'

Macrae went to his office and closed the door carefully behind him. There was a pile of messages on his desk. He stood with his hands behind him staring from the dusty window at nothing. There was a knock at the door. 'Give me a few minutes, Harry,' he called.

But it wasn't Sergeant Laker. 'It's me,' Silver said.

'What is it?'

Ever since Silver had picked up Macrae that morning he had kept his mouth shut and his eyes down.

'There's been another sighting.'

'Is that all!'

'This one sounds right. Guy who works in Kensington Gardens. Says he saw a coloured boy, light-skinned, wearing a green knitted hat – beret he called it – on Wednesday around dusk. Said the boy was running like he was an athlete. Trainers. Track suit. That sort of thing.'

'Go on.'

'I got his address. He's not working today.'

'OK. I want to make a couple of calls.'

He waited for Silver to leave the office and then he dialled.

'Norman?' Macrae said, when the phone was answered.

A man's voice said, 'No, sweetie, it's not Norman.'

'Who's that? Lionel? It's George Macrae here.'

'You're an early bird,' Lionel said. 'I'll get him.'

While George waited he visualised the flat off Baker Street. He'd been there many times.

Norman wasn't your usual crime correspondent. The days of the Hollywood old sweats with their fedoras and their pencils behind their ears were long since gone. But even by today's standards Norman was odd. They'd known each other for years. In fact, Norman Paston had once made a pass at George, the only male person in the entire world so to do.

'Call me a queer, call me gay, call me a bender. Doesn't bother me a bit,' Norman had once said to him. 'Just so long as you don't call me straight.'

He was tall, in his forties, and elegant in a 1950s kind of way. He wore charcoal grey suits which he bought at Harrods and had his shirts made in Jermyn Street. As far as Macrae knew he originally came from the sticks, somewhere in Suffolk where his father was a farm worker. He didn't talk about his background.

Macrae tolerated Paston, indeed liked him. And the same could be said for Norman. They often drank together, or had

151

a meal. Paston had an encyclopaedic knowledge of crime, not only contemporary but also historical. He had excellent contacts and was respected both by the police and by his fellow journalists. If Norman Paston said something in print it was usually eighty per cent right.

Once, and George had known him in those days, he had been married with two children. But for some reason George had never discovered, Paston had decided to come out and revert to what he really was.

He had written several excellent books on recent murders and another in which his research had led to the release of an innocent man. He made a lot of money out of books and the *Chronicle* paid him a handsome salary which he could have doubled had he wanted to go to a rag.

He and Lionel, a young bricklayer from the north of England, had lived in connubial bliss for several years.

'Morning, George,' Paston said. 'I've been waiting for you. Just as well there's no paper today.'

'There's nothing definite,' Macrae said. 'You know almost as much as we do, probably more.'

'Remember our agreement, George.'

'I'm remembering.' It was said harshly.

'Rough night?'

'So, so.'

'You should watch it. Age and all that.'

'You can talk.'

'Me? I was in bed by ten last night with a box of chocolates. Oh, and Lionel. And we watched *Come Dancing*. You should have seen some of the frocks, George. Just gorgeous.'

'Yea, OK,' Macrae said. It was all part of Paston's spiel.

Over the years they had formed a useful partnership. Macrae fed Paston titbits for the *Chronicle* and Paston passed on what information he had to Macrae.

'I'll fill you in when I've seen a couple of punters later today but I need some line on Foster's private life here in London. I've been down to see his wife.'

'Lucky you.'

'You know her?'

'We've got a man down there. And I saw her on the

152

box when she slagged you lot off for being racist bastards.'
'Yeah, well if you believe that you'll believe anything.'
'Sure. What d'you want to know?'
'Well, was he playing around? That's the big one. And, if he wasn't, what the hell was he doing with his spare time? I mean he was up in town all week and he couldn't be working on the programme every bloody minute.'
'Hang on a sec.' There was a pause and he heard papers being ruffled. 'I've got a note here. There was a girl. A researcher on the programme. It's just a whisper. Maybe nothing in it. I was going to check it out today.'
'I'll check it out for you.'
'Got a pencil? Sheila Gant. Forty-three Lighter Lane. Twickenham. Just a whisper.'
'Thanks, Norman. I'll get back to you today.'
'Do that. We've got a paper tomorrow.'
Macrae rang off and dialled another number.
'Linda?'
'George? You sound—'
'My throat's a little rough. It's the chilli sauce.'
'I told you last night. God knows what it's doing to your stomach.'
She paused, waiting.
Macrae cleared his throat. 'I just wanted to say,' he began and uncharacteristically felt tongue-tied. 'I'm just phoning to say I enjoyed last night.'
'I should be doing that. I was the guest.'
'Are you up?'
'Sort of.'
'Dressed?'
'Not yet. Why? You're not suddenly dropping in are you?'
'Would you like me to?'
He heard the clink of a spoon on a cup and felt suddenly embarrassed. 'You having coffee?'
'You haven't been to this flat, George. I'm sitting in the bay window, looking out on trees and a pleasant street of terraced houses. It's really very nice. And I'm having a coffee.'
He felt an ache in his chest at the thought of her. Jesus, what a bloody fool he'd been.

153

'I wish I could drop in. I'd like to sometime.'

'That would be nice.'

Her voice was cagey, but underneath it he thought he could detect a faint note of warmth.

'Once this Foster thing is over.'

'How's it going?'

'So, so. We're getting there – I hope. Otherwise they'll have my b— They'll be down on me.'

'You can say balls, George. I told you, I'm a big girl now.'

'I'd like to come round and talk about Susan,' he said.

'Oh?' Her voice suddenly hardened.

'I want to do what's best for her.'

'I told you what's best for her last night.'

'That's what I want to talk about. What we talked about last night.'

'George, I don't want you coming to tell me you don't think it's a good idea or anything like that. I'd rather you just stayed away from both of us.'

'No, no. It's not like that.'

'Well . . . I don't . . . '

'I'll work something out,' he said. 'But I'd like to talk to you about it.'

'OK, if that's what you want.'

'I'll ring you later today. Maybe tomorrow. This weekend may be good, if I can get rid of the Foster thing. I mean, if you're not doing anything.'

'I don't know what I'm doing yet,' she lied. 'But give me a ring.'

As he put down the receiver it rang instantly.

'Macrae,' he said.

A woman's voice said, 'I meant what I said last night, George. You better have the cheque here by Monday or I'm going to start making problems for you.'

'It's a holiday weekend. There's no way.'

'Well, Tuesday then. If not you'll have to bring it round.'

'I'll post it.'

'You do that.'

'Listen, we've got a new man on the desk. He doesn't know you. He's logging every call.'

'So?'

'Les is getting itchy.'

'To hell with Les. Anyway, if you paid prompt I wouldn't be calling. I've got much better things to do with my time than sit on the phone trying to get hold of you. Just get your act together, George.'

21

Jack Benson watched the waiter fuss with the trolley and begin to lay out the breakfast on a table by the window. Breakfast in his room, a sleep, a long hot bath, a late lunch with a bottle of something really good. And then he'd be feeling tremendous. The heat and lassitude of early summer in Hong Kong was already being replaced by the vigorousness of northern Europe. Every time he returned he felt full of energy and zip for a while, but then he began to pine for warmth and sun and lotus eating.

'Aren't you having a holiday?' Benson said to the waiter.

'No, sir. They giving me Tuesday off.' He was young and dark and by his accent Benson would have said he was Greek-Cypriot. They made the best waiters, he thought. Greek-Cypriots and Italians. The Brits were no bloody good at all. Britain just wasn't a service nation.

'I want my jacket and pants valeted. And I've got some things for the laundry. Can you take them?'

The waiter finished laying out the breakfast. 'I send a chambermaid, sir.'

'Not your department?'

'No, sir.'

'OK, thanks.' He tipped him and after the waiter had closed the door Benson sat down facing the window. It looked out over Piccadilly and Green Park. The morning was clear but cold. There was hardly any traffic in Piccadilly and he could only see one old man in the park feeding the pigeons.

He lifted the covers of the dishes: crisp bacon, creamy scrambled eggs, two country pork sausages. Toast. Seville marmalade. Tea. He had stipulated Darjeeling. Now he poured a cup. It was strong, just how he liked it. He began to eat. There was nothing, he thought, like an English breakfast in a good English hotel.

There was a discreet knock on the door. Benson pulled the dressing gown round his body and called to come in. A middle-aged Pakistani woman stood in the doorway.

'You have clothes for valeting?' she said.

He gave her the jacket and pants and the shirts and underwear.

'I must have them after lunch,' he said.

'All right.'

She took them from him and disappeared. Benson went back to his breakfast.

Greek-Cypriot waiters, Pakistani chambermaids, the receptionist had sounded Swiss and the Japs had taken over the car industry. What would be left of the Brits, he wondered, the next time he came back? *If* he came back. Came back from where? He wasn't sure yet. But there was no hurry. He had enough money to sit quietly and think it out. Talk to Richard when he came back. No, that wouldn't be a good idea. Not Richard. Just Maria. He smiled in anticipation.

When he finished his breakfast he opened the bag containing the money and placed the bundles on the bed. In the sunshine entering the windows from the park, they made a pretty sight. He began to count the notes.

Just then the phone rang. He paused as though caught in the act of something disgusting. He was about to throw the counterpane over the money when he thought: Don't be bloody silly, no one can see down the telephone.

'Hello?' he said.

There was no answer at the other end.

'Hello?'

Irritated, he replaced the receiver and went on counting the money. When he finished he placed the bag under the bed.

'Johnnie! John-*eee*!' Mrs Porteous stood at the back door of her house and shouted. She was a small white-haired woman in her seventies, seemingly made entirely of gristle and bone.

She turned to Macrae and Silver and said, 'He's either gone to the snake place or he's down there.' She waved at the jungle that was the long and narrow back garden. 'If he's down there he can hear all right, only pretends he can't. Doesn't want to hear his mother. You best go down and see.'

They were in one of London's northern fringe suburbs. The kind of place few people ever go to except the people who live there. The house was built next to a railway line and just then a train went thundering past.

'You get used to 'em,' Mrs Porteous said in a shrill voice. 'When Johnnie was a boy he knew where every one went. Glasgow, Edinburgh, Newcastle, Manchester. Just had to look at one and he knew.'

Macrae and Silver picked their way along a path bordered by cracked plastic buckets and weed-filled beds. At the end was an old pigeon loft. A muscular, track-suited bottom stuck out from one of the small doors.

'Mr Porteous?' Macrae said.

There was a violent movement and then the head and torso were drawn back and a man of about thirty-five, with a weather-beaten face and thinning, sandy hair stood before them.

In his hand he held a sky-blue mouse.

They showed him their warrant cards and Silver said, 'What's that?'

'A mouse. Blue mouse.' Then, with heavy irony, 'It's not illegal is it?'

'You been dyeing it?' Macrae said. 'That's cruelty to animals.'

John Porteous stroked the mouse and said, quickly, 'No. No. Never. You must be joking. I've got blue . . . ' He turned back into the hutch and picked one up from the straw. 'Chocolate. Black. These are show mice.'

'Show mice?' Silver said.

'You don't think they come like that in the wild do you? Oh, no. It takes years. Look,' he pointed to the claws on the black mouse. 'See those? Natural black. Some in the fancy paint them black 'cause they can't breed them properly. Always get found out though.'

158

Silver looked at the three mice with fascination. 'You mean there're mice shows like dog shows?'

'All over the country. I used to breed ferrets until one got into mother's bed. Then bantams. But the cockerels kept the neighbours awake.'

'Why not dogs?' Macrae said.

'You got to exercise dogs,' Johnnie Porteous said. 'And I get enough exercise during the day. I'm a physical education teacher. No, mice are sedentary little things. I don't have to take them for runs.'

He dropped the mice back in their cages.

'What do you do with mice that don't make the grade?' Silver said, looking at one that had come burrowing out of its straw, it was black and tan with an orange belly.

'Take them down to the pet shop. They buy them for snake food. Especially the constrictors. But you haven't come to talk about mice, have you?'

'Terry Collins,' Macrae said. 'He's one of your pupils.'

'What's Terry done now?'

'Gone missing.'

'Is the school still standing?' He smiled at them, showing perfect white false teeth.

'He's an athlete, isn't he?' Silver said. 'Anywhere he might have gone to? I mean, a track or a club. Something like that?'

'Not that I know of. Anyway, he hasn't done any running for months.'

'Not since his grandfather died?' Macrae said.

Porteous looked at him sharply.

'You know about the old man, then?'

'We've spoken to his mother,' Silver said. 'Tell us about the old man. He was an athlete too, according to his daughter.'

Porteous shook his head slowly. 'That was just his story. Said he'd run for Jamaica. But I checked it out. He never did much. At one time he was a member of the British Railways Sports Club, but that was years ago. But he was keen all right. Keen for Terry to go in for it. I think he thought it'd keep the boy out of trouble. And it did for a while.'

Silver said, 'I can understand Terry being upset when his

159

grandfather died, but if he was doing well, I mean at school, winning things, I'd have thought . . . '

'You must be joking.' He picked up a chocolate mouse and stroked it. 'Just look at that.' He held it on his palm. 'See? Tail and body about the same length. And those petal-shaped ears and wide skull. Just like a piece of sculpture.'

'He won a cup,' Macrae said, impatiently. 'We've seen a picture of it. He's holding it up. The old man's with him.'

'Oh, that. His grandfather bought it. Gave it to me to give to Terry. I was supposed to say it had been given to him by the school for "endeavour". I suppose that meant training hard.'

'You mean, he never ran for the school?'

'We don't have athletics. We don't have any competitive sports at all. No money to pay the teachers. Just gym – that's me.'

'Did he realise?'

'What?'

'That he was being conned.'

'Why should he? He was as happy as a cricket when I gave it to him. So was the old man. It wasn't an expensive cup you know, just electroplate.'

'What about friends, other hobbies?' Silver said.

'I dunno.'

'Anything outside school? What did he do in his spare time?'

'Set fire to classrooms.' He caught Macrae's expression. 'Sorry. I didn't really mean that. To tell you the truth I don't know.'

'You don't know much, do you?' Macrae said.

'Listen, our union says we don't do anything except teach. No coaching, no after-hours hobbies. OK? We do what we get paid to do. You don't like it, you take it up with them.'

22

Before Huntsman Collins, the amazing fourteen-year-old, became the Second Greatest Athlete in the World, which is to say before his grandfather came to stay on the Douglas Garden Estate, he used to sleep a great deal. Each day he wasn't at school he would sleep until noon and then lie in a half wakeful trance until two or three in the afternoon when the children's programmes would start on TV.

His mother, who was usually entertaining new friends, did not care what he did as long as he did it in his bedroom. Sometimes she would start entertaining them in the lounge and then go to the bedroom. These were usually old new friends. They often brought along a bottle of Bacardi or a few joints and Mrs Delilah Collins would have a little party in the lounge.

The new new friends she took straight to the bedroom.

Sometimes, when Terry was going out he would find several new friends waiting on the doorstep. Some of them were not much older than Terry himself and were in the gangs that roamed the Douglas Garden Estate.

These had formed along racial lines. The Greens and the Nazis were white; the Rastas and the Bikos were black.

Terry had tried to join a gang when he was ten but had been rejected by the former because he was too dark and by the latter because he was too light. After that he stayed in bed as long as he could because it was dangerous for a boy without affiliations to walk through the estate.

It was now mid-morning and Terry was in bed in the upstairs bedroom of the mews house in Bayswater. He was fully dressed in his track suit and trainers with a blanket over him. He was in his trancelike state, lying on his side and staring at the wall.

161

He did not want to get up because that would mean action and action would mean thought and Terry's mind was blank.

What thoughts he had were of Gail. He thought of sitting with her in the partly demolished building, holding her cold hand, willing her to come back to him. But she had not come back. Like Garner Maitland, she had left him for ever.

Why?

They could have got a flat or a little house. That's all Gail talked about. A place of their own. She had wanted a sofa where she could sit and watch TV and talk and drink tea.

His grandfather could have come and lived with them. Just the three of them in a little place somewhere nice, the country perhaps.

Now there was no one – except Daley. He was the Greatest Athlete in the World. Maybe if Terry could find him. Maybe if he could talk to him. Why shouldn't they be friends?

He got out of bed. The morning was sunny and cold, the great city quiet on this Easter Friday. He looked from the bedroom window and saw that the mews was deserted. The man must have fixed the station wagon for it was no longer there. He could not ever remember London being this quiet.

He went downstairs and ate another tin of baked beans and one of pineapple slices. Then he had another stale cigarette. How long could he stay here? How long would it be before the owners came?

He decided to carry the TV set upstairs. It was only a portable so he managed well enough. But the flex wouldn't reach any of the plugs from the little landing. He put it in the bedroom. He knew that as long as it was daylight no one outside would be able to see the blue-green light of the screen.

There was a church service on one channel, a choir singing on another, a nature programme on the third and a Bugs Bunny cartoon on the fourth. He watched the cartoon. Half his mind watched it but the other half still asked the question: *What am I going to do?*

And when there was no answer, that half of him became

162

frightened. More frightened even than when the man came to look for him.

That had all been over so quickly he had hardly had time to be afraid.

'Use your brains, mon,' his grandfather had always said.

OK, so use them.

Maria was in Hampstead. The plan had been that she would kill the remaining hours before meeting Jack by going to a movie where she would not have to think. But it was only when she came into London she remembered that because it was Easter Friday the movies would begin late in the afternoon.

So that plan was up the spout, as Jack used to say, and she had a long time to fill and nothing to fill it with.

London had always meant Hampstead to her. It was still a village, the last remaining village in the megalopolis. She had driven up and parked near the Heath. It was a sunny day and families were out taking a brisk pre-lunch walk with their children and their friends and their dogs.

She envied them.

She walked down to the swimming ponds then up towards Highgate, and back along Spaniard's Way. It had been a favourite walk of Richard's and hers. She decided she would have lunch, then see if there was a gallery or exhibition open in the West End.

She cut through to Heath Street and looked for a restaurant. Most were closed. She had more or less decided not to got to Dahlman's but it seemed the only one open.

It was a small Swiss restaurant where she and Richard had often eaten. Herr Dahlman made a fuss of her and told her how much he had missed them. He was fat and elderly with a plump baby face. She ordered a veal chop, rösti and a green salad. She was about to order a glass of white wine and then changed her mind and ordered half a carafe.

When she finished she went to Gun Place and looked at the house where she and Richard had lived. They had been happy there. She stopped in front of Christchurch, its great

163

steeple glinting in the March sun. This was where they had been married.

She fought the memories unsuccessfully. The most insistent was the holiday. That was when she had realised what Jack really was.

They had taken a house in Brittany in August. It had been Jack's idea. The way he had described it he had made it sound like Arcadia.

'We'll eat oysters and drink Sancerre and play golf and make love. How does that sound?'

It had sounded wonderful except she didn't play golf. But he would take care of that, he said. He would ask an old friend, Richard Dunlap, who did play golf. And Richard would bring a girlfriend.

She had hoped it might just have been the two of them but when he saw the look in her eyes he said, 'Don't worry, *liebchen*, we'll have lots of time to ourselves.'

Jack was to organise the villa. He left it late and had to accept what was left. It wasn't much. It lay between St Malo and Cancale near the Pointe du Grouin. It was high on the peninsula and was supposed to have fantastic views of the sea. In fact, they hardly saw the sea for the fog and the rain, and the wind almost flattened them when they stepped out of doors.

The house was too small, the bedrooms alongside each other and the walls thin. But even that might have been acceptable if the weather had not been so bad and the women had been able to get out.

Richard and Jack went to Dinard and played golf most days, despite the weather, and Maria was left with Birgit.

She had never met anyone who irritated her more. Birgit made it quite plain that she had favoured going to Spain. She said Swedes liked the sun. This place was like some remote peninsula on Heligoland and thanks very much but she could do without it. She got up late, well after the men had gone out, cooked herself large breakfasts which she did not clear away, and then set about the task of painting her toenails or washing her hair. Her conversation was limited to clothes and men.

But she was very beautiful, a grey-blonde with a skin like milk and light blue eyes. They had taken the villa for three weeks, but by the end of the first week Jack was bored by golf and fed up with the weather and the house and the general lack of excitement. He wanted to gamble. He wanted night clubs and bars. Birgit wanted water skiing, hot sun and topless beaches. The talk was of moving south. St Tropez was mentioned. So was Nice and Biarritz.

But Richard was firm. They had taken the villa and there would be little chance of finding anything else at this time. Why not make the best of it?

That was the first time Maria really noticed Richard. Jack and Richard had a kidding relationship. Out of this banter Jack emerged as the more amusing and interesting personality and it was only later that Maria realised this had happened because he was always trying to put Richard down.

Richard was tall and slender with a thin face that in repose wore a worried frown. But when he was amused his slow smile would wipe the worry from his face and he would display a highly developed sense of humour. The worry, Maria discovered, was because his father was seriously ill and was, at that time, undergoing tests in London.

By some sleight of hand Jack managed to make it seem as though it had been Richard's idea to come to Brittany.

'We should have gone to Iceland, then he'd have been really at home,' Jack said.

The weather made them all irritable and the banter became more pointed and there was a sharp edge to Jack's sarcasm.

'It's only a few hundred quid,' Jack said, when they were discussing again the idea of abandoning the house and moving south. 'It can't matter that much.'

'It's not the money,' Richard had said, with irritation.

'What is it, then?'

'Look, it's August. Everything'll be booked out. The roads'll be packed. The whole of France takes its holiday now. We'll spend half our time trying to find somewhere to stay. And the other half trying to get away from people. The beaches will be awful. It'll be like a package deal without the security of the package.'

165

'But we will have sun,' Birgit said. 'Do you not like the sun?'
'You could always wear a hat,' Jack said.

'I think we should give it a few more days,' Richard
said. 'The weather might clear.'

That evening they decided to go into St Malo for dinner
and then on to the casino in Dinard. By midnight Jack had
lost over three hundred pounds and when Richard suggested
they leave, Jack said, 'For Christ's sake, don't be so wet.'

They stayed another two hours during which time Jack
lost another fifty pounds. He left in a sullen mood. Suddenly
in the car park he said to Richard, 'I'll race you back. Birgit
can come with me.'

'Don't be stupid,' Richard said. 'If we're picked up and
breathalysed we've had it.'

But Birgit was already getting into Jack's car. 'Come on,'
he said. 'Get your finger out.' He took off in a shower of
loose gravel.

The night was misty and Richard drove with exaggerated
care. Maria sat hunched up at the door, angry and bewildered.
She took it out on Richard. 'Can't you go any faster?'

'No, I can't.' It was like a slap in the face.

Jack's car was not at the house when they got back.

Maria wasn't sure how to react, everything had happened
so fast.

'Would you like some coffee?' Richard said.

'No.'

She went to her room and got into bed. The minutes ticked
by. There was no question of sleeping. Every sense was alert
to the noise of Jack's tyres on the drive. What if they had had
an accident? It was just the sort of thing that might happen
with Jack in that mood and after the amount he had drunk.

She got up at first light. The clouds had rolled away, the
fog was gone, the sea was calm and the sun was beginning
to rise on a perfect day.

She found Richard in the sitting-room. 'We should go
and look for them,' he said.

Just then Jack's car pulled up outside the house and Jack
and Birgit got out. They were laughing and he put his arm
about her shoulders.

166

'Where were you?' Richard said. 'What the hell happened?'
Jack seemed rather drunk and so did Birgit.

'We stopped to see the sunrise,' Jack said.

Birgit gave a low, gurgling laugh, and went to her room.

At breakfast Jack said, 'What about it? What about going south?'

'What for?' Richard said, pointing to the window and the bright yellow sunshine.

'Birgit wants to and so do I.'

The tension was almost palpable. Maria had wanted to talk to Jack in private but he had avoided her and now suddenly it all boiled over.

'What the hell's going on?' she said. 'We came for a holiday! There's been nothing but fighting and bad feeling! And now you and Birgit . . . '

'Don't say anything you'll regret, *liebchen*.'

Birgit was looking at her with a small smile on her lips and suddenly Maria knew it was all over.

She gathered what she could of her dignity and went to the door. 'I'm going for a walk,' she said. 'You go where you like.'

She walked right out to the Pointe du Grouin. The tiredness had all gone and she was stiff with anger. When she came back only Richard was there.

In her bitterness she turned on him. 'It's your bloody fault,' she said. 'Why did you bring someone like her?'

He nodded slowly and then said, 'As the man said, it seemed like a good idea at the time.'

She went to her room and began to pack. Richard stood at the door watching her. 'If you'll take me down to St Malo, I'll get the ferry,' she said.

'Look, we've nearly two weeks of the holiday left. Are we going to let them ruin it?'

She turned and lashed out at him. 'What do you think, that I'm going to leave his bed and get into yours?'

'No. I didn't think that for a moment. But we're in France. We've paid for the house. The sun's shining. There are restaurants and drives and things to see. Couldn't we just do it on that basis?'

She said, 'I don't know how you could even—'

'For Christ's sake!' he said harshly. 'You aren't the only one with dented pride. I've been humiliated too. What I'm suggesting is a salvage operation.'

He walked to the window and looked at the sea. 'I should never have brought her. He can't keep his hands off. Never could. You just have to accept that with Jack. It's like living with a drunk and hoping he won't find the cooking sherry. Either you accept it, or you don't have anything to do with him.'

Suddenly she felt completely drained. Her love for Jack sat like a lump in her stomach. What should she do? Go back and sit in her small London flat and cry her eyes out? Or take the plane to Berlin and sit in her parents' flat in Charlottenberg and cry her eyes out there?

As if reading her mind Richard said, 'You'll get over it and so will I. People always do. Look, the ferry sails every day. You can go any time you like. Why don't you leave it until tomorrow and see how you feel then?'

The thought of sitting up all night in a ferry made her flinch. What she wanted was to be by herself. She crawled into bed and cried herself to sleep and didn't wake until the afternoon.

Now, wandering unseeingly through Hampstead she remembered those two weeks with an intensity she had not felt before.

What she remembered most was Richard's kindness when she was going through her withdrawal from Jack. What made it special was the fact that he was raw himself.

They spent the remainder of the holiday doing the things they should have done all along: going for drives and finding little restaurants and bars off the beaten track, going to Finisterre and standing in the wind by the old lighthouse and taking photographs, walking round the ramparts of St Malo, lying in the sun, just sitting and reading.

He had suggested a salvage operation and that's what it was. They lived in the house like brother and sister.

She saw him in London. But it was a bad time for him. His father was not expected to recover although no one could tell how long it would take. Richard spent hours each day by his bedside and Maria was filled with admiration for his selflessness.

Jack turned up like the proverbial bad penny. His idea was to kiss and make up and for the first time Maria saw him as he really was. He was one of those men who proposition every attractive woman they meet and when they are refused, proposition the next one that comes along.

Maria had taken a long time to get over Jack and had no intention of being sucked back into a repeat performance. When she said she wasn't interested, Jack at first could not understand the reason. She had to explain that you don't leave your mistress flat and go off with another woman and expect things to be just the same.

'Are you seeing much of Richard?'

There was no use lying. 'Yes.'

'He's a good bloke is Richard, a hell of a lot better than me.'

A good bloke.

Yes, he was a good bloke. She had grown to love him in a different way, with a depth she had never felt for Jack. Jack had been her first lover and she knew there was always a special place for first lovers. But Richard was more than a lover: he had been, for a time, all things to her.

And they'd had such a wonderful time! Sure the work was hard, but that's what made the rewards so sweet.

Then she had wanted the icing on the cake. She had talked him into selling the house he loved so much. The move to the country. The ultimate happiness.

But it didn't happen.

And *she* was to blame.

The thought came like an electric shock. Up to now she had blamed circumstances, she had blamed outside factors, she had blamed Richard. But it was *her* fault. She knew that now. Her fault that he was having an affair, her fault that he did not want to come home, her fault that he was spending the Easter weekend with someone else.

She was standing in the middle of the pavement. Passers-by were looking at her oddly. She was right down at the bottom of the Heath but had no memory of having got there.

169

23

Jack Benson lay in the bath, his head nestling between the taps, a glass of wine in his hand. He had had a late lunch of Dover sole off the bone – there was nothing like it in Hong Kong – and now he was sipping the last of a bottle of Pouilly Fumé and thinking of Maria.

He wondered if she had ever had a real debauch. When they had been lovers she had been innocent, not much more than a schoolgirl. She used to tell him how much in love with him she was but he supposed it was not much more than a crush. Well, now she was grown up.

His thoughts touched briefly on Richard. He felt no sense of guilt at what he was going to do. Any man who left his wife alone on the Easter weekend deserved all he got.

He wondered if the situation between Richard and Maria was serious. If it was he foresaw many such pleasant meetings.

He also wondered what would have happened if they hadn't gone for that disastrous holiday in France where he'd ended up with the Swedish bird. What a bloody nuisance *she'd* become.

He had handed Maria on a plate to Richard. It had been a stupid thing to do. She was like a little puppy in those days. You only had to snap your fingers and she'd come running. It was just a pity that she had been serious about things. Ah, *liebchen*, you had a lot to learn.

There was a knock at the door. Benson remembered the chambermaid. The bathroom door was ajar and he pulled the shower curtain along the bath so that he was hidden.

'Yes?' he called.

A man's voice said, 'Your clothes, sir.'

'OK, bring them in.' He heard the door open. 'Hang them

170

in the wardrobe, please.' Then, 'I thought this was women's work.'

From the bath he could look into the mirror above the handbasin. In it was reflected part of the interior of his room. The waiter passed close to the bathroom door. He was carrying the clothes over one arm. His other hand was held behind his back. Light from the bathroom streamed out into the bedroom at that point and for one split second only Benson saw what the waiter was holding in that hand, something he was not meant to see. It was a piece of brass wire shaped into a loop and at either end there were two small wooden handles.

He had seen such a thing twice before in his life. In Hong Kong a police acquaintance had shown him one in their 'Black Museum', and told him it was a weapon used by the Triads. The second time had been very early one morning in Manila. It had been lying on the pavement next to a dead body. They were called death loops or killing wires. They strangled in a matter of seconds.

The waiter dropped the clothes on the bed and turned towards the bathroom door.

Benson's mind was still in shock but moving at the speed of a mainframe computer. He saw the man's features for the first time. He had never seen him before but he was unmistakably Chinese.

Two thoughts crashed together. The first was that he had never seen a Chinese waiter in a British hotel; the second was that he was looking at the long arm of Mr Shao.

The Chinese did not realise he could be seen in the mirror and he stood in the doorway holding the wire loop in his hands. He spoke to the shower curtain. 'I put 'em away,' he said.

Benson had begun to move slowly down through the hot soapy water to the bottom of the bath. 'Put it on the bill,' he said, hearing his voice crack. 'I'll sign for it later.'

He looked round desperately for a defensive weapon but there was only a piece of soap.

In the mirror, he watched the man come forward to the tap end of the bath. The Chinese had his hand on the shower

171

curtain to pull it back when Benson reared up, grabbed the curtain rail, and brought the whole thing down.

The Chinese was not a big man and Benson's weight and the enveloping shower curtain threw him off balance. His foot slipped on the wet tiled floor and in a second he had fallen forward into the bath.

Benson, with the strength that comes from terror, fell on top of the writhing mass, pushing him down into the water. There was a splashing and thrashing, but his arms and legs were entangled in the curtain. His head was covered. He could not see. Now, with Benson's weight on top of him, he sank beneath the surface.

He fought and kicked but Benson pressed down with all his power.

The kicks and jerks gradually lessened. There was a noise of a blocked pipe unblocking as he coughed great gouts of air into the water, then gradually he grew limp.

Benson did not relax. He'd seen the movies of bodies suddenly rearing out of bath water. He lay on top of the man for fully five minutes until he was sure, absolutely sure, that no life remained.

Then he slowly pulled away and stood in the middle of the bathroom floor, shaking like a jelly.

The room was a complete mess. The shower curtain hid the man's body except for his feet which stuck out in the air. Benson backed away, terrified, but something made him stop and gather himself. He pushed the feet into the water. Now the curtain hid the body completely.

He ran across the bedroom and locked and chained the door. Then, still naked and dripping, he stood in the centre of the room and tried to think.

He had not the slightest doubt that Mr Shao had organised this little reception for him. If he had taken a little longer over his lunch, if he had not been in the bath ... If ...

He had a bottle of duty-free whisky and gave himself a large measure. Then he lit a cigarette and drew on it heavily. He had to think! But the computer was freewheeling. He tried to get it under control.

The first thing he had to do was get away from the hotel.

But where? Did the trains run on a holiday? He could hire a car. But if Mr Shao's friends had already traced him to the Ambassador why wouldn't they have contacts in the car hire business? That was the *first* place they'd check.

Maria.

She had a car. She could pick him up and take him to the airport or to one of the Channel ports and he could be out of the country by evening.

He dialled her home. He let the phone ring and ring but there was no answer. She must have left already. He phoned the house in Bayswater. Again the phone rang and rang. She must be on her way, he thought.

There was only one thing to do, get to the Bayswater house, wait for her there, and the moment she arrived, take off.

But how the hell could he tell her what had happened? How would she react? *I'm sorry I can't have dinner tonight I've just killed a man. Oh, and by the way, I want to leave the country NOW!*

Christ! What a mess!

He'd been running and running ever since the golf game with Mr Shao. He thought of him, cool in his brown tropical kit, cool in his air-conditioned house, cool in his bloody swimming pool. Cool and laid back, reaching for the phone and issuing a few orders and then sitting down and counting his bloody money until one of his boys came in and said, 'It is done,' or Chinese words to that effect.

And while Mr Cool was counting his money he, Benson, was running for his life all over South-East Asia.

They hadn't bothered! That was the bloody point. He'd thought he was so clever covering his tracks and they hadn't even bothered to try to follow him. They'd just organised the reception at the other end.

Mr Shao had probably figured it would be either New York or London. Both had large Chinese communities which meant that they also had Triads who, for a fee, or just for Auld Lang Syne, would erase anyone with whom Mr Shao had lost patience. All he had to do was pick up the phone. Even now, Benson imagined, there would be someone alerted

173

and waiting in New York. And there might be others in Paris and Amsterdam and Rome – and Timbuktu for all he knew. The mills of Mr Shao ground exceeding fine.

Well, who the hell was Mr Shao anyway? He was only a bloody Chinaman after all. He, Benson, also had a brain.

First of all he had to get clear of the hotel. He began to dress hurriedly in his newly pressed clothes.

No one must suspect *anything*.

What about the body?

What the hell could he do?

What if the real chambermaid came back to turn down the bed? Did they still turn down beds in good hotels? They did in Hong Kong. But here?

And where could he hide the drowned man? He looked at the bed but there was no space beneath it. He opened the wardrobe door. But the man was sopping wet and the water was bound to run out on to the floor. He could hear the woman's scream ringing in his ears.

He opened the bathroom door. He could leave him in the bath but only if he put back the shower curtain.

He examined the rail. Several plugs had come away from the wall with the screws still in them. He untangled the curtain from the corpse and tried, at the same time, not to look at the man's face. He pressed the plugs back into the holes in the wall. The rail held.

The body lay on its back, eyes open, staring at the ceiling. Benson carefully pulled the curtain along the bath and stepped back. It was of a heavy plastic material with London scenes printed on it. It hid the body completely.

He dressed quickly.

The money? He didn't want to be seen leaving the hotel with a suitcase. All he could see was the bag from the duty-free shop in Karachi. He stuffed the money into it. On top he placed pieces of French bread which had come with his lunch.

He'd go to the house, wait for Maria, and if she gave him a hard time he'd take her bloody car and to hell with her. He wondered how he should leave. By air or by sea? He'd be easier to trace by air. No one bothered to take the name of a foot passenger on a channel ferry.

He looked once round the room. It gave the appearance of having been left briefly by its occupant who would return. He closed the bathroom door. Then he went out into the corridor put his food tray on the floor and placed a DO NOT DISTURB sign on the handle of his door. There was nothing more he could do. He was buying time. By tomorrow he could be in any one of five or six European countries.

But which?

He took the lift down to the foyer. A uniformed policeman was talking to the receptionist who looked harassed and upset. An ambulance was standing at the front door and the driver and his assistant were wheeling in a stretcher.

Benson went to the porter's desk. 'What's happened?' he said.

'There's been an accident. One of the chambermaids.'

'Oh.' Benson felt himself go cold. 'Bad?'

The porter looked at Benson with the faint contempt of his calling and said, 'I wouldn't know, sir.'

Benson pointed to the bread visible in the top of his plastic bag. 'I want to go into the park to feed the pigeons. Is there a short way?'

The porter said, 'If you go past the dining-room, you'll find an exit there, sir.'

'Thank you.'

Benson, carrying his duty-free plastic bag, went along the passage, past the dining-room and out into Green Park. He did not look round but ambled west towards Hyde Park Corner, throwing small pieces of bread to the pigeons that clustered round him.

24

Number forty-three Lighter Lane was a small cottage in a small road that ran down to the Thames at Twickenham. Sheila Gant, who might have been twenty-five or forty-five or anywhere in between, let Macrae and Silver into her sitting-room after they had shown her their warrant cards.

She was small too, a shade under five feet, Silver would have said, and was dressed in a Laura Ashley print, with puffed shoulders and a ribbon at the waist, that came down to her ankles, giving her a Victorian appearance. Her hair was caught in a bun.

The room was also Victorian and so stuffed with knick-knacks that both men stood quite still fearing any sudden movement would send occasional tables crashing to the floor.

'I know what you've come about,' Miss Gant said, forming her words with exaggerated care. 'But I can ash . . . assure you that it was not my fault. Assure you of that.'

It was apparent that Miss Gant was very drunk.

'What wasn't your fault?'

'The accident. Isn't that why you've come? It was only a shcrape . . . a little paint. I assure you.'

'No it's not about any accident,' Macrae said. 'It's about Henry Foster.'

'Oh God. Please. I can't talk about Henry. Don't you understand? He's dead!'

'That's why we're here,' Silver said.

'But I . . . '

She was swaying lightly and Macrae said, 'I think you'd better sit down.'

'I ashure you I am quite cabaple . . .' She suddenly sat

176

down. Then immediately rose again. 'May I give you a drink? A little madeira? Some sherry?'

'It's a bit early,' Silver said.

'Early?' said Miss Gant vaguely. 'A glass of wine? Men like whisky and soda.' She crossed to a small table on which stood a bottle of gin, the only alcohol Silver could see. She poured a good shot into a wine glass and sipped it as though it was Chardonnay.

'You knew Mr Foster quite well?' Macrae said.

'Of course. I worked with him. A drop of port?'

'As a researcher?'

'That is correct. Title: Research Assistant. First Grade. Programme: *Focus*.' She sat down, rose shakily. 'A biscuit? Tea? Coffee?'

'Nothing, thank you,' Silver said.

Suddenly she said, 'Don't you just *hate* Good Fridays? I do. I hate Christmas Day too. I hate the shops being closed. I hate the trains not working. I hate the offices all still and quiet. I like people, movement. I mean, if you're not religious Good Friday's just a desert. Twenty-four hours of absolute hell.'

'Tell us about Henry Foster,' Macrae said.

'What's there to tell?'

'We have information that you were often in his company, not just for reasons of work. Were you having an affair with him?'

'Christ!' she said. 'That's subbley put! An affair?' Tears began to run gently down her cheeks. 'How can you ask me that?'

'We have to be sure,' Silver said. 'We're investigating a murder.'

She pulled a handkerchief from her sleeve and dabbed her eyes. 'Of course. I realise that. An affair?' Abruptly she began to laugh. It was such an emotional change that Silver stared at her in amazement. 'You think Henry would have an affair with someone like me?' She held up her left arm. 'I would have given that for Henry.'

She pushed herself up. 'Henry was superb.' She gave herself another neat gin. 'I once saw him naked, you know.

177

At his flat. He didn't realise it. I was in the living-room and he walked from the bathroom to the bedroom. Naked black men are the most beautiful things in the world. There is a unity about their bodies which whites don't have. And he was well hung. He had a cock like a donkey.'

'You didn't have an affair, then?' Macrae said, calmly.

'I would've if he'd wanted me to. But he'd never have been disloyal to that bitch—' She caught herself. 'To his wife.' Then she said passionately, 'I would've walked on broken glass for him.'

'What was your relationship, then?' Macrae said.

'I was teaching him.'

'What?'

'Look around you. I'm just a magpie.'

The walls were covered with miniatures and framed samplers. Tables groaned under snuffboxes and paperweights, ivory letter knives. In two display cupboards Silver saw cups and plates and small jugs.

'Collecting?' Silver said, and he felt a frisson cause his hair roots to prickle. 'China?'

She nodded. 'English china. Spode, Chelsea, early stoneware. Some Doulton. Worcester. He'd begun a collection. Only a few pieces, but quite good.'

Silver was remembering the rubbish bin in the area below Foster's apartment. The broken pieces in the plastic shopping bag.

'What was his collection worth?' Silver said.

'Difficult to say. Eight or nine thousand, perhaps.' There was a knock at the door. It was Eddie Twyford. A call had come in on the car phone – which Macrae had bullied Wilson into giving him – for Silver.

It was Laker, who was in charge of the Incident Room. He said the same man had called for Silver three times. The first two calls he had simply asked for 'the Jewish detective'. When told that Silver wasn't there he had hung up. The third time, which was now, he had said he had information about a 'young person in a green woollen hat' but he would only give it to the Jewish detective.

'Is he on the line now?'

'Yes.'

'Can you transfer him on to this phone?'

'Hang on.'

After a few moments a voice said, 'Is that you Silver?'

'Yes.'

'You know who's speaking?'

The Scottish lilt was unmistakable and Silver's memory flashed up the picture of the young street kid with the blood running down his nose and Macrae standing over him with a balled fist.

'Rattray, isn't it?'

'Yeah.'

Behind the voice Silver could hear the noise of traffic so he assumed it to be a public phone.

'Laker said you wanted me.'

'Yeah.'

'He said you had information about the youngster we're looking for.'

'That all depends.'

'On what?'

'On the money. You pay for information.'

'Sometimes.'

'Don't give me that shit. You got a special fund.' He sounded strung-out.

'It depends on the strength.'

'This is top strength. The best.'

'You tell me and I'll know if it's top strength. Everyone thinks they've got top strength.'

'I'm not gonna go on chatting here while you trace the bloody call, Silver. I'm not gonna be taken in and get my head beaten in by that bloody Celt. Just believe me. Top strength. I know where he is 'cause I followed him.'

'Listen, you tell me and I'll—'

'Forget it. I'm going to hang—'

'All right, hang up!'

'What?'

Silver wondered if the Rat needed a fix. 'I've got some cash. Not a lot. I could let you have a tenner.'

There was a pause.

'Can you get to Fulham?' Silver said. 'I could meet you there.'

'If you pay for a taxi.'

'OK. I'll pay for the taxi.' He gave the Rat the address of Henry Foster's flat. 'Wait for me outside. I don't know how long I'll be, but not too long. OK?'

'Why there?'

'Because I've got to pick up something. It's the dead man's flat.'

'The black guy's flat? Hey, that's terrific!'

As Silver ended the call Macrae came out of the house.

'Christ, what a stupid cow,' he said.

'Listen, guv'nor—'

'If I was a betting man, I'd say she was halfway round the twist. Just the sort of crazy who'd stick a knife into someone who wouldn't give her what she wanted. But, and it's a hell of a but, how did she get him up there on that ledge after she'd killed him?'

'Fork-lift truck?' Eddie said.

Macrae ignored him. 'No, she didn't kill Henry-bloody-Foster. But I wouldn't feel safe with her, myself. Well, what's it all about, laddie?'

'It was the Scotch kid, Rattray. The one we had in for questioning.'

'You got a good degree, didn't you?'

'A two-one.'

'That's good, is it? Well let me teach you something they never taught you. There's Scotch whisky and Scotch salmon and Scotch broth. But for most of the rest its Scots or Scottish. OK? Now what the hell does he want?'

Silver filled him in quickly.

'Why at Foster's flat? Why the hell doesn't he come into the station?'

Silver forbore to point out that Rattray was unlikely to place himself in a position where he could take another beating. Instead, he told Macrae about the broken china.

'Christ, why the hell wasn't that picked up before?'

'The bin was in a different place from the others. It was

180

easy to miss. The bits may have prints on them. I mean
we're assuming this kid killed him and . . . '
'We're not *assuming* anything of the bloody sort.'
'OK, sorry.'
'And don't be *sorry*, laddie! Only girls are sorry.'

'Dear Daley Thompson,' Terry wrote (or rather printed, for
he had never mastered looped handwriting) 'I am writin you
becos I want become a great atleet.'

He was lying on his stomach on the bed. It had taken him
a long time to work out this first sentence. He had found the
paper and pencil in the room downstairs while getting to
know his territory. The desk and the filing cabinet and the
drawer in the coffee table had all so far been unknown quan-
tities. Now he knew he could not open the filing cabinet,
nor the desk. But in the drawer of the coffee table he had
found a dozen more sheets of white paper and a propelling
pencil. He had never handled a propelling pencil before.

It was then he had decided to write to Daley Thompson.
He had never met him, of course, but he had seen him so many
times on TV and cheered for him so often and spoken about
him to his grandfather so frequently and had thought of him
just about every day that he felt a kind of bond between them.

He had heard somewhere that Daley Thompson helped
young people to get on in athletics, to become track stars,
and that he went to schools and encouraged young athletes.

This was what Terry wanted above everything. He wanted
to go to a school where there was proper athletics, where
they didn't give you a cup just for trying. He wanted to run
for his school and then for his country and then perhaps in
the national junior side. Then one day he wanted to run and
jump and vault and throw in the Big One. The Olympics.
Huntsman Collins. Number One.

He read the sentence again and struck out the word 'great'.
It just looked too much. But then he thought that Daley
Thompson might not be interested in people who wanted
to be ordinary athletes, so he put the word 'star' above the
scratching out.

181

Then the next sentence formed in his mind. This was meant to reassure Daley about his intentions. He wrote laboriously. 'I does not take drugs or anythin like that. I am no Ben Johnson.'

He read the two sentences over and was pleased with them. Now came the problem of what to say next. He thought he would tell Daley about how his grandfather had run for Jamaica with Arthur Wint and Herb McKenley and, as he was working out the words in his head, he heard a key in the front door.

For a second he was frozen, then he flung the paper and pencil aside, straightened the counterpane and even before whoever it was had relocked the door Terry had come out on the upstairs landing.

When he had brought the TV set upstairs he had had to push the loft ladder into the roof and the trapdoor had closed. His secret place was unreachable at the moment.

There were only the two rooms upstairs. The bedroom and the bathroom. The bathroom had an airing cupboard which contained the immersion heater. There was just enough room to squeeze in if he did not quite shut the door.

On the ground floor Jack Benson locked the front door and stood for a moment just inside it. Then he released his breath in a shuddering sigh of relief.

He was safe.

For a while anyway.

He looked around the sitting-room/office. It was much the same as when he had last been here. There was a smell of dust and stale cigarette smoke and Richard had clearly given up a maid because there were cigarette butts in the ashtray. Benson lit a cigarette of his own with a shaking hand.

He had made himself walk slowly along Green Park expecting any moment someone, no, not someone, a Chinese person, to step out from behind the trunk of a plane tree, and . . . Well, best not dwell on that.

Then he had crossed Piccadilly near Hyde Park Corner and walked up Park Lane. London was quiet but what traffic there was went up and down this artery and what pedestrians were abroad also seemed to favour Park Lane.

182

So he had walked towards Oxford Street seeking out other pedestrians and matching his stride to theirs, always trying to keep someone between himself and . . . and what? A bullet probably. They wouldn't try anything else in a London street.

He'd found himself sweating in spite of the cold and was full of resentful anger. What had the world come to when you could be bloody nearly murdered in your room in one of the best hotels and were in danger on any of the main thoroughfares?

He reached Marble Arch and crossed over to the far side of the Bayswater Road and was soon in Broadhurst Mews. There was not a soul in sight. Even the sounds of London seemed muted.

Now he finished his cigarette as he looked out between the slats of the venetian blinds, watching for her. Then with a start he realised he had been so taken with his own safety that he had forgotten the money. He wanted a safe place for it temporarily. He looked around, pulled the drawers of the filing cabinet but found them locked. The desk was locked too. He went into the little kitchen and put the money in the food cupboard.

Then he sat down in the front room and stared at the wall. That's when the terror really gripped him.

25

'I'm not sayin' a bloody word,' the Rat said to Silver. 'Not while he's there. That's not the deal.'

'What difference does it make? You get the money anyway.'

'Not him. The bastard! I said *you*! I said I wasn't gonna—'

'All right. Hang on.'

They were arguing in the doorway of Foster's apartment block in a bitter wind. Macrae was standing by the car. Now Silver went over to him and said, 'He's shy in front of you, guv'nor. Says he's scared of you.'

'Silly wee boy,' Macrae said. 'All right.' He got back into the car and lit a slim cheroot.

Silver went back to the Rat. 'He's not coming. Let's have it.'

'Got the money?'

'Of course.'

'Well, not here.'

'Come on, don't be stupid. There's nothing there.'

'He's famous. I never been inside anyone's place who's famous.'

'You can't go inside.'

They went out into the rear area and Silver took the broken china in its plastic shopping bag out of the dustbin.

'Thievin' from bins? Whatever next?' the Rat said.

'Never mind,' Silver said. 'Let's have it.'

'OK. I saw him last night. He was up the West End. Dunno why or what he was doing, but anyway I followed him back to Bayswater. And he went to a stables.'

'A what?'

'Where they keep horses.'

'I know what stables are.'

'Well, there're stables in Broadhurst Mews. That's where he went. In at a window and he never came out.'

'Stables? You sure?'

''Course I'm sure. Broadhurst Stables. Says so on the door. I bet he's sleeping on the straw. I know I would.'

Silver gave him the money.

'Aren't you even gonna give me a kiss?'

'Some other time.'

Silver went up the back stairs carrying the plastic bag of china. He unlocked the door and entered the flat. Nothing had changed.

Again he had a strong feeling that something had happened in the flat, that it was trying to tell him something if he only had the eyes to see it.

He went from room to room but was drawn back to the bathroom. Suddenly he knew what was bothering him, what had bothered him from the start. It was the bathroom itself. It was out of character. *Out of character?* He could just imagine Macrae's contempt. *Only girls talk like that, laddie.*

But it *was* out of character. With its oversize bath and its mirrors and mock-gold fittings it did not fit in with the severity of the other rooms.

He looked up at the shower bracket again. It didn't seem possible for a shower to be aimed into the bath from that position. Maybe Foster had had the bathroom redecorated and refitted and decided just to leave the old shower fitting where it was.

And maybe he didn't. That wouldn't fit his character either.

The closer he looked the more the bracket didn't seem to have anything to do with a shower. He went out into the sitting-room to get a chair to stand on to examine it more closely.

'Not much for a famous TV person,' the Rat said. He was standing in the middle of the sitting-room.

'I told you not to come in here!'

'Jesus, look at all those videos. They all of him?'

'Never mind. Get going.'

'You stealin' chairs now?'

Silver turned to place the chair in the bathroom. The Rat pressed the play button on the video recorder.

185

'Is that him?'

The picture showed the final seconds of one of Foster's shows, the one Silver had already watched.

'Christ, you stupid nit!' Silver called over his shoulder. 'Don't touch anything!'

'He'd look better without glasses.'

Silver placed the chair in the right position. Then he heard the Rat swear. He went back into the sitting-room.

'I told you not to . . . '

They were looking at a home-made black and white video. It was a high shot of a boy in a bath.

The bath in this apartment.

The boy was about fourteen and his skin was the colour of milky coffee. He lay back in the soapy water and another figure knelt by the side of the bath. He was gently rubbing the boy's body with soap and then sponging it.

Both Silver and the Rat looked on in fascinated silence.

The kneeling figure rose and they saw it was Henry Foster. He was wearing only a towel. He moved out of shot but in a moment he entered it again. Now he was naked. He said something to the boy and laughed. Then he too got into the bath. He began to stroke the boy's face. But the boy turned away and Foster playfully splashed a handful of water at him. The boy splashed back. There was a splashing contest for a few moments.

Foster was obviously enjoying himself, but the boy's expression was angry. Then suddenly Foster grabbed him and tried to kiss him. There was a struggle. The boy, still soapy, slipped out of Foster's hands and out of shot. Foster climbed out of the bath and he too moved out of shot. The camera played on the bathwater as it gradually became still. Finally, all they saw was a shot of the bath and the taps.

Silver pressed the fast-forward button. The tape whirred on, but the picture did not change.

They waited in silence until the tape ran out. 'Is that him?'

'Yeah. That's him. That's Huntsman.' Then suddenly the Rat said, 'I'm off!'

'Wait!'

But he slipped out of the back door and Silver heard

186

his feet racing down the stairs. For a moment he thought of running after him, but he'd never catch him and anyway what more could he add?

He went back into the bathroom and looked at the bracket. He knew now it was used to hold a video camera. He wondered if all the other videos on the shelves would show similar scenes. He thought it highly likely. Put your own show on first then hide personalised porn on what was left of the tape. Clever Henry Foster.

He went down in the lift and fetched Macrae.

Dark clouds had come up during the afternoon and turned the day to dusk. Benson sat in the living-room of the mews house and chain-smoked, lighting one cigarette from another.

His thoughts reflected the sky; they were ominous, portentous and confused. One second scenes from Hong Kong flashed into his mind, the next he was seeing again the dead, staring eyes of the Chinese man he had drowned.

Killed a man! God, he never thought that would happen. Never ever. He'd never seen himself in a role like that. Nor in the reverse. He'd never . . . well, not until he'd played golf with Mr Shao, he'd never seen himself in the role of victim.

He was a businessman, nothing more, nothing less. Businessmen were known to have their ups and downs. Christ, if every businessman who owed money was murdered, the place would be littered with bodies!

Did they know about the money in the food cupboard, the money that had come from his safe? They couldn't have. Not even Mrs Feniman knew. So this was pure revenge. Not that they would see it that way. Rather *pour encourager*. Not good business to have people get away with owing money. Spoils your reputation.

And she wouldn't have been able to tell them where he'd gone either because he didn't know himself until he started. But they had ways. There was the American Express payment and the passenger lists. It wouldn't have taken them long.

He began to pace up and down the room.

Where the hell was *liebchen*?

Even as the thought went through his mind he heard a discreet knocking at the door. He strode to it and flung it open.

'*Liebchen!*' he said, his eyes alight with relief.

But it wasn't *liebchen*, it was another Chinese man. He was young and slender but dressed, like Benson, in a suit. He was wearing a trilby on his head.

Before Benson could react, the man pushed the door and Benson backwards and had come into the room. Now he slammed it shut. But Benson was already running. He ran up the stairs and into the bedroom. His knowledge of the layout gave him just the smallest start.

He closed the door and locked it, sprang across the bed and grabbed the phone on the bedside table. Nine . . . nine . . . nine . . .

'Hello! Hello!' he shouted.

But even before the phone could be answered at the emergency services, the line went dead. He sat on the bed with the useless receiver in his hand. His eyes sought the telephone wire. It was stapled into the bedroom wall just above the skirting board and disappeared under the door.

He threw down the phone and ran to the window and began to wrestle with the catch. It had recently been painted and had stuck. At that moment the door burst open.

'You want money?' Benson said, shrilly. 'I give you money!'

He heard his voice but hardly recognised it. He was speaking as though to a primitive savage.

'Plenty money!'

He began to move towards the bed. Then he saw the pistol in the man's hand. The barrel was elongated and thickened by the silencer that had been screwed into it.

'You don't want to do this, old chap,' Benson said, holding out his hands. 'Be reasonable. I'll give you everyth—'

The man shot him in the chest.

'Oh!' Benson said, as he half fell. He looked down at his chest. 'For Christ's sake don't do that! Can't you understand English? Me give to you—'

The man shot him in the head. Benson's last view of the world was the counterpane on the bed. He reached for

188

it. His fingers gripped it. Then slowly he toppled sideways and pulled the counterpane on top of him.

Had he survived for another few seconds he might have lived to be a grandfather for, as the Chinese put away his gun, a voice called to him in Cantonese from below.

He ran swiftly and quietly down the stairs. Another Chinese man was waiting for him. He nodded in the direction of a car outside the stables. It was parked with its rear to them. They could see someone at the wheel and they could also see a blue police light on the roof, now switched off.

They kept to the darkness on their side of the mews and got into a small white car and drove out the other end. Eddie Twyford heard the car start and leave. But they weren't looking for someone with a car. They were looking for a boy who had got here on his two feet. Eddie was not interested.

In the stables Macrae and Silver were questioning the owner. His name was the Hon. Evelyn Biggs-Stratton. He was a slender man wearing a long tweed hacking-jacket, white pin-cord riding breeches, long highly polished riding boots and a monocle. He smoked a cigarette in an amber holder. He was old and grizzled and Silver had never seen anyone like him.

'Fit?' said the Hon. Biggs-Stratton, who was deaf and had misheard one of Macrae's questions. "Course I'm fit. Eighty-six next year and I can still ride to hounds twice a week. Try that when you're my age and then you can come and ask impertinent questions. What the hell's it got to do with you anyway?' His bloodshot eye glared at them through his monocle.

Macrae decided to let it pass. He pointed to a window high up on the wall. 'Is that window kept locked?'

'Kept what?'

'Locked.'

'How the hell should I know? You want to ask Veronica that.'

The horses had turned their heads towards the three men as though fascinated by the encounter.

'Who's Veronica?' Silver said, facing the owner of the stables and speaking loudly and clearly.

'Stable girl. She's the one who's supposed to know things like that. How the hell do I know if a window's left open or not?'

Silver stood on one of the boxes underneath the window and was just able to see that the catch was not closed. He tried it and said, 'It's stiff and hasn't been used for years.'

'As the bishop said to the actress.'

The Hon. Biggs-Stratton gave a rasping laugh. Then he said, 'I don't know what you fellows think you're after, but you're not going to find it here. There's never been the slightest hint of impropriety about these stables. Clean as a whistle except for one sod who lived down the mews. Said he couldn't stand the smell of the manure and got the health inspectors. I said the stables had been here since 1831 and been owned by my family for most of that time and if he didn't like the smells he should bugger off and live somewhere else. Bloody sight better for him than exhaust fumes.'

'We're looking for someone who might have slept here last night,' Macrae repeated loudly. 'A young boy. We think he may have got through that window and slept in the straw.'

'In the straw? If you ask me it's the best place. Better than a bed. Oh, much better. More comfortable. Healthier too. Better for the back. Nothing like it. I've slept up there many a night. Had my first stable girl up there. First of many. There's something about horses that does something to women, thank God. Otherwise I'd have packed it in after the war. Not sex. Horses.'

'Do you mind if we look around?'

'Do what you like. Only don't ever say I'm not fit. What about a point-to-point in the morning, a three-mile slog in the afternoon and a couple of sets of racquets in the evening? Think you could manage that? Fit? Christ, you don't know what it means.'

Macrae and Silver had climbed the stairs into the hayloft. Several bales had recently been moved nearer to the top of the ladder and others had been pushed back against the wall. There was no evidence of anyone using the place as a refuge.

Silver picked up the stalks of a bunch of grapes. 'Yours?' he said to Biggs-Stratton.

'Grapes?' The eye swivelled in the monocle like a red beam. 'I'm not a bloody invalid. That's the sort of stuff Veronica eats. Yoghurt . . . bananas . . . dried fruit . . . Horrible.'

He fitted another cigarette into his holder and lit it. He caught Silver's glance. 'You think it's unhealthy, do you? You come along and tell me that when you're eighty-six.'

They went outside. Macrae stood on the tub of dead geraniums. He saw several small marks on the window-sill that might have come from hands or feet or both – or they might not. If it was Terry Collins he was miles away by now.

'He was conning you,' Macrae said angrily to Silver.

'Who?'

'That bloody layabout Rattray. But I'll watch for him. You'll have that money back or he'll go inside.'

26

Maria parked her car in the mews directly in front of her house and went in. The long walk in Hampstead had cleared her mind. She knew now that she was not going to have an affair with Jack, but it still left her with the problem of what to do about him. She knew him well enough to know that he hadn't invited her to London just to play pat-a-cake. He knew and she knew what the arrangements were. They were the same arrangements that had pertained in Berlin when he would fly in from London and phone her from Tegel airport.

'Feel like a dirty weekend?' he would say.

And she would ham it up in her thickest German accent, 'Please, I do not understand. What is that?'

And he would say, 'An old English custom. Like morris dancing lying down.'

It had amused and excited her. Just as his phone call coming out of the blue had excited her this time. Now she was no longer excited in that way. She was brittle and febrile and wished it was all over and that she was safely back in Hampshire listening to the rain dripping off the eaves. Already she had begun to look forward to getting home, to preparing for Richard's arrival. She'd get in something special to welcome him back; and make herself look as attractive as she could.

She would erase any thoughts of what he had been doing that weekend. She would go after him with everything she knew. She'd be a mistress to him as well as a wife.

But in the meantime there was Jack. She had thought of telephoning him at his hotel to say she had broken down, developed 'flu, picked up a stomach bug, anything. But then she thought: what if he came down to look for her? What

192

would Richard think of that? And in any case it was pure cowardice.

No, the best way was to face it. Go out to dinner and a movie and pretend that was all she had ever had in mind.

'Good God, Jack, that was all over a long time ago,' she would say.

And Jack would shrug and say, 'OK, *liebchen*, just testing.'

Would he?

Or would he become drunk and unpleasant and make a scene?

This is what worried her.

She lit a cigarette and dropped the match in the ashtray and noticed there were several butts in it already. Richard must have failed to tidy up before he left. At least none of the butts had lipstick on it.

She carried the ashtray to the kitchen and emptied it into the pedal bin. Frowning, she looked more closely. There were several empty tins in it. This was unlike Richard. Anyway, who would eat baked beans and apricot jam and pineapple slices? You'd only eat a mixture like that if there was nothing else. But there were lots of other things. She knew because she kept an eye on the food cupboard. She opened it to check and the first thing she saw was a plastic bag with 'Duty-Free Shop' printed on it in large letters.

Then she knew what had happened. Jack had been here. Those had been his cigarette butts. But had he eaten two tins of baked beans, one of pineapple slices and a pot of apricot jam? Not unless the Far East had dramatically changed his habits.

The bag had been pushed into the cupboard squashing some of the packets on the shelf and now she pulled it out to replace it more tidily. As she did so she looked inside it and found herself staring at three pieces of French bread and wads of various currencies kept together with rubber bands.

She couldn't believe it. She thought it must be Monopoly money. Then she looked more closely, taking out several bundles and riffling through them. They were real enough.

She felt her stomach clench with tension and a kind of nameless, free-floating apprehension. Why? Why would Jack carry all this money around in a plastic bag? And why would he hide it here?

She pushed the bag back into the cupboard and closed the door. Her mouth was dry with fear. She took down a glass and filled it at the tap and was raising it to her mouth when there was a tiny plop and she found herself looking at what appeared to be red smoke gradually staining the water.

She looked up but all she could see was a dark spot on the ceiling. Someone had been in the bedroom above, she thought. Someone had spilled red wine.

A scenario formed in her mind. Jack had come early. He had brought a bottle of wine, drunk some of it, and knocked over the glass or the bottle.

And the money? That was typical of Jack, he had always skated on the edge of the law.

Was he still there, she wondered? Had he gone to sleep?

'Jack?' she called up the stairs. 'Jack, are you there?'

She went up and looked into the bedroom. It was something of a mess. The bed was empty, but clearly Jack had been there. The counterpane had been flung on to the floor on the far side. He must have had a sleep and gone out again. She straightened the pillows and then pulled up the counterpane. It seemed to be caught. She pulled harder. A white hand, the fingers crooked into the material, slowly rose on to the bed as she pulled.

'Jack, are you—'

She saw him. His face was covered in blood and there was more blood on his shirt.

She was horror-struck. Frozen.

'Jack!' It was just a whisper.

She forced herself to go to the other side of the bed.

'Oh, Jack!'

She stood looking down at him, willing him to answer, to get up and tell her it was really raspberry jam and that it was his little coming-home joke.

But there was something about the way he was lying, with one arm caught in the counterpane, that was not a natural position for any living person to take. And then there was his skin. The parts not covered by blood were strangely white, almost phosphorescent. She knew she was looking at a corpse.

Every instinct in her body made her want to scream and run. But she told herself that would be impossible. This was a friend and sometime lover, a partner of her husband. He had been killed in their house. She could not run. She must do something. She must telephone the police. She picked up the bedside phone and hit 999. Nothing happened. She turned away from Jack's body and stared hard at the wall as she tried once more for the dialling tone. She did not get it.

This was an extension phone, there was another downstairs. She turned – and saw in the doorway the fantasy that frightened her most, the image that had gone some way to making her decide to leave London, the image which paralysed young women and old alike – and most men too. In the doorway crouched a black man wearing a knitted cap and holding a knife in his hand.

Whatever courage had brought Terry this far had drained away like water in a desert. From his position in the bathroom he had seen most of what had happened and what he had not been able to see he had heard. Now he wanted support. He wanted his grandfather or Gail or both. He needed *someone*.

He himself was not conscious of holding the knife as he crouched in the doorway and everything that happened now seemed to happen in slow motion.

He knew she was going to scream and he didn't want her to. He didn't want to draw any more attention to the house. He knew he had to stop whatever train of events had started. He needed time to think. But first of all he wanted to tell the woman that whatever had happened in this house, in this room, had nothing to do with him. Nothing, nothing, nothing.

He began to walk towards her. She backed away. She opened her mouth to scream.

And then he saw the body. The face. The blood.

His own blood surged into his head. Here it was again. The nightmare. The man under the bridge.

'You little bastard!' the man had said, climbing up into

the den below the railway tracks. 'You smashed them, you little shit, and now I'm going to make you pay.'

That was when Gail had passed him her knife. The TV man hadn't seen it in the half darkness because he had come on with his hand outstretched to grab Terry.

If you trap a ferret or a rat, if you block all exits so that they cannot escape, then they'll fight. Terry was trapped in his territory. There was no way past the man. So he had fought. As the man reached for him he had got to his knees and struck one blow. He had thought he was striking the man's legs but at that moment the man crouched to get at him. Just one blow. That was enough.

In those split seconds, as the tape was running through Terry's head, Maria pushed him. He fell against the bed and rolled on to the corpse. She was past him in a flash, making for the stairs.

But there vanity caught up with her. To make herself look as inviting to Jack as possible, she had worn a pair of very high-heeled black patent courts. They were shoes which showed her ankles and legs to advantage, but they were not the shoes to go rushing about in, especially on staircases.

She went down like a nine-pin. Ceiling, walls, carpet, spun through her vision, and then she was lying at the bottom of the flight. She was conscious for a few seconds and aware that the black man was crouched above her.

'Don't hurt me,' she whispered. 'Please don't hurt me.'

'I ain't gonna hurt you,' Terry said, but the woman did not hear him for her eyes flickered and he saw the whites as they closed.

27

'I'm getting too old for this sort of lark,' Macrae said.

He and Silver were standing in the foyer of a tower block in London's East End. As with the Douglas Garden Estate, this was suffering from blight. The difference was that, although the elevators had been out of order when they went to see Mrs Collins, they had only to walk up a few floors. Now they had to walk up twelve.

'You want me to go, guv'nor?'

'I said I was getting too old, laddie. I haven't got there yet. C'mon.'

Silver started off as though he were racing up Everest. Macrae followed slowly. By the fifth floor Silver could taste pennies in his mouth. By the seventh he thought his heart was going to burst. He stopped and waited for Macrae to catch up with him.

The older man was hardly breathing. He plodded past Silver and went on slowly up to the eighth and then the ninth floors. Silver came after him. Macrae, half-turning, said, 'You watch a good man on the hill. He goes up slowly. There's no prize.'

Finally, they came to the twelfth floor. Here the wind was fierce, howling along the corridors and rattling doors and windows. Silver thought the top of the building was probably swaying. He tried not to think of a similar building less than half a mile away, like this one built in the 1960s, which had simply fallen down one day killing forty-three people.

Macrae, holding his hat on with one hand, knocked at a door with the other. The door was covered in a protective wire screening and had a fish-eye security lens. A light came on inside the door and a voice said, 'Yes? Who is it?'

197

'Is that Mr Woods?'

'Who is it?'

'Police, Mr Woods. You telephoned us.'

There was a rattling of chains and the door opened slightly. 'Have you got any identification?'

Macrae held his warrant card at the narrow opening. Silver thought how much like his own door this was.

Macrae withdrew his hand and more chains rattled. The door swung open. 'Come in,' Mr Woods said.

'Who is it, Charlie?' came a woman's frightened voice from a room on the right.

'It's all right, love. Just friends from the club.' He put his finger up to his lips then whispered, 'I don't want to scare her.' He led them into a small sitting-room.

He indicated a couple of chairs but did not sit down himself. He was a small man with a lined and weather-beaten face which looked as though it had been out in all weathers, which it had.

'Excuse me.' He went into the room next door and they heard the low murmur of voices. In a few moments he was back.

'I told the wife you was from the fishing club. The season starts next month. She'd go into a panic if she knew you was coppers. Anything puts her into a panic. It's because she can't get out, see. Got a bad back and the lifts don't work. Hasn't been out of these walls for three years or more. Doesn't even go out on the balcony because the height makes her dizzy.'

Macrae said, 'You phoned us about a young boy you saw in the park.'

'That's right. Day before yesterday.'

'What time?'

'Just getting dark. I remember that because the gates had been closed. He came running along like he was lost.'

'What was he wearing?' Silver said.

'What I said on the phone. Those things the athletes wear.'

'Track suit?'

'That's it. A black and green track suit and a green beret on his head.'

'A beret?'

198

'Ain't that what they call them? Those knitted things. A lot of blacks wear them.'

'All right,' Macrae said. 'Sounds like the boy we want.'

'And he looked like him,' Mr Woods said.

'Charlie!' came the voice of Mrs Woods from the bedroom. He went to the door. 'What, love?'

'You ain't going out are you?'

'No, love.'

'What do you mean it looked like the boy?' Silver said.

'The picture on TV. You know, the one the police artists draw. It was in the papers too.'

'The photofit?' Silver said.

'That's it.'

'All right, Mr Woods, what happened?'

'Well, the gates were closed, see. I was late myself. Now, when the gates are closed, you got to go right back to the Serpentine bridge to get out that way. But I catch my train at Lancaster Gate station so I was going to take a short-cut.'

'And?'

'Well, I says to the kid he can come with me, otherwise it means he's probably going to climb over the fence and we don't want that. It's high and it's got spikes and last month a geezer tried to climb over in the dark and he slipped and the spike went through his thigh and he stuck there and someone had to call the fire brigade. Lucky it didn't get him, you know, in the other place.'

'Go on.'

'So, I says to him, I know a way out but he's not to say a thing about it. There's this loose railing.'

'Where?'

'Near the station. Opposite the pub.'

The moment he said it he looked away as though he had made a mistake.

'What pub?'

'The Duke of York.'

'Go on.'

'That's it. I let him through. Told him to forget about it. I went over the road to catch my train. I never seen him again.'

'Charlie!'

199

'Right here,' he called.

'You sure you're not going out? You said you wouldn't.'

'I'm not going out, love.' He turned to Macrae. 'See what I mean?'

Macrae said, 'The problem is we'd like you to come and show us.'

'Show you what?'

'Where you first saw the boy. Where the loose railing is.'

'Listen, mate. You can see how it is. I'm in for the weekend. Told her so. She's been looking forward to it. I can't go an' leave her now. Not at night.'

He looked appealingly at Silver.

'I mean it's the least I can do. Especially if I want to go fishing next month.'

'All right,' Macrae said wearily. 'Let's go over it again. This time in detail. Everything.'

Terry crouched over the woman. At first, he thought she was dead. The clatter of her falling down the stairs had frightened him badly. And, if she *was* dead, would they blame *him*?

This was what preoccupied him now. Blame. It lay on him like a great black animal. When they caught him would they say he had done it?

And it was no longer *if* but *when*, for beneath the layers of anger and resentment and rebellion, beneath the tough street-wise exterior, beneath the skin of Huntsman Collins, the World's Second Greatest Athlete, there was, and always had been, Terry Collins of twenty-eight Thackeray House, the Douglas Garden Estate, London. And that Terry Collins was confused and scared as hell.

When someone had a problem his grandfather used to say, 'Mon, he up de creek widout a paddle.'

Terry knew he was up the creek.

Without a paddle.

And yet nothing . . . nothing . . . had been *his* fault.

He felt tears of anger and injustice come into his eyes. That was the thing. He hadn't *started* anything.

The man had come up to him near the bridge and said, 'Hello, you look lost.'

Well, he wasn't lost. But Gail was zonked out. He had no money. He was hungry. And the man had spoken in a deep and reassuring voice.

'Would you like a cup of tea?' the man had said.

Terry hadn't replied.

'I'm sure you could do with one. And a bacon sarnie?'

It was the thought of the bacon sandwich that had done it. He hadn't *said* anything, but his look must have spoken for him, for the man said, 'I make the best bacon sarnies in London. And when we've had tea I'll show you some videos. You like videos?'

Terry had nodded. The man had smiled. The smile was reassuring too, full of dimples and white teeth. But what had reassured Terry most was that the man was black.

He remembered the Rat pointing out a man in Soho and telling him that if he went with him and did what the man wanted there would be a tenner in it for him.

This man didn't seem like that. He was a brother. The same colour as Terry's grandfather.

And so they had got into a taxi. It was the first time he had ever been in a taxi. The man had asked him his name and Terry had told him it was Huntsman.

'What a marvellous name!' the man had said. 'You can call me Bobbie.'

They had gone to Bobbie's flat and he had made tea and bacon sarnies and Terry had watched the afternoon children's programmes. A feeling of cosy nostalgia had come over him. This is what he had done sometimes after he and his grandfather had finished the training. If his mother and sister were out they would make tea and watch children's TV. His grandfather had liked *Sesame Street*.

And Bobbie was kind. He had said to Terry, 'You watch the TV and I'll do a little work and then maybe you'd like a bath and then we can talk. OK?'

And Terry had watched TV and Bobbie had worked at his desk and then after a while he had said why didn't Terry have a bath because there was a lovely bath and lots of hot water.

Terry could take bathing or leave it. But he thought

201

it would be nice to be clean again. So he'd had a bath and Bobbie had come in and said, 'I bet you haven't been bathed for a long time. Did your father bathe you when you were little?'

And he'd soaped his hands and used them to rub Terry's body. All over his chest and neck and arms. He was pretending it was a game. And then, whoops, down under the soapy water to what Terry's grandfather had called his 'privates'. Terry had pretended it wasn't happening and so had Bobbie. It had felt pleasurable. He had lain there in the hot water and allowed Bobbie to rub him wherever he liked but then Bobbie had got into the bath and it was as though Terry had woken from a dream. For Bobbie was big in more ways than one and he began to try and kiss Terry, to get his large pink tongue into Terry's mouth. And Terry hadn't liked that so he had got out of the bath and Bobbie had come after him.

Terry couldn't remember in exactly what order things happened next. He was trying to get dressed and Bobbie was trying to stop him and they were wrestling – Bobbie pretending it was still a game. But after a moment or two the pretence vanished and it became real.

And then, slippery with soap, Bobbie had fallen and hurt himself and had started shouting at Terry and Terry had seen the china and smashed it.

He didn't know why.

It was like setting fire to the project he had built. It had just happened. He had swept it from the table-top where it was displayed and it had smashed to pieces on the floor.

Bobbie had been shocked and angry and had started to pick up the bits and Terry had grabbed the rest of his clothes and run. And no one was going to catch Terry when he was running.

Not Arthur Wint. Not Herb McKenley. And surely not Bobbie.

He had finished dressing in an alley and then begged small change from passers-by and taken a bus back to the West End.

Gail was awake when he crawled back into the den. He told her what had happened. And they had talked about it for a long time while trains rumbled over their heads and

202

darkness came. Gail had said he was stupid for not knowing what was in Bobbie's mind.

And then suddenly Bobbie was there, under the bridge, climbing up into the den, and the nightmare had begun.

He saw the woman's eyes flicker and for a moment he was reminded of Gail. This is how she looked coming out of it: eyes flickering and trying to focus. In many ways the woman reminded him of Gail; same size, same shape of face, same short hair.

'You all right?' he said.

She pushed herself up slowly to a sitting position. He wasn't a black man. He was a black *boy*! She looked for the knife but did not see it. Then she looked at his face and thought there was something vaguely familiar about it. She moved again and groaned with pain. Her left shoulder had taken the brunt of the fall and she felt as though she might have broken her collar bone.

'You all right?' Terry said again.

'What do you care?'

The nature of her fear had changed since she had seen him more closely. She realised that her first view of him had been through eyes already programmed with terror. Then he had seemed the very stuff of nightmare. Now she could see he was a boy, maybe a dangerous boy, but a boy.

'Why don't you run?' she said. 'While you've got the chance?'

'I didn't do it.' Terry said, with a mounting sense of injustice.

She tried to rise but couldn't. There was something wrong with her left leg. She had only one thought: to get this black boy out of the house, then to get help. Even though he was a boy he was a murderer and every second he was there she was in danger.

Why in God's name had he killed Jack? Impulse? It could hardly have been planned.

But . . . and this thought came to her on the heels of the others . . . if he had wanted her dead too he had had the perfect chance.

203

While she lay momentarily stunned at the bottom of the stairs he could have ... Her mind baulked at the thought of what he might have done. But he had certainly had the opportunity.

'I swear on my dying solemn oath,' he said.

'What?'

This was the most portentous and awful declaration in Terry's lexicon. It too had come from his grandfather.

When you swear on your dying solemn oath God can strike you dead!

Maria was engulfed for a moment in pain. 'OK. I believe you.'

Humour him, she thought. It was always best to humour them. *Them?* Who were *they?* She began to rub her leg and gradually feeling returned to it.

'You stayed to tell me you didn't hurt the man upstairs? Is that right?'

'Yeah.'

'OK, you've told me. I believe you.'

He looked confused. 'And because you was hurt.'

A bitter smile twisted her lips. 'You stayed because I was hurt?'

'Yeah.'

Bullshit, she thought. Bullshit.

She said, 'That was good of you. Kind of you.'

Did he want her? He looked young to be a rapist but how could you tell these days?

'Well, I'm OK,' she said. 'You can go. You're free.'

'You think I killed the man?' Terry said. The way the light fell on his face she *knew* she had seen him before.

'No. No.'

'Yeah. You think so. I goin' to show you sometin'.'

He took out his knife. There was a snick and the blade shot out of the handle.

'For God's sake!' she said, throwing up her hands.

But he wasn't threatening her.

'This a knife, right?' Terry said.

'Yes ... yes ... '

'I mean he ain't dead from a knife. I seen it. I was

204

in the bathroom. He got shot. He got bullet holes in him.'

He rose. 'You want to come and see?'

'No! No! I believe you!'

She struggled up on to the sofa.

'Listen,' she said. 'You better get out of here before the police find you. I've got some money. I'll give you lots of money.'

'I don't want money,' he said.

She could not take her eyes off the knife.

Keep him talking!

'What *do* you want?' she said.

'I dunno.'

'You don't know? There must be something. I mean what do you want here in my house? This is my house you know!'

'Yeah.'

'What's your name?'

'Hu . . . Terry.'

'Mine's Maria. Did you think you could hide here?'

'We was looking for a place to live.'

'Who?'

'Gail and me. And my grandfather.'

'Gail?'

'Yeah. She and my grandfather. We goin' to live together.'

'Here? In my house?'

'Just while I looks around.'

'So you were already in the house when Jack . . . when the man came?'

'I heard him. So I hid.'

'And?'

'He sittin' and someone comes to the door and he runs up the stairs and the man breaks down the bedroom door and – you all right?'

She felt waves of sickness and pain break over her body. For a moment she thought she was going to black out again.

Keep him talking!

'Is Gail your girl?'

He paused for a moment and said, 'Yeah. She my girl.'

'Tell me about them.'

205

He told her about Gail. He told her about his grandfather and how he had run the four hundred metres for Jamaica. He told her about Arthur Wint and Herb McKenley and Harrison Dillard and Daley Thompson until Maria's mind became fogged and bewildered. His speech became feverish. It was as though he could not stop.

Then he began to talk about a man called Bobbie. The rushing pattern of his speech slowed. He began to pick his words. It was as though he was actually telling himself what had happened. Explaining. Arguing. Justifying. Rationalising.

Halfway through this strange mixture Maria realised she knew who this boy was. The green woollen hat. There had been a description of him on TV and radio. And, as it clicked into place, she felt doubly afraid, for even if she had begun to believe him about Jack, she knew now that he had already killed a man.

She realised he had stopped talking and had fixed her with a penetrating stare. Hastily, she said, 'You say his name was Bobbie and he took you back to his flat. What then?'

'He give me a sandwich and a cuppa tea. It's cool.'

'And?'

'I'm watching TV and he's working at his desk. And then he says does I want a bath, right?'

'And?'

'So I gets in the bath and he wants to . . . Listen I can't say no more.'

'Yes, you can. For God's sake I'm old enough to be your mother.'

He thought about that for a moment and said, 'So he starts messin' with me, right?'

She thought: *Do I want to hear any more?* But there was something in his eyes, an appeal, a need, to which she found herself responding.

'Oh, God, Terry!' she said.

'Yeah.'

'And?'

'I don't like it. So I get out and he comes after me so I break his cups and saucers. And he looks *mad*! Really mad!'

'And?'

206

'So I split and goes back to Gail. But he comes there. He wants, you know, to beat me. So Gail, she gives me the knife.'

'Oh, God, Terry,' she repeated.

'Yeah.' Then he said, 'I didn't mean it. He coming at me, right?'

'Listen, I'll help you.'

'How?'

'Do you trust me?'

'I guess.'

'Well, then we'll talk some more. We'll think of a way. But I'll help you. I swear it. Just trust me.'

'There's nothing you can do.'

There was something in the way he said it, a hopelessness, a finality, that touched her.

'It was self-defence,' she said. 'They'll find Gail. She'll be your witness. Don't you see? She'll tell them everything!'

'They never going to find Gail,' he said.

This time the emphasis was unmistakable. Oh God, she thought, he's killed her too.

'Terry.' She tried to keep her voice calm and warm. 'Terry, would you do something for me? Would you get me a glass of water?'

He looked doubtful.

'Please,' she said. 'Then we'll talk some more. Then we'll think of a way to help you.'

'OK.'

He turned slowly and sadly and went into the kitchen. She heard him turn on the tap. She pulled the phone from the coffee table and began to press nine . . . nine . . . nine . . .

Suddenly the cord was ripped from her hand. Terry sawed at it with the knife blade.

'I seen that on TV,' he said. 'They always doing that on TV.'

They looked at each other. The light in his eyes had gone out.

She felt a savage pain in her chest. 'I'm sorry, Terry,' she said. 'I'm so sorry.'

He shrugged and went slowly over to the window and looked out. He turned back to her. 'I'm going now,' he said.

Her heart lifted.

Then he said, 'The man who kill your fren'. He out there.'

'What d'you mean?'

'He waitin' in the car. The Japanese man.'

He began to move to the stairs.

'Japanese?'

'Yeah.'

'Why do you say Japanese?'

She rose and went to the window. Twenty yards along the mews on the other side was a Toyota station wagon. A man was standing next to it and he was wearing a trilby hat.

The machinery inside her head was buzzing. Putting things together. The voice on the phone. Jack. The money. Nothing to do with Japan. Everything to do with Jack. Everything to do with Hong Kong.

'Terry! Listen to me!' Suddenly the scenario was all different. 'I believe you! I really do!'

He was halfway up the stairs.

She came to the bottom.

'Where are you going?'

'I going before the man come back.'

'There's no way out that way! There no back door either!'

'I know a way.'

'Terry, don't leave me!'

'I gotta go.'

'Terry!'

'What?'

'Please. I beg you. If you know some way out of here then take me.'

'Why should I?'

'Because I believe you.'

He stared at her.

'For God's sake, would you have believed me if I'd come to you with that sort of crap? Four hundred metres. Daley Thompson! Don't you understand? How *could* I believe?'

But nothing had seemed confusing to Terry.

'Listen. I think I know who the man is. No, not know *who*, but why he's there. Why he did it. He wants money, a lot of money. And he's going to come back into the house to look for it. We've got to get out of here. If you help me, I'll help you. I promise. I swear it.'

Terry looked at her with contempt.

'OK,' she said. 'I know what you must be thinking. You trusted me. I let you down. But listen. That's what happens between people. We're not perfect. We let each other down from time to time. What about Gail? Was she perfect all the time? We make mistakes, Terry. We're only human!'

He shrugged. 'OK,' he said. 'But you better be quick.'

She followed him up the stairs. He pulled down the trapdoor and the loft ladder swung down. Her left leg buckled as she put weight on it.

'Help me!' she said.

He went up first and got his hand under her arm and used all his strength and slowly, like a sack of maize, she came up into the roof space.

'Stay behind me,' he said, bringing up the ladder and closing the trapdoor.

She followed him blindly in the dark, scraping her knees and hurting herself on joists and pipes. She could not see him but touched his leg and crawled on. She heard him moving something, then suddenly she smelled the countryside: horses, manure, hay. In a moment she was deep in the hay itself and looking down on the broad backs of several animals.

'Come on,' he whispered.

She followed him down the ladder from the hayloft. He paused and stroked one of the horses. He climbed up to a small window and looked out. Then he indicated that the man outside had gone into her house.

There was a smaller door within the large stable door which was held by a bolt. He opened it and they slipped out into the mews.

'Quick!' he said.

She began to run as best she could. The end of the mews was almost blocked by a car. It was a small white car and a man, also in a trilby hat, was sitting in the front seat. She had to squeeze past it. Their eyes met. They both knew where she had seen him before. She heard him shout, then Terry was pulling her arm and they were running across the Bayswater Road, dodging the traffic. 'Here! Get through!'

Terry was showing her a hole in the park fence. She managed to get through. He followed. Then he caught her hand and was dragging her across the dark wet grass.

28

They had not gone fifty yards before they knew they were being followed. They had run past the fountains and the statue of Jenner and on to the west side of the Long Water, taking the path that would lead them to the Peter Pan statue, when they heard the sound of running footsteps.

Maria was already dragging on Terry's arm. Her breath was coming in painful gusts and there were spots in front of her eyes. She knew if she let go now she would collapse.

Terry sensed this too and he pulled her off the path to the right. A low wall loomed up. It was exactly where he hoped it would be, where he had remembered it.

'I can't!' she said, as Terry scrambled over the top. He tugged at her. She scraped her knees and shins. Then they were over the top and into the half-acre of rubbish and grass cuttings.

Some of the grass piles were burning slowly, just wisps of smoke coming from them. Every now and then, as the icy wind blew out of the north-east, a section of one would light up for a moment and then die as the wind died.

The grass cuttings had been brought in by a dozen powerful mowers and then heaped up by a bull-dozer. Some stood six to eight feet high. There was an eeriness about the area, as though fumiroles were venting steam in a volcanic landscape in the middle of London.

'I can't go on,' Maria said. 'I can't.'

'OK. We can stay here.'

In his mind was his original plan, before the park worker had surprised him. Here was a sanctuary, a place where they could burrow down in the fermenting grass. Normally it would have been damp but the cold wind of the past few days had dried it out. He picked an area where there were no fires and they went in like hamsters burrowing into straw.

'We be all right here,' he whispered.

She nodded. She was listening for the footsteps. Her mind was a jumble of thoughts and memories. Even as they had been running, her subconscious had been reminding her of the telephone calls to the house in Hampshire, the man in the street in the white car.

Jack must have stolen someone's money. It didn't even surprise her. It had always been on the cards that he would do something criminal. That's what had made him exciting. So now he'd stolen money and they had come after him. From what she knew of Hong Kong this did not surprise her either. Like most people she had heard of the Mafia-like organisation, the Triads.

She longed to run out into the park and find one of the men and tell him exactly where the money was so that he could take it and leave her alone.

But she knew that they were not the kind of people to say, 'OK. Let's shake on it.'

It was like some awful Victorian cautionary tale of the fallen woman: a moment's weakness and it was purgatory for ever.

'You OK?' Terry whispered.

'Yes.'

'It's safe here.'

'Yes.'

Safe. It didn't bear thinking about. Safe with a street kid who had knifed a man.

The wind came again and she could hear the fire crackle in a great pile of dry grass to their right. She had a vision of Richard burning garden rubbish. Often he would leave a pile and it would burn like this, off and on all night, and in the morning there would only be ash.

If only he hadn't gone away. If . . . if . . . if . . .

On the Bayswater Road, Eddie Twyford said, 'There's the Duke of York, guv'nor.'

'OK, pull up on the pavement.'

212

Before they'd opened the door Silver had seen the gap in the railings.

'It looks like a bloody highway,' Macrae said.

They squeezed through.

'If he's sleeping rough he could be anywhere,' Silver said.

'Woods said he'd first seen him behind the Peter Pan statue, in that waste disposal area. He was sheltering from the wind. Let's try there.'

Maria heard a voice. Just a snatch of a shout on the wind. Then she thought she heard shoes scraping on the wall. Terry heard it too for he seemed to burrow down more deeply. She knew they were invisible to anyone without a torch.

Then suddenly, so suddenly that she almost screamed, the pile of grass on her right burst into flames. One of the Chinese men was silhouetted against the orange light. He had a piece of wood in his hands and was lifting the grass so that the wind could reach into the heart of the mound.

Flames shot up illuminating the area for several yards all around. Another mound spurted flame. Then a third. Grass and old newspapers and pieces of cardboard and plastic, all were catching alight now.

There were several grass and rubbish piles which had not originally been burning, but the men began to throw lighted matter on these and soon they began to burn. It would only be a matter of moments before their own was burning.

'We gotta go,' Terry said.

She flinched at the thought of movement. Her arm was aching, her legs felt weak. A stronger gust of wind blew across the park and the pile next to theirs went up with a woosh.

'Now!' Terry said.

They scrambled from their hiding place and began to run towards the wall. A second Chinese man came from nowhere. He was almost on top of them. He dropped into a crouch, holding a gun in the professional way, with his two hands locked on the butt.

Terry suddenly jinked like an antelope and, before the man could decide which was the target, Terry had pushed

213

him with all his strength. His feet tangled with rubbish on the ground, he swung his arms like a windmill to regain his balance, then, in a series of tripping backward steps he over-balanced and, with a scream landed in the burning grass.

The second man raced to him and managed to grip his coat. He struggled for some seconds. The man came out of the fire like a burning scarecrow.

Terry, pulling Maria, scrambled over the wall. Ahead was the statue. But then he saw two men running towards them from the direction of the Bayswater Road.

'This way!' he said.

But Maria could run no more. 'I can't!'

There was only the water. He remembered the park worker pointing to the far side where there were reeds and over-hanging branches and saying, 'That's where the ducks sleep.'

He and Maria waded silently into the black water making for the shelter of the far side.

Tendrils of weed slung to their bodies, under their feet was soft mud. Ducks quacked in fear and irritation and fluttered away.

She wanted to say, 'Leave me. They don't want you.' Then she thought they probably did. She had involved him. No, that wasn't true. He had involved himself.

'Oh God!' She felt an underwater branch scrape her leg.

'We nearly there.'

'You go on! You can run.'

'In here,' he whispered, parting the long branches of a weeping willow. 'They never find you here.'

But she no longer believed that. They had found them in the grass piles.

'Terry, go now.'

'But what you goin' to do?'

She was silent. She didn't know. The water was up to her waist and she was beginning to freeze.

Macrae and Silver had seen the flames coming from the burning grass and, as they had run towards the wall, had seen two people, a woman and a boy, cross over in front of them and enter the water.

214

'Terry!' Macrae shouted. 'Terry Collins!'

Then Silver had shouted, 'Watch out!'

A man came out of the darkness on their right, his clothes alight. A second man, also burning but not so severely, raced past him. He was carrying a gun and fired once at Macrae then flung himself into the water.

The burning scarecrow never made it. As he ran he created his own wind, and that, combined with another strong gust, caused him to go up like a torch. His steps faltered. He stood. And then, like a Guy Fawkes rocket that has not lifted off, he fell forward in a shower of sparks.

Macrae and Silver ran down to the water's edge. The first man was on his knees, the gun in his hand. Macrae hit him on the side of the head and Silver grabbed his gun arm. They dragged him from the water.

'I don't know what the hell's going on, laddie,' Macrae said. 'But whatever it is, it's disturbing the peace on Good Friday.'

Silver waded into the water. 'Terry!' he called. 'Terry Collins!'

There was a movement under the trees on the far side.

'Terry, listen! My name's Leo. I'm a policeman. It's all right. Nothing bad's going to happen to you. Terry! Are you there?'

There was a sudden splashing on the far side. Then the sound of running footsteps. Then a woman's voice said, 'Please help me!'

Silver waded into the black water. 'Where are you?'

'Here. Under the tree.'

The water gripped him icily round the scrotum and then up his back. Macrae stood on the bank. 'To your right!' he called.

Silver went on. Branches shook and he saw the white blob of her face.

'Give me your hand,' he said.

She stumbled forward and he caught her, then pulled her up on to the far bank.

'You're all right now,' he said. 'I've got you.'

She began to shake with relief – then she began to cry.

215

*

For Maria the remainder of the night and most of the early part of Saturday morning passed in a dream – but at least it was a dream and no longer a nightmare. The two Chinese men, one dead and one groggy from Macrae's blow to the head, were removed. Then Maria took Macrae and Silver to the house in Broadhurst Mews where Benson's cold body still lay tangled in the counterpane. She gave them the money and tried to explain it as best she could.

They sealed the house and called in the lab liaison officer, the police photographer, the coroner's officer, the doctor, and the district fingerprint officer. By the time they took her to the station to take her statement she was wearing Silver's leather jacket and Macrae's heavy woollen scarf.

And by that time Terry was a long way away.

29

'Half the holiday's gone,' Zoe said, 'and we haven't seen each other yet. Never mind an orgy.'

'I know,' Leo said, coming out of the shower and towelling himself.

It was breakfast time on Easter Saturday and he had just got home.

'It's the only time in the day I see you. Either now or late at night. What do ordinary people do?'

'We're not ordinary.'

'You want some more coffee?'

'Listen, I've got to be back in the office in a couple of hours. The whole thing's blown wide open.'

'I thought you'd solved it. I thought it was a kid.'

'It was until yesterday. Now it's ... well ... ' He explained it to her as best he could but the look on her face told him she did not understand and he knew too little about what was going on to make it any clearer.

'But what about the kid?'

'We lost him in the park. It was as black as pitch. By the time we'd dealt with the other two and found the woman, he'd split.'

He got into his pyjamas and crawled into bed. He was so tired his head felt numb.

She got in with him and put her arms round him. 'This is platonic,' she said hastily. 'Just hold me. It's better than nothing.'

She was warm and living and breathing and her skin felt wonderful under his hands. Slowly he began to relax. Slowly his brain rejected the images of the night: the burning man, the dead man. Slowly, in her arms, he became Leopold Silver, human being.

Sleep began to creep into his brain.

'Leo, what'll happen to the kid?'

'We'll pick him up. Probably today. He can't get far.'

'And?'

'We'll check his story. I'm pretty sure I know what happened. It was probably self-defence.'

'Poor kid.'

'Yeah.'

Macrae sat on his unmade bed and dialled Linda's number. She answered almost immediately, as though she might have been waiting for the call.

'Oh, it's you, George.'

Did she sound just that little bit disappointed?

He said, 'Sorry to ring early like this. You up?'

'Yes, I'm up.'

'I was going to suggest we meet.'

'That's right. You said so.'

'But things have . . . well, they've got a bit, you know . . . '

'Oh. Well, never mind.'

She sounded so brisk. She was probably going out with someone else anyway.

'Could I ring you tomorrow?' he said.

'Tomorrow?'

'I might be clearer tomorrow.'

'Let's see. Yes. Why not? Why don't you ring me tomorrow?'

'I'll do that. Oh, and, Linda . . . '

'Yes.'

'Tell Susie it's all right. I mean about the money. I'll get it somehow.'

'That's good of you, George!'

'Yeah, well. Listen, I've got to go. I just thought I'd tell you.'

'Thanks, George. I'll ring her today. She'll be thrilled.'

'OK, then. I'll try to ring you tomorrow.'

He put down the phone and gave himself a belt of whisky then stretched out on his bed fully clothed. The whisky tasted

good. If he was going to become like his father at least he was going to enjoy it.
But he wasn't.
No, he wasn't.
Because if he wanted to make the sort of money he clearly needed to make he was going to have to keep the whisky bottle out of sight. And he was going to have to be a good boy.
Christ, what a prospect.

At the other end of the dead line Linda Macrae went and got herself a cup of coffee and looked out over the silent suburban street.
She would have two cups and then a long bath with a book. And then? Well, the shops were open at least. She could go and do the weekend's food shopping. But that wouldn't take long. She was shopping for one now.
And then?
She didn't know.
The weekend was halfway gone but it was still a long time to Tuesday.

At the same time as Linda was pouring herself a second cup of coffee, Maria was unlocking the front door of her house in Hampshire. She hadn't fetched Caesar. She wanted to have a few hours' rest first. She closed the door behind her and thought: home. For the first time it *felt* like home, like her territory.
She threw her things down on the hall table. She wanted a bath and bed. She had been up all night with Macrae and Silver. She'd told her story half a dozen times and each time it had sounded like she was describing some dirty weekend that had gone wrong.
Which it was – but in a different way.
She walked to the bottom of the stairs and as she did so she heard a noise at the far side of the house. It seemed to be coming from the kitchen. It came again. A scraping noise. As though someone had moved a chair.
The house was gloomy and silent. She was gripped by the terror of the night before.

219

Who was this? Another man? Someone who was coming for her alone?

She saw a figure materialise at the end of the passage. He seemed to be coming towards her. She turned and ran for the front door, wrenching at the handle.

'Maria!'

She stopped and turned. She could see him now.

'Oh God, Richard!'

She threw herself at him, feeling his arms come round her body, squeezing the breath from her lungs.

'Oh, God. I'm so glad to see you! When did you get back?'

'Half an hour ago. Where were you, and where's the dog? Nothing happened has it?'

'I'll tell you in a minute,' she said, already beginning a mental editing process. 'You first. I thought you were going to be away the whole weekend.'

He gave her a cup of coffee in the kitchen where he had cooked himself breakfast. The smile disappeared from his face as he talked. As he told her where he'd been.

'Hong Kong!' she said. 'But you said . . . '

'Lisbon. I know.'

And then he told her why.

'Stealing?' she said. 'From the business?'

'I'm afraid so. It's been going on for some time. Mrs Feniman alerted me. You remember her?'

'Chiffon scarves.'

'Right.'

'Then it was Mrs Feniman who was telephoning. I thought . . . '

'What?'

'Nothing.' She lit a cigarette and said, 'I always knew Jack was dishonest but I never thought he'd steal from us. From you.'

'Us. Well, he did. I didn't want to tell you until I was sure and I couldn't be certain until I'd been out there. He's disappeared. Run for it. And he's taken everything he could.'

'Darling, there's something you should know.'

When she had finished telling him his face was white and drawn.

220

'God, what a mess,' he said. 'And I haven't told you the worst. Mrs Feniman. By the time I got there the police had found her body in the office. She'd been tortured then killed.'

'Oh, Richard!'

'The police think they know who organised it, but they say it's going to be difficult to prove. Things are always difficult to prove in Hong Kong when big money's involved.'

'Talking about money . . . ' she said, and told him about the duty-free bag.

He listened in silence, chewing at the side of his cheek, then he said, 'Mrs Feniman told me he was salting it away somewhere. That's last year's profits, and the year before that, and before that, and God knows what else. And I was pouring money in from this end. It was like an open wound.'

'We'll get it back, won't we? I mean, the police will understand?'

'I'm not sure I have your faith. Anyway, we'll give it our best shot.' He was silent for a few moments and then said, 'What about the boy? The one who helped you?'

'The police don't think he'll get far. Richard, I want do to something for him.'

'What?'

'I don't know yet. But something.'

'Sure. We'll do something. But in the meantime I'd better get in touch with this superintendent what's-his-name?'

'Now?' She rose and put her arms around his neck.

'Well, perhaps not just at the moment,' he said.

Terry was only truly happy when he was running. And he was running now. One foot after another, his soft-soled trainers making a light thud . . . thud . . . thud . . . on the cold London pavements.

Day . . . lee . . . Day . . . lee . . .

He kept up the rhythm of his running. Left . . . right . . . left . . . right . . . Day . . . lee . . . Day . . . lee . . .

He ran towards Shepherd's Bush. The sign on the road said White City Stadium.

221

People were out shopping. The streets were busy. Terry's green woollen hat bobbed along, jinking in and out of the crowds.

White City Stadium!

It was where his and his grandfather's kind of people came together. Maybe that's where Daley would be. Preparing for the new season.

He couldn't think of anywhere else to go.

Or anything else to do.

So . . . OK . . . Hundred metres final. Daley Thompson. And Barney Ewell. And Harrison Dillard. And Haseley Crawford . . . and Huntsman Collins.

Everybody nervous. Yawning a lot. Belching.

'Better out than in,' his grandfather always said.

Everybody getting down to their blocks and kicking their feet backwards to shake the dirt from their spikes.

On your marks . . .

Get set . . .

Wait for it! Don't false start.

And the gun . . . !

Huntsman out of his blocks like a racehorse.

And racing now over Shepherd's Bush, between the cars and the people.

And it's Huntsman Collins . . .

'He coming through like a train . . . '

Huntsman . . . ! Huntsman . . . !

Here's the tape . . . !

Last great effort . . . ! Chest out . . . !

And the cheering and the shouting were in Terry's ears as he ran as fast as he could up Wood Lane and into the cold north-east wind.